L. C. Tyler was born in Essex and e̶ ̶̶̶̶̶̶̶̶̶̶̶̶̶̶
Oxford and City University. His con̶ ̶̶̶̶̶̶̶̶̶̶̶̶
author-and-agent duo Ethelred Tressider and Elsie Thirkettle
has twice been nominated for Edgar Allan Poe Awards and
he won the Goldsboro Last Laugh Award with Herring in
the Library. His latest crime series is set in the seventeenth
century and features lawyer John Grey.

He has lived and worked all over the world, but has more
recently been based in London and Sussex.

To find out more about L. C. Tyler visit www.lctyler.com or
follow him on twitter @lenctyler.

Also by L. C. Tyler

Too Much of Water

A JOHN GREY HISTORICAL MYSTERY

L. C. TYLER

CONSTABLE

CONSTABLE

First published in in hardback in Great Britain in 2021 by Constable
This paperback edition published in 2022 by Constable

A CIP catalogue record for this book
is available from the British Library.

ISBN: 978-1-47213-506-3

Typeset in Caslon Pro by SX Composing DTP, Rayleigh, Essex
Printed and bound in Great Britain by Clays Ltd, Elcograf S.p.A.

Papers used by Constable are from well-managed forests
and other responsible sources.

Constable
An imprint of
Little, Brown Book Group
Carmelite House
50 Victoria Embankment
London EC4Y 0DZ

An Hachette UK Company
www.hachette.co.uk

www.littlebrown.co.uk

For Reggie

'Too much of water hast thou, poor Ophelia,
And therefore I forbid my tears'

Hamlet, William Shakespeare

Some Persons in this Book

John Grey – myself, currently a magistrate in the fair, if rather flat, county of Essex, formerly a spy but definitely not, as amply demonstrated by my red velvet coat and breeches, a Puritan, contrary to anything that you may be told by . . .

Aminta, Lady Grey – that is to say my wife, a playwright and poet, who insists on the superiority of her ancestry over my own, in spite of being the daughter of . . .

Sir Felix Clifford – a reprobate Cavalier, who features no more in this story than he has to, and who is (in my absence) currently teaching our two-year-old son how to drink hard and seduce actresses, but who in his younger days rode headlong into battle alongside **Prince Rupert**, as did . . .

Jacob Cavendish – impoverished in the past by fines imposed by Cromwell and by loans to the previous King, and more recently by his own folly in contesting the forthcoming Eastwold by-election in which he was originally to stand against . . .

Admiral Sir Robert Digges – a brutal and foul-mouthed sailor, who has fought with great impartiality both for Cromwell and the present King (but almost always against the Dutch), and whose inexplicable death, just as he was about to bribe his way to victory in the said election, is a matter of great concern for . . .

Mister Samuel Pepys – Clerk of the Acts to the Navy Board, who has to ensure that Eastwold's next Member of Parliament is willing to support the government of **His Gracious Majesty King Charles II**, especially in respect of the onerous and much resented taxes that are needed to build ships and fight the Dutch (see above), and whose sudden arrival in Eastwold is inconvenient in so many ways for . . .

Mister Digby Digges – son of the late Admiral Digges, a magistrate like me and deeply grateful (he says) for the strict puritanical upbringing and righteous chastisement provided, after the death of his mother, **Venetia**, by **his uncle Alexander Digges and his aunt Barbara Digges**, and now the fortunate husband of the beautiful . . .

Silvia Digges – the daughter of the impecunious Jacob Cavendish (whom you've already met briefly) and thus connected closely to both parliamentary candidates until the strange and unexpected death of her father-in-law, which was initially investigated by . . .

Mister David Larter – the local Coroner, who may not have been entirely impartial, since his uncle . . .

Solomon Larter – is Eastwold's other MP (and no particular friend of the Digges family), formerly Mayor until, under the Republic, he was replaced by . . .

William Peacock – whom my wife is completely at liberty to call a Puritan if she wishes, a piously gaunt man in black, who farts Psalms and looks down his long nose at everyone including . . .

Elijah Spratchett – a very self-satisfied rogue, who in turn replaced Peacock as Mayor when the King came back ten years later, and who now owns most of Eastwold's fishing boats, though he employs others to actually risk their lives at sea, just as . . .

James Tutepenny – daily risks his, being a poor but undoubtedly honest fisherman and one who formerly served under Admiral Digges, along with . . .

Ezekiel Benefice – a man with a rather strange name, even for this part of Suffolk, innkeeper and part-time smuggler who lost a leg as a direct result of the Admiral's overly enthusiastic battle plan at the Battle of Scheveningen (against the Dutch, obviously), and thus wouldn't tell you who killed the Admiral, even if he knew, rather like . . .

The Reverend George Wraith – vicar of a church that is about to fall into the sea, who hates Peacock, Spratchett, Cavendish, both Larters and all of the Diggeses, though that may simply reflect his contempt for the rapidly shrinking town of . . .

Eastwold – a place with which you will become at least as familiar as you are with any of the above personages, and towards which I shall shortly be travelling in a coach in the rain, but which you will first view, as is wholly appropriate, from the choppy North Sea.

Prologue – February 1670

The ragged grey sky promised nothing good. The coast, bobbing erratically in the middle distance, was a smudged line, badly drawn with an ochre crayon – low cliffs of soft sandstone that crumbled to the slightest touch. The sea that slapped against the boat's tarred planks was shallow, at least by the standards of salt-water sailors, but Aaron knew that a man incautious enough to fall in could still drown twice over before he reached the soft, dimly lit bottom.

His frozen fingers tugged again at the fishing net, as he turned his envious gaze on Dick, whose only duties were apparently to puff away at his short clay pipe and keep the little sailing boat on course.

'It's caught on something,' he called out. The wind, whistling through the rigging, whipped his words away into the sky. He shouted the message again.

'What?' said Dick, taking his short clay pipe out of his mouth and theatrically cupping an ear.

'The net. Must be caught on something. Can't be just fish. Too heavy.'

In the brief, unnatural calm that followed these words, Dick's answer came to him with conversational clarity. 'That'll be the church spire,' he said. 'Most likely it's snagged on that.'

Aaron looked at the older man. Was it senility or was this just another joke at his expense? 'Spire? We're half a mile from land, almost.'

'St James's church. We must be right above it. See where the cliffs are now, boy? Well, back in King John's time, the land stretched all the way out here. There was a whole town between where we are and where dry land begins today. A town bigger than London, so they say. Ships came to it from all over the world – timber from Norway, wine from France, spices from India, purple cloth from somewhere out of the Old Testament. Then there was a great flood, like Noah's but without any instructions to get the animals yoked pairwise, and the whole blessed place was lost under the waves. On a calm day, you can stand on the beach and still hear the ghostly bells ringing in the steeple of the drowned church.'

'You ever heard them?'

'Might have done.'

'When?'

'Afore you was born or thought of.' Dick stuffed his pipe back between his brown teeth, which was his usual way of concluding an argument that he believed he had won.

Aaron frowned. His mother was paying Dick to take him under his wing as an apprentice and teach him fishing. What he got in practice was a bit of advice on how to cast the nets and gut fish, and a great deal of misinformation on life in general. There was plenty of time on a fishing boat to tell tall stories and this seemed to be one of them.

'That's squit,' he said cautiously. 'There's no church down there.'

'True as I'm at this tiller,' said Dick. 'I knew a fellow once who came here at low tide – one bright spring morning when he could walk out for miles across firm, damp sand. He said he saw house after house, covered in barnacles, and, in the very middle of it all, the great dead church of St James, with bunches of emerald seaweed draping the brick walls. He walked up, cautious-like, and pushed the church door open on its rusty hinges. Inside, there was rows of pews, with the parishioners still sitting in them – all skellingtons they was, with their prayer books in their bony hands. And in the pulpit, in his white surplice, was the skellington parson, scraps of wet hair hanging from his skull, grinning with his clenched teeth and pointing with a raised arm at the Ten Commandments on the wall. For the flooding was God's verdict on the town of Eastwold, and the parson's wise words came too late, as is sadly so often the case where wicked sinners are concerned.'

'How sinful were they, exactly?' asked Aaron, hoping to learn about more than gutting fish.

'They offended the Lord grievously,' said Dick, 'though not as grievously as you and Bessy Waldegrave offended the Lord behind the cockle sheds last Tuesday. So, I'd be careful, if I was you.'

'It couldn't happen now, though, could it? That was all in King John's day. It's almost as long ago as Adam and Eve or when you was born.'

Dick ignored this last slight. He'd never claimed to be young and gullible.

'On the contrary, young man. There's still houses falling into the sea. The waves nibble away at the bottom of them

3

cliffs, and anything perched on top tumbles bit by bit onto the beach. You can just see that house over there – one half already gone and the other half hanging over the edge, like a broken piss-pot. There are great heaps of bricks and tile on the beach where others fell, not so very long ago. You and your Bessy aren't safe by a country mile. God sees all things and He bides His time.'

Aaron considered this. 'You're saying the houses fall bit by bit?'

'That's what I just told you. You'd better clean your ears out, boy, so I don't have to repeat myself all the time. And if you don't, I'll give you a clip round one of them to remind you that cleanliness is next to holiness.'

Since Dick couldn't easily leave the tiller, it was unlikely that threat would come to very much. 'I meant, if the houses fall like that, then the church would as well. It would just be a heap of bricks on the beach. The tower would've collapsed, with its bells inside it. So the bells wouldn't ring. And the parishioners couldn't still be sitting in rows. They'd be all mixed together like sprats in a basket. So, whatever this net's snagged on, it's not a church steeple.'

Dick paused for a moment, then said: 'That's as may be. But the tide comes up pretty fast behind them cockle sheds all the same.'

Aaron gave the net another tug. Even if he could drag it to the side of the boat, he'd never get it over the gunnels.

Dick watched him with the satisfied smile of a man who knows that there is more than one way of punishing sin. 'Yes, just the last few houses now, up on the cliffs. Soon there'll be nothing left of Eastwold, except a couple of inland farms and the old manor house – I mean the Priory. The town still sends its two MPs to Parliament, of course. That was in King John's charter, and they can't take the right away, not ever. Once the ink is dry on the parchment, it's like holy writ. A dozen or so burgesses, as they calls themselves, elects two members. Profitable business that, now people are willing to pay good money to get elected. Easy living in Eastwold, these days, I'd say. Better than fishing, though that's true of most things.'

'Who's going to pay to be a Member of Parliament?'

'Bloody Digges is one of them. That's Admiral Sir Robert Digges to you and me. One of Cromwell's Generals at Sea, he was, and the King's Vice Admiral of the Blue after that. Lives in Eastwold now, on dry land, lucky beggar. He don't have to go near a boat if he don't want to. Not even in fine weather. He bought the manor house from whichever Cavalier owned it before. Cavendish, I think he was called. They're a big family in these parts – or was.'

'So, this Digges – he'd have fought the Dutch, then?'

'That he did, young man – both for Oliver and for the King, because the Dutch are a powerful and cunning nation and only hard knocks will keep them away from our fish and our womenfolk. Digges was a fearless enemy of the Hollanders and an even harsher one to his own crew. Ordered his ship straight into the Dutch fleet, where it was torn apart by shot and holed beneath the waterline. Did he flinch? Not Digges. Got himself rowed to another and did the same with that. Watched them both sink from a third and cheered his men as they vanished for ever beneath the waves, they not being able to swim and he having taken the only seaworthy rowing boat from both ships. The hero of the Four Days Battle, they called him, but I know a few sailors who wish he hadn't lived to be knighted by the King. How's that net coming along?'

5

'It's no good. It's too heavy for me on my own.'

Dick swore softly, stuffed the pipe in his pocket and lashed the tiller in place. Then he inched cautiously along the pitching boat to Aaron. He didn't much want to fall in either.

'You're just cack-handed,' he said. 'And that dratted wind's getting up again. Pull away, boy. I haven't got all day to do your job for you, and this pipe is like to burn a hole in my second-best fishing coat.'

Together they dragged the net and its sodden contents into the boat. As Aaron had predicted, it wasn't a church spire or a herring or anything else they could sell in Ipswich.

'Bloody hell,' said Dick. 'What was you thinking of, catching that?'

'I wasn't thinking of nothing. I didn't invite him into the net.'

They looked at the pale face that stared back, glassy-eyed, through the strands of thin rope.

'He must have been in the sea a day or two,' said Aaron.

'Maybe less. He's not much eaten,' said Dick. 'Just a bit nibbled at the edges. Dragged one up once – you wouldn't want to know what he looked like. And he'd been missing less than a week.'

'That's a fine coat he's wearing,' said Aaron. 'Velvet. Gold lace. A bit spoilt by the water but it might brush up. He's lost his periwig though.'

They both looked at the short grey hair that remained. Neither of them would ever be able to afford a periwig, but it would have been the first thing the tide ripped from their catch. It would have been nice to have at least tried one on. Just for fun. 'And his shoes,' said Dick, thinking sadly of the silver buckles they would doubtless have had. 'The sea's had the best of him, my lad, and left us nothing but human clay in all its frailty.'

They untangled the dead man very carefully from the net, which was valuable, and went through his pockets, just in case. They were in luck. Even on a cloudy day like this, the gold snuffbox that Dick now held gleamed and spoke of riches beyond their usual fish-blighted dreams. It could be worth a whole year's haul of herring, that could. And nobody would know, when they landed the body, that the box wasn't at the bottom of the sea with the periwig and shoe buckles. But whose property had it been before it had become rightfully theirs?

'There's words on the lid. Do you want me to read it to you?' asked Aaron.

'Who says I can't read it for myself?'

'Fine. You read it to me, then.'

Dick reluctantly handed the box across to him. 'Don't drop it,' he said. 'Unless you want to dive in after it.'

Aaron scanned the inscription slowly, his lips moving, his finger tracing the words.

'Well?' said Dick. 'I thought you was a scholard?'

'It *says* it was presented to Admiral Digges by his comrades-in-arms to mark his victory at the Four Days' Battle.'

They looked at the white, sea-wrinkled face again. They looked at the sparse grey hair. They looked at the fine velvet coat, from which the seawater still streamed. Their man did not have the appearance of somebody who would steal a gold snuffbox from an Admiral. And it would have been a brave man who would have risked stealing from Bloody Digges anyway. In which case . . .

'It seems they'll need somebody else to stand in the election, then,' said Dick.

'You'd have thought an Admiral would have a sword,' said Aaron, thoughtfully.

7

'Swords are ten a penny,' said Dick, pocketing the snuffbox. 'Just be grateful for what we've got, eh? No more fishing for us today. Or tomorrow. I don't like the look of them clouds, boy. They're heading for nasty weather round Eastwold, and no mistake.'

Chapter I

In a carriage, still slightly too far from Eastwold –
March 1670

It is not my fault that rain lashes the windows of our coach,
but Aminta thinks otherwise.

'You could have stayed at home,' I say.

'I am a dutiful wife,' she replies. 'Look at me meekly sitting
here, saying nothing. Where should I be, John, except at my
husband's side? Silent and uncomplaining.'

As a renowned playwright, she is aware of irony and all
of its possible uses. She pulls the heavy woollen cloak more
closely round her shoulders. Modern and well sprung though
our coach is, it admits draughts in too many places to count.
We are at least better off than our coachman, up on the box,
or than the four horses, floundering along the muddy road
with the urgent spring rain lashing the flesh of beast and man.
This unfamiliar countryside is low and misty. Phantom poplar
trees haunt its overflowing dykes and rivers. Everything here
in Suffolk is damp and clinging.

'I would have been away only a few days,' I say.

'If the rain continues, it might be weeks before the roads are passable again.'

'Then we could not have gone to London anyway,' I say. 'I am sorry that my having to travel to Suffolk has delayed our leaving for the capital, but this is at the request of the Sheriff. And I am of course delighted that you are able to accompany me.'

Should I point out that last year she was urging me to cut the last of my ties with my legal practice in London and spend more time in contented domesticity in Clavershall West? Should I point out that she has always said that she can write her plays as well in the countryside as in town? Should I point out that she too was born in the Essex village in which we now both live? Should I point out that leaving for London once the roads were fit to travel on was merely a proposal on my part – an idle thought on a rare sunny afternoon a fortnight ago – not a contractual obligation?

But it has been a hard winter. And a small Essex village in the pinched first quarter of the year has little to offer any woman who does not wish her dress to become caked in mud as soon as she steps out of doors or descends from the carriage. Much of the time, she must feel a prisoner in her own house, from the last of the leaves falling to the emergence of the first apple blossom. Yes, I can see why she now wishes to be in London and why my acceptance of this sudden request from the Sheriff that I should visit a small town on the Suffolk coast seems like a broken promise on my part. I can understand why accompanying me is better than remaining at home, though not very much better. All of that is true. But the rain is still not my fault.

'I am very pleased that you were able to come with me,' I repeat. 'And I am sure that Digby and his wife will entertain you well while I am working.'

'Is your Mister Digges not to work with you? He is after all the magistrate there, albeit very young and newly appointed. I'm sure he was much looking forward to his first investigation into a death. If he's anything like you.'

'The Sheriff's instructions are clear,' I say patiently. 'Since it is sadly Mister Digges' father who has died, he is conflicted. The services of another magistrate are required. Me, in this case. I am to investigate, as well as I can, the cause of Admiral Digges' death.'

'And there was no magistrate living closer to Eastwold who might have been sent for?'

'I don't know.'

'Did you think to ask?'

'No.'

Aminta nods significantly. Had I really wished to take her to London – something any reasonable husband would have done with demur – I would have at least insisted on knowing why no other magistrate was available, demanded that one *should* be made available without delay.

'Perhaps those living nearer were busy?' I say.

Aminta raises an eyebrow. Other magistrates are clearly more attentive to the wishes of their wives.

'Or perhaps I have some knowledge or skill that other magistrates lacked?' I continue.

Aminta shakes her head.

'Well, it is a simple enough task, to be sure,' I continue. 'I have only to ask a few questions and confirm the cause of death. So, it is unlikely to detain us for very long.'

'But from what you have told me, I think as we were passing through Saffron Walden, the Coroner has already ruled that the cause is drowning? An accidental death. Is it not customary to accept that?'

'Indeed. And if Admiral Sir Robert Digges had been merely Master Bob Digges and a catcher of herring, then that would indeed be that. But he is an admiral and was about to be elected to Parliament.'

'And the Sheriff normally overrules Coroners if the deceased happens to be an officer of flag rank?'

'Of course not.'

'Then it must be for some other reason.'

'Digges was not a popular man in Suffolk or anywhere. Under those circumstances there is always a risk of foul play. I assume the Coroner's verdict did not entirely rule that out.'

'And so, on the basis of that vague possibility, you decided to drag your wife to Suffolk in the pouring rain.'

'I mean that must be the case, or the Sheriff would not have needed any help.'

'No, you mean that you were so flattered to be asked to interfere in another county's business that you did not think to question the Sheriff's request, odd though it was.'

I decide not to say again how pleased I am, nevertheless, that she has chosen to accompany me. It is unlikely to help.

For a while Aminta is silent, then she says: 'If Digges was that unpopular, why are you so certain he would have been elected?'

'There are just a handful of electors – the burgesses of the town. His unpopularity would not have stopped them voting for him.'

'Because they will always elect whoever pays them most?'

'Yes. It would be perverse to accept the lower of the two offers. The town of Eastwold returns two members. By tradition, the burgesses are free to select one from amongst their own number. The other, after suitable payment has been made to all of the freemen, is nominated by the Admiralty. And that is that, unless somebody decides to waste money standing against the Admiralty candidate.'

'An Admiralty candidate nominated by your good friend Samuel Pepys?'

'By the Duke of York – though doubtless based on Pepys's carefully considered recommendation. And he is neither my friend nor good.'

'So, Pepys recommended Bloody Digges? The man who bears responsibility for the death of more English sailors than the Dutch and French combined?'

'And the Spanish, though their contribution is relatively small. The question, for Pepys, is not a candidate's moral character or ability as a naval commander, but whether he can be depended on to vote in the interests of the Admiralty. The same applies to the voters. Their Member of Parliament does not need to be a native of Eastwold or even to know exactly where the borough is. They certainly don't have to like him. It is simply a matter of whether he will pay enough and then use his influence in their interest. And, however unpleasant he was, Digges came doubly recommended: he was not only backed by Admiralty cash but he was also a local man. He had been a burgess of Eastwold for several years, ever since he bought the manor from the Cavendishes back in '54 or '55.'

'Ah,' says Aminta. She looks at me significantly.

'I'm not saying that the King shouldn't have restored

the estates of Cavaliers who were forced to sell them during the late wars—'

'Aren't you, my dear husband?'

I say nothing. Her father, an impoverished but unrepentant Cavalier, also lost his estate to a roundhead Colonel in much the same way and at much the same time – an estate that Aminta has recovered through a succession of marriages, that is to say my mother's arguably bigamous marriage to the aforementioned Colonel Payne and Aminta's subsequent marriage to me, as my mother's heir. The Big House in Clavershall West is, in Aminta's view, finally back in the right hands. Other Royalists, like the Cavendishes of Eastwold, still petition the King for redress, on the grounds that forced sales, brought on by loans to the King and fines imposed by Parliament, should be set aside. But His Gracious Majesty continues to look with equal favour on old Royalists and on former supporters of Cromwell, which is as well for the many people who once served the Republic. Like me. And Pepys. And Lord Sandwich. And the Duke of Buckingham. And the Duke of Albemarle. And indeed the late, lamented Admiral Sir Robert Digges. We are inconveniently many, and the King likes an untroubled life, free of difficult decisions.

'The rain seems to be easing off,' I say. 'See how the sun shines on the willows yonder. That is a good omen for our journey, wouldn't you say?'

'Jacob Cavendish was to stand against Digges?' asks Aminta, less interested in willows than I had hoped.

'Yes. Though the Admiralty candidate is normally given a free run, Cavendish chose to oppose him. Perhaps he thought he could, if elected, use his influence in Parliament to help restore the family's estate. Perhaps, along with most other

14

people, he just disliked Digges. But he would have lost anyway. He couldn't have afforded to pay more than the Admiralty.'

'But with Digges out of the way?'

'He is, for the moment at least, the only candidate. His daughter, Silvia, recently married Digby Digges. And Digby has of course now inherited his father's estate, following the Admiral's death. So, perhaps the more general question of restitution is no longer so pressing for the Cavendishes as it was a few weeks ago. In effect, they have the estate back. If the Admiralty does send another candidate, and I expect they will, then Cavendish may choose to stand down and avoid any further expense.'

Aminta smiles. She approves of Silvia's methods. 'So, the roundhead uncouthness of the Digges family will have been mitigated by a judicious addition of Cavalier finesse. That is always a good idea. In my experience.'

I shake my head. 'My mother was always a Royalist,' I say.

'And you think that doesn't make you a puritanical Republican?'

'I am not puritanical.'

'Only because I watch your Puritan tendencies day and night. If it wasn't for me you'd have nothing in your wardrobe that wasn't black.'

'I am immensely grateful for your advice on my costume,' I say. 'But even if I were a Puritan, it doesn't mean that our own domestic situation is anything like that of Digby and Silvia Digges. Admiral Digges was a brute by any standards. My father – also a Royalist, I would remind you – was a surgeon in the King's Army. A gentleman of taste and discretion.'

'Not according to your mother.'

'My mother's view of my father was unfair in many ways, especially since she was at least as unfaithful to him as he was to her. But none of that makes the Greys uncouth roundheads. My stepfather, Colonel Payne, was of course a roundhead. But he was the only one in the family. Unless you count me.'

'I do count you. Let us be absolutely clear on that: you are an unrepentant Republican and a Puritan. But I apologise to your mother's family,' says Aminta. 'The Wests are of ancient lineage and moderately well bred. It was only the upstart Greys I wished to disparage.'

'Thank you,' I say.

'Of course, Silvia and I will still have much to talk about,' says Aminta. 'I'm sure that you and Digby Digges resemble each other in many ways, and I should be interested to know what she has done about it. I'm really looking forward to meeting her. If we ever get to Eastwold, that is.'

I stare out of the window. I think we have at least another hour's travelling and there is no guarantee that, just round the corner, we shall not find an impassable stretch of flooded highway. The rain has started again, harder than ever. But it is still not my fault. Not in any way whatsoever.

Chapter 2

Hospitality at the manor house

Eastwold Priory is at least warm and dry. The fire blazes in the hearth and the light of many candles ripples across the bright new tapestries on the walls.

'My father rebuilt the house some fifteen years ago,' says Digby Digges. Digby is a muscular young man with a straw-coloured periwig and a cheerful, ruddy face. I am sure he would have liked to follow his father's career at sea, but Admiral Digges determined that his only son should be a country gentleman, of exactly the sort that had always looked down on the Admiral himself. That's why he bought the estate. That's why he did not discourage a marriage into the family of the former owners of the house. I suspect that Sir Robert Digges hated the old gentry and longed to join them in equal measure.

'What he bought from the Cavendishes was a ruin,' Digby continues, 'scarcely habitable. Of course, the old house had been badly damaged during the siege of Eastwold. Cromwell's troops never left more of a Royalist mansion standing than they had to. The comfortable, well-built residence of a supporter of the King enraged them almost as much as a stained-glass window in a church. My father wanted to knock down all that remained and start again but my mother persuaded him to keep the monks' dining hall and the cloisters. Some people now admire these broken stones of barbarous ages past. My father did not and I do not myself, but they are becoming fashionable, I'm told. Well, 'tis done now and there's an end on it, Sir John. Can I refill your glass?'

I hesitate for a moment and find my glass has been replenished generously. Digby is an obliging and enthusiastic host and visitors here are rare.

'I think that the ruins of past ages are beautiful,' says Silvia Digges suddenly. 'All of them. As for Cromwell and his vile minions – it is a pity that some people know only how to destroy and not how to build.' She is a slight young woman, very pale and dark haired. Two of her would scarcely weigh as much as her husband. This is the only thing that she has said this evening, other than to agree politely with Digby or to plead with us earnestly to eat more. She is dressed in midnight blue, which in this candlelight seems almost black. A long rope of very small pearls is looped three times round her neck and hangs down languidly over her chest. Nothing suggests that she is competing in any way for our attention, but her porcelain fragility demands it nevertheless.

Digby smiles at her approvingly and nods. 'Silvia has excellent judgment, Sir John,' he says. 'I fear that I do not appreciate the finer things in life as she does. Nor, I think, did my late father, in spite of his many other virtues. But I am proud to say Silvia has learning and good taste enough for us both.'

'My husband says much the same about me,' says Aminta, 'though he often needs prompting to do so.'

'You do have excellent taste and judgment,' I say. 'I have never disputed that.'

'Thank you, John,' says Aminta. 'And, if I thought for one moment that you knew what taste and judgment were, I would take that as a great compliment. But your father certainly created a beautiful house, Mister Digges – I mean the new parts of it as well as the old.'

Digby laughs. 'Oh, that was my mother too,' he says. 'In my father's absence, she dealt with everything – ancient and modern. Sadly she died almost as soon as the work was completed. She never lived to see the house as it is now – warm, happy, comfortable.'

'I'm sorry,' I say. 'It would have been a privilege to have met her. Like your wife, she clearly had good taste in abundance. What was her name?'

'Venetia,' says Digby. 'I think it sounds rather aristocratic. I was little more than a child when she died, of course.'

'You must miss her terribly,' says Aminta.

'I have done so most of my life,' says Digby. 'Or that's the way it seems. A mother snatched from me and a father who always seemed to be away at sea.'

'So who brought you up?' she asks.

'My uncle and aunt a great deal of the time. They live not far from here – they have a farm a little inland, less than half an hour's drive in a coach. My family have always lived in Suffolk – though not in Eastwold until my father bought this house. But, like my mother, he did not live to fulfil his dreams – I mean becoming the Member of Parliament for Eastwold. He saw it as a duty incumbent on him as the biggest landowner in the area, and also as a great honour.'

'Even though Eastwold no longer exists for all practical purposes?' says Aminta.

'Oh, but it does,' says Digby. 'It has a legal existence that is as real as anywhere in the country. It has a Mayor and a Recorder and a Sergeant of the Mace and a Water Bailiff and a First Freeman. Somewhere, on the seabed admittedly, it has a Guildhall. And under the water too are many stately mansions, which may still be bought and sold, because possession of a freehold within the walls of the town is necessary to be a burgess. Eastwold, you see, has a charter from King John that gives it the status of a borough in perpetuity. If such rights, bought with newly minted gold from a King who badly needed money, could be revoked arbitrarily by his successors, what value would any city's charter have? True, a charter may be forfeited if a borough fails in its obligations to the King. But we have not done so. That Eastwold has vanished under the sea is not its fault. Not in any way. There is no reason why the burgesses should be punished for an act of God.'

'But nevertheless it cannot require two Members of Parliament,' says Aminta. 'There is nothing of any value to represent.'

'The charter doesn't specify that there should be evidence of need in order for Eastwold to retain its status as a borough or its representation in Parliament. It is true that there are large towns now without any Members of Parliament, but that has no bearing on our charter. Let Birmingham serve the King as well as we have over the centuries if it wishes to be represented at Westminster as we are. In any case, what would be the merit of making all constituencies the same? If all boroughs had many electors to bribe, only the richest men would ever be able to afford to stand. Once, it is true, the burgesses of towns and cities would go cap in hand to a worthy candidate and beg that he should do them the signal favour of representing them in Parliament. Boroughs would even pay towards a member's expenses, since the King does not, and give him a horse on which to ride to Westminster. But it is not so now. After the Restoration, men saw how many decisions were to be made by Parliament – who might be excused punishment for supporting Cromwell, who might be ejected from office, who should and should not be compensated for their losses during the late wars. Suddenly gentlemen started approaching both boroughs and counties and to bid for the support of their electors. Thousands of Pounds are now distributed routinely for beer and beef for the voters or for a new dry dock or a town hall for the general good. A dry dock is not cheap, my lady. Would you have only London goldsmiths and bankers able to become MPs?'

'And the burgesses of Eastwold will give their votes freely to a worthy man, regardless of how little is in his purse?' she asks.

'We are not one of those boroughs controlled by a single landowner who will forgo payment of any sort to assist a talented young man,' says Digby, 'but we are cheap by today's standards, if not by yesterday's. When Larter and Paston were first elected in 1660, they entertained the burgesses after the event, down on the beach, as was customary – a roast ox, a basket or two of loaves, a cask of ale, a few dozen bottles of wine. No more than that. But in the last ten years prices have risen in the market. Now Paston has bought his way, fairly and openly, into the House of Lords and there is a by-election to fill his place, the burgesses of Eastwold will want more substantial compensation for their brief visit to the hustings. And my father would not have been unwilling to pay as a gentleman should.'

'Is that not wrong?' Aminta asks. 'To buy votes like so many eggs or pounds of salted butter?'

'Wrong in what way? Who loses from it? The electors are satisfied. The successful candidate is satisfied. A town with so few voters troubles Parliament little. It has no possible objection to new laws banning the import of Irish cattle or to restrictions on Catholics, of which it has none. Larter and Paston have, with minimal effort, made sure that no act of Parliament has been passed that in any way inconveniences Eastwold – either the part above water or the part below. Few Members can claim such success.'

'You will not stand, now your father cannot do so?'

'Against my own father in law?'

'He still intends to be a candidate?'

Digby looks slightly embarrassed. 'Of course. Why not? His candidature was never a matter of self-interest or animosity toward the Admiral. He believes, as an article of faith, that Parliament must persuade the King to remember the old Cavaliers – not just his family, but all of them. So, if I did choose to stand in my father's place, it would be a matter of a Pound from one side of the family cancelling out a Pound from the other. But the Admiralty always wants a candidate with some knowledge of naval affairs. They will send another man of their own. I would have served in the Navy had I been permitted to do so, but my father, wisely I'm sure, declined to use his influence to gain me a commission. He saw my future differently. Perhaps my son – if we are ever blessed with a child – will continue the family tradition at sea.'

Silvia gives us a very thin smile. The subject of children is perhaps an awkward one. I try to recall how long they had been married. A year? Two? Not long. She reaches out and takes Digby's hand. 'It pains me that neither of your parents lived to see their grandchildren,' she said.

'I wish my mother had done so,' Digby says. 'I am not sure that it troubled my father. He preferred the sea to his family in all respects.'

He smiles to indicate that his father did in fact prefer his wife and son in some ways that he cannot now describe. I am not in a position to contradict him. Admiral Digges was famous for flogging the seamen who served under him – everyone spoke of it in tones of hushed awe. His home life was less well documented.

In the thoughtful silence that follows, I ask: 'How did your mother die, Mister Digges?'

'She drowned. As my father did. Her body was discovered on the seashore, almost exactly where he later kept his boat.'

'It is terrible to lose a mother in a tragic accident of that sort,' says Aminta.

'It was tragic, but it wasn't an accident,' says Digby bitterly.

'Really?' I say.

'She was murdered,' says Silvia to nobody in particular. 'My uncle murdered her.'

Chapter 3

Beneath a crumbling cliff

Today, nobody is suggesting I may be responsible for the weather. The sky has cleared. A warm sun shines, both on the wide, rippling, early morning beach and on the soft, sandy cliffs that rise forty feet above our heads. I offer my arm to Aminta as she gathers up her skirt and petticoats and steps lightly over a slab of somebody's house, an irregular mass of buff-coloured brick, stubbornly held together by mortar. A little further off is a sea-washed square of stone, bearing the date 1542 and some initials, now illegible but still lovingly intertwined.

'Houses fall from above all the time,' says Digby, shaking his head at their carelessness. 'Yesterday's rain will have weakened the cliff and brought down a little more of that one. It won't last much longer.' He looks up. 'Then, after that, it will be David Larter's house next, I think. He's the nephew of Solomon Larter – the other Member of Parliament. Only a few feet now separate his front door and the cliff edge.

The sea is sadly no respecter of rank, Sir John. It attacks the dwellings of common fishermen and of gentlemen with Cambridge degrees. At least it does in these parts. I know of nowhere else in the country where the ocean takes such voracious bites out of the land and returns the next day with an unsatiated appetite.'

'How much land has been lost over the years?' I ask.

'Who can tell? Who can possibly tell? The position of the coastline in King John's time is a matter of pure conjecture. Nobody living now knows where it was and the sea has taken many of our records as well as our land. The church of St James lies almost half a mile out there, so they tell us. You've heard the stories of the ghostly congregation? The skeletons with prayer books in their hands?'

'Yes. And the phantom bells,' says Aminta.

'They say the ringing of the bells presages a death,' says Digby. 'I've never heard them myself, but others, more fanciful than I, have done so. And if I ever do hear them, it will not trouble me. Not at all. War, old age and disease kill. Ghosts do not.'

'Isn't that a skull over there, by the way?' asks Aminta.

Digby looks down the beach to where a round object of surprising whiteness lies half buried in the fine, golden sand. He smiles. 'I imagine so. They are not uncommon on this shore. As the sea drives into the churchyard, it exposes one grave after another, high above us on the cliffs. If the coffin cannot be rescued in time, or nobody cares to do so, then our fellow parishioners fall onto the beach, like their houses, little by little, a bone or two at a time.'

'Perhaps we should inform the churchwarden?' I say. 'He could rescue and reinter that reminder of our mortality.'

'Churchwarden? There isn't one at present. He died a few weeks ago.'

I raise my eyebrows.

'No, not another drowning,' says Digby with a grim laugh. 'He died of a fever. As it happened, I was with him when he passed away. I hope I was able to give him some comfort as he breathed his last. Edward Catch, his name was. He lived in a tiny cottage near the church – one room, warmed by an open fire in the centre of the floor, and the smoke rising through the roof. But that was all he required – his earthly possessions scarcely fitted into a small oak chest. He must have been somewhere between sixty and eighty. People are careless about their ages here. He said he could remember Queen Elizabeth's time, but people here also like to tell a good story, so that is not to be relied on. Still, at the moment of death, a man will usually speak the truth, wouldn't you say? *Nemo moriturus praesumitur mentire.*'

He looks at me, as if anxious for confirmation, in Latin or English, as I prefer.

'I've seen men die,' I say, 'but most of the time they didn't get a chance to say anything of significance.'

'My husband formerly worked for Lord Arlington,' says my wife. 'He was a spy. Men often died quite suddenly in his presence.'

'Arlington never called my work spying,' I say.

'But that's what you did?' asks Digby. There is a note of respect in his voice that I have never noticed in Arlington's.

'Yes, I suppose it was. When I had time.'

'Arlington is the one person I am certain will contradict your maxim and expire with an untruth on his lips,' says Aminta. 'He will serve the King with his dying breath. Unless he has changed his allegiance in the meantime.'

'In any case,' I say to Digby, 'I have given up that line of work completely, just as I have my more profitable London legal practice. I am now merely a country gentleman and a Justice of the Peace.'

I pause, wondering if Digby, a country gentleman and Justice of the Peace, will bridle at the word 'merely'. But he just nods. Either he does not take offence easily or he holds the position in no greater esteem than I do. I think he would prefer to be commanding even the smallest of His Majesty's frigates, sailing nimbly between palm-fringed islands, offering his men kindly encouragement or gentle reprimands.

'Yes, of course,' says Digby with a sigh. 'I truly envy you the adventures you must have had in Lord Arlington's service. But how do you propose to go about your more prosaic investigations here? I mean, we have a Coroner's verdict. That is usually sufficient, if the jury comes down in favour of accidental death. What reason did the Sheriff give for wanting to reopen the matter?'

'The Sheriff's letter was brief, and his messenger was unwilling or unable to elaborate on it. I must assume that the jury's verdict left open the possibility that there might have been foul play?'

'I was there at the inquest. I do not recall anything of the sort. The verdict was accidental drowning. It was perfectly clear and left no room for doubt. None at all.'

'Then I cannot say what can have caused disquiet, other than your father's elevated position as an Admiral and parliamentary candidate.'

'It is an unusual request for the Sheriff to have made.'

'Indeed,' I say.

'Unprecedented, in my admittedly limited experience.'

'And in mine,' I say.

'A slur on the judgment of our hard-working Coroner.'

'I doubt the Sheriff meant it as such.'

'No? Well, I have no wish to tell you how to conduct your business, Sir John, but I am certain that the Sheriff did not intend that you should spend long here, when the matter has already been investigated by the proper authorities. I have no objection on my own part, of course, but I am anxious that we are wasting your time.'

'His time is less valuable than you might imagine,' says Aminta, 'but he had very much hoped to be setting out for London shortly. He deserves a visit to town and I am reassured that you wish to delay him as little as possible.'

'Much though Silvia and I enjoy your company, I shall do everything in my power to ensure you both get to London as soon as you can.'

'That is kind of you, Mister Digges,' I say. 'Having talked to you, I must admit I am puzzled as to exactly what the Sheriff expects of me. Perhaps there has been a simple misunderstanding as to the Coroner's meaning. If so, I'm sure I can clear things up quite quickly and be on my way. I shall talk to the Coroner, of course, and also to any witnesses, if that seems necessary. That much cannot be avoided. Then I shall write a report for the Sheriff, containing sufficient legal Latin for him to believe my conclusions must be true. After which, Aminta and I shall travel back to Essex and onwards to London as we both intended. Where will I find the Coroner?'

Digby looks upwards. 'The Coroner is David Larter, the nephew of the Member of Parliament. I have pointed out his house to you. But he is away from town at present, dealing with a case a few miles inland.'

'That is inconvenient.'

'I hope he will be back before you have to leave us. But he would be able to tell you little that I cannot tell you myself – indeed I was the main witness at the inquest. The evidence I gave was very straightforward: on the evening of his death, my father informed me that he had a mind to take his sailing boat out – though he had retired from the Navy, he liked to remind himself of the feel of the waves beneath him. It was a simple craft, constructed to his own plans, easy enough to launch, easy to sail single-handed if you are strong enough, though it would carry two men if needed. It was late in the day when he set off, just at the turn of the tide. We waited for his return, getting more and more anxious. At some point, upon my wife's prompting, I went down to the beach, but I did not see him there, though I walked a considerable distance. The boat was found beached a mile or so down the coast the next morning. My father's body was brought in by two fishermen a few days later, minus periwig, gold snuffbox and every item of value he usually had about him. He was taken to the church, where he lay until he could be properly identified by me.'

'Thank you. That is admirably clear. But are you implying that the fishermen robbed his body?'

'I do not begrudge them a fee for bringing my father home to rest. The loss of a trinket or two was nothing in comparison to the loss of a father.'

'I could make enquiries,' I say. 'I am sure that the items could be identified if they have been sold on.'

Digby waves a large, soft hand to decline my offer to have some fishermen hanged. 'No, no. Let us be charitable and believe their story that they took nothing. In any case, I wish to bring matters to completion, not start some new hare running.

I shall of course give you every cooperation in your work. But, as an especial favour to me and to my wife, I should prefer all to be concluded as soon as possible. My father was well liked in the town. He would have made a very popular Member of Parliament. I cannot conceive that anyone would have wished him ill. But ... you see ... it must have occurred to you that, if people start to call it murder, then my father-in-law will be blamed. My father deprived him of his estate and looked set to deprive him of what he sees as his rightful place in Parliament. I do not believe for one moment that Jacob Cavendish did kill him – our families are now joined by marriage, after all. But it would be forgivable if some of the town thought like that, do you understand me? I want suspicion to hang over Jacob for as short a time as possible. For Silvia's sake. She has suffered enough. I mean, her uncle and my mother ...'

'Of course,' I say.

'This is the second strange death in the family,' Digby continues, 'and the first still hangs heavy on my wife. This is no novelty, to be drawn out and savoured.'

'Indeed,' I say.

'That it was your wife's uncle who killed your mother must have been horrible for both of you,' says Aminta.

'My mother and Isaac Cavendish were very close – unwisely close, I'm told, though I was too young then to form a judgment myself. And my father was away at sea at the time a great deal. My mother was a beautiful woman and I think she increasingly regretted marrying ... well, a coarse sailor ... I cannot deny that is what my father was. For all his other virtues, obviously. Good hearted – everyone agrees that – but, even on land, he never forgot that he was a ship's Captain and he expected to be obeyed as he was at sea. He meant no harm – it was just his way.'

'I am sure your mother took it well,' says Aminta.

Digby looks at her uncertainly, swallows hard and continues: 'Isaac Cavendish had been the owner of the manor house, but had suffered a cruel reversal of fortune during the war. You must understand that this part of the country had been solidly for Parliament all through the conflict. But Eastwold, with its royal charter, was a small pocket of support for the monarch, led by the Cavendishes. Parliament eventually sent Oliver Cromwell, then merely a captain, to bring Eastwold under control with a couple of cannons and a troop of horse. It won't surprise you to learn that Eastwold could muster scarcely a dozen men armed with eight muskets between them. It wasn't the longest or most glorious of sieges. By the time the town and the manor house had been taken, two of the defenders had been killed and another two slightly wounded. None of the attackers suffered so much as a scratch. Afterwards there was little sympathy for Isaac Cavendish, who had led them into the folly of opposing the good Captain Cromwell. Informers sent word to London of his continuing support for the King and he was fined, as so many were, ultimately to his utter ruin.

'For my mother, though, he seemed a romantic figure. Brave. Loyal. Well read. Handsome. Doomed. She would slip away to walk with him on the shore or the heath. And so on.' Digby smiles apologetically for the behaviour of his mother a dozen years ago. 'Then, the day before my father was due to return from his latest campaign, she was found dead on the beach. Actually he returned almost a week later, but the fact that Isaac and my mother would have *believed* that evening was their last chance to flee together was later held to be significant. It was assumed that he had asked my mother to run away with him before her husband returned, that she had refused and that he had killed her in a jealous rage. The Coroner had no doubt that something of the sort had occurred, especially since Isaac chose to leave the town the very same night. A warrant was issued for his arrest. The ports were doubtless watched. But he was never heard from again. It's likely he went to the King's Court in exile in Brussels, as so many Cavaliers did, and died there.'

'I am sorry,' I say.

'But you see the problem, Sir John?' says Digby. 'I now have a father and mother discovered drowned scarcely half a mile from each other. I thought the inquest, painful though it was, had cleared up the matter of my father's death. What I don't want is week after week of needless speculation that another Digges has died at the hands of another Cavendish. I should like to shield my father-in-law, if I can – not from justice but from false accusations that would cling to him for ever, regardless of actual evidence.'

'Yes,' I say. 'I can see that. But, if the Coroner recorded no reservations, then somebody who was at the inquest must have chosen to write to London in order to cast unwarranted doubts on the verdict. Do you have any idea who might have done that or why?'

'None at all,' says Digby. 'Nobody could have believed that it was anything but an accident. My father was loved by everyone here.'

I look at Digby to see if he really believes what he has just said. Yes, I think he does. But somebody else here thinks murder is more likely.

'Yes, of course,' I say.

The three of us turn and watch the waves crashing against the shore. The sea has crept a little closer since Mistress Digges' body was found on the beach, and will creep closer still before my work is done. That is one thing I can be certain of.

We climb back up a steep path that brings us out by St Peter's church. It is built out of hard, shiny, black flint, with windows and doorframes in sandstone. The nave is low and the tower unimpressive, but it was one of the lesser churches of Eastwold in its better days. At least twenty larger churches, dedicated to other saints, now lie out of sight beneath the water, together with the old Guildhall and market square, the warehouses and quays, the grand and still marketable houses of the burgesses and the forgotten hovels of the poor. The Church of St Peter, patron saint of fishermen, walled with plentiful flint and roofed with a great weight of lead, is simply, by pure chance, the last to survive.

'The churchyard is much reduced from what it was,' says Digby. 'You will see that one corner of the church already stands right at the edge of the cliff. Another five years – maybe less – and the rose window and the altar will be in the sea. Small pebbles of red and blue and yellow glass will appear on the beaches of Essex, to the wonder of those who live there. Five years more and the tower will start to collapse. But, for the moment, I think it is a pretty little church, is it not? Well, there is a pleasant walk back to the manor through the heather, just beyond the gate. Shall we go that way?'

'I should speak to the vicar about your father's death,' I say. 'I'd have preferred to talk to the Coroner first but, in his absence, the vicar, to whom your father's body was first taken, may have some light to shed on why anyone would object to the jury's verdict. You and Aminta can return together. I shall find the vicarage and rejoin you as soon as I am able.'

'I can accompany you, if you wish, Sir John. I could introduce you to him. If it would help you in any way.'

'If I am to maintain some sort of independence in my investigations – or at least the superficial appearance of it – I should go alone,' I say.

For a moment Digby's duties as a host seem to wrestle with those as a magistrate. I think he may be about to insist that he comes with me, but the procedural arguments eventually win the day. 'Very well, Sir John,' he says a little reluctantly. 'It is entirely as you please. He's called George Wraith. The vicarage is also just beyond the churchyard and on our route home. I suppose we can walk with you that far without influencing you unduly?'

'I am sure we can arrive together at the vicar's garden gate with my magisterial integrity intact,' I say. 'I doubt that I shall learn much from your vicar, but I can at least alert him to the presence of one of his flock, half buried in the sand. He may wish to do something himself, in the absence of a churchwarden.'

The vicarage is also built of flint but this time roofed with faded orange-brown tile – a neat little house and a garden in front that is full of daffodils.

George Wraith looks up as I am shown into his sitting room by his maid. His face is thin and his skin almost like parchment. His hair is white and wispy. He stretches out a bony hand, more in defence than welcome.

'You are . . . ?'

'John Grey,' I say.

'Ah, Sir John – the magistrate sent unto us from out of the rich and famous county of Essex.'

'Indeed. From Essex, as you say. I don't need to take up much of your time, Vicar.'

'As much as you wish, Sir John. I am completely at your service. Young Mister Digges has already informed me of who you are and what it is that you have to do. But I can tell you little about the death of Admiral Digges. As for his life, he was a cruel man, Sir John. He studied cruelty as others study natural philosophy or the gospels. A veritable Doctor of Cruelty. Loyal to the King, I suppose, but hated by everyone else.'

'By everyone? His son implied otherwise.'

George Wraith pulls a face and considers this. 'You have met somebody who liked him? Since you were come hither, has anyone said a kind word about him?'

'I have really spoken only to young Digby,' I say. 'He would naturally be prejudiced in favour of his father.'

'Prejudiced certainly, but surely not blind to his failings? How could he be? Does he not have eyes as other men? Does he not have ears? The Admiral was the most hated man in Suffolk, Sir John. Perhaps also elsewhere, but I cannot speak for Norfolk or Lincolnshire. Never been there, you see. Nor Essex. All sorts of monstrous cruelties may be practised in Essex. You would know better than I do. But I was brought up here. Entirely on this piece of shitty, crumbling coast.'

'There is cruelty everywhere,' I say. 'I have certainly seen it in my native village, much to my shame.'

He looks startled, as if I have outmanoeuvred him by the clever trick of being born somewhere. 'Of course, I did not mean to disparage your own county,' he says. 'I simply tell you what I have been told by others. Forgive me. I forget why I mentioned it.' He picks up a quill pen and studies it, as if a feather will aid his memory.

'I'm told the Admiral liked to sail a small boat from time to time,' I say.

He turns suddenly. 'Yes. Yes, that is true. I would've thought it nothing like the ships he was used to – so much smaller and with no great brass cannons to rip out men's guts and splatter them over the deck. But there you are. We must make do with what God gives us. And it was all he had, after he was dismissed from the Navy.'

'Dismissed?'

'The Admiralty now wants gentlemen of good lineage, not old tarpaulins from Cromwell's time.'

'But they still want men who can defeat the Dutch.'

'He won victories, of course – but at what cost? I ask you, Sir John, at what cost? Look out to sea, if you please. Look out there. How many of his sailors lie under those gentle, foam-flecked waves? Too many. Far too many. They do not rest in peace, Sir John. No comforting words were said to them as they slipped beneath the surface, many without their arms or legs or heads. They died troubled, for want of limbs. They could not raise their hands in prayer. They could make no confession. Their drowned ghosts must drift for ever across the surface of the water like sea mist. Who shall pray for them? *Dona eis requiem sempiternam.* But I do not even know by what names to call them in order to summon up their souls from the worm-riddled mud.'

Wraith looks at the pen in his hand. He has just snapped it in two. He can't remember doing that.

'If Digges was so hated,' I say, 'hated contrary to what his son clearly believes, could somebody here have killed him?'

'Is that what they think in London?'

'I have no idea what they think in London – only that

the Sheriff asked me to come here, for reasons I do not yet understand.'

'I see. How inconvenient for you.' He puts his head on one side and smiles.

'You say that many of his sailors died unnecessary deaths? Could he have been killed in revenge for that? Do any of his former crew live here?'

'James Tutepenny does. He's a fisherman and a decent honest man. And then, conversely, there is Ezekiel Benefice, the innkeeper. He lost a leg fighting under the Admiral's command.'

'And Benefice resents the loss?'

'Perhaps. He has another leg, of course. But I think he would have preferred to have two.'

'Tell me about Benefice,' I say.

'As I say, he runs the inn. He has almost no customers, because there are so few of us now. But he makes up for that by smuggling. I think Admiral Digges may not have approved greatly of smuggling. Many naval men do not.'

'Digges took a boat out the night he died. Could he have been murdered trying to prevent Benefice landing a cargo?'

'Admiral Digges believed himself capable of most things,' says Wraith. 'That he should single-handedly intercept a gang of smugglers in a small boat – yes, he might think he could do that. Ha! Vanity of vanities, saith the preacher. All is vanity.'

'Thank you. I shall speak to Benefice, and see what he knows. By the way, when we were on the beach earlier, we saw a human skull that had fallen from the cliff.'

'Yes, they do that all the time. The churchwarden would sometimes make a collection and take them down to the crypt. He would pile them in a heap like cannon balls. He liked doing that, I think. He had little else to do, the churchyard growing smaller and smaller all the time and each day growing longer and longer for him. Sometimes the sea would take the bones before he could. Sometimes he would snatch them from the ebbing tide. Edward Catch and the ocean divided the spoils quite happily. Neither grudged the other their proper share.'

'I was sorry to hear he had died.'

'Poor Catch. A fever. They are common on this coast. We buried him just outside the churchyard.'

'*Outside*? You buried your churchwarden outside the churchyard? Surely that is for they who die beyond hope of salvation?'

'So he is,' said the vicar. 'So he is. Utterly beyond hope. He must be in Hell by now. I don't know exactly how long it takes to get there, but less time than it takes to get to London, I would imagine.'

'Mister Digges was with Catch when he died,' I say. 'That was a charitable act. I hope he was able to offer Catch some comfort, whatever his sins may have been.'

'You think so?'

'You do not?'

'Digges has not come to church since we buried his father.'

'But that is not long. He can scarcely have missed three Sundays.'

'He will not be back,' says the vicar. 'Not young Digges. Not until we bury him. Then he will come. He will have nowhere else to go but into the ground. Is there anything else I can do for you, Sir John?'

'No,' I say. 'No, you have been very helpful.'

'Have I? Then I must apologise. That was not my intention. You'll find your own way out? Thank you, Sir John. I'd be grateful if you would shut the door as you leave. The sunshine is bright out there but, inside, it is still as cold and bleak as Heaven.'

From my Lady Grey's most excellent poem,
The Election

On Suffolk's low and sandy shore,
There was a town in days of yore
Whose walls encircled many a dwelling,
With wharves to which sleek ships came sailing,
Loaded down with silks and satins,
Wine and brandy bottles that inns
Needed for the population
Of Eastwold Town, toast of the nation.
Though no one there gave half a fart for
Bad King John, he sent a Charter
To that town. He acted rashly?
No! He needed all the cash he
Reasonably could stash away
For kings have many bills to pay.
Thus when, at length, a Parliament
Was called and first the country sent
Its envoys to Westminster Hall
(For reasons not yet clear to all)
How many of that motley crew
Sent Eastwold? Why, no less than two!

Chapter 4

At the only inn in the town

The inn too sits on a cliff top, though that was not the intention of its builders. Once it was far inland. On a calm day in the distant and mostly forgotten reign of Henry III, you might not have known you were in a coastal town at all. Like St Peter's church, it was not made to be the grandest of its kind in town, but now it is the only example to be found. You drink here or you drink at home. The other inns – larger, cleaner, busier, serving better ale – have all crumbled away, and there would be no trade for them if they were still here. Their customers have gone with the land they lived on. The last inn in Eastwold is meanly constructed of slabs of wattle and daub with thin, grey, cracked timbers in the interstices. The ragged bundles of reeds with which it is thatched are black with grime, and streaked bright green with damp moss, but there is no point in replacing the roof when the supporting walls may soon fall into the sea. A fire burns petulantly in the grate, sending out more smoke than heat. At this time in the morning nobody is drinking at either of the greasy tables, but there is a sour smell in the air, of beer spilt copiously in good company. A man hobbles out from a back room. He is short, his face is weather-beaten, his long hair is grizzled and tied back, and he has only half the legs he was born with. A wooden peg and a crutch supply the deficit.

'You are Ezekiel Benefice?' I ask.

'I might be. On the other hand, I might be the Grand Sophy of Persia.'

'Might you? You're a long way from home then.'

He does not smile. 'Do you want beer?'

'No,' I say.

'Well, we serve nothing else, so piss off.' He turns slowly, manoeuvring peg and crutch in jerky stages.

'My name is John Grey,' I say. 'I'm the magistrate charged with investigating the death of Admiral Digges.'

Benefice reverses his previous turn, the crutch sounding angrily on the floorboards. He's in no hurry. It's not as if he has dozens of customers shouting orders at him. And I don't think keeping me waiting distresses him in any way whatsoever.

'A magistrate? Are you now?' he says. 'And do you think I have any reason to love magistrates?'

'Probably not,' I say. 'But you are obliged to answer my questions anyway.'

'How do you plan to make me do that?'

'I can if necessary get the constable to arrest you,' I say.

'And lock me up where exactly? The jail went under the sea in 1590.'

There's no point in asking who the constable is. With so few inhabitants, they've probably not appointed one for years. Unless Benefice is the constable, of course. That's more than likely. He'd find it convenient to combine the roles of constable and smuggler.

'I take it you didn't like Digges, then?' I say.

'Nobody liked Digges,' he says.

'He disapproved of your activities?' I say.

'Which activities are those?'

'Smuggling.'

'Who says I smuggle?'

'The vicar. I hope it's true. I might need some brandy.'

He laughs. 'I thought so. You're gentry, and gentlemen who come here don't usually drink my beer.'

'How much for a bottle?'

He looks me up and down, taking in my new red velvet coat and red velvet breeches, my gold pocket watch and beaver hat. He pauses for a long time over the hat.

'To you, my good sir, the very reasonable price of one Shilling.'

'I can buy it for less than that in London, duty paid.'

'You can't here though. If you want it before you get back to London, it's a Shilling. If you'd like to pay the duty, then I'm sure you can give it to the King when you next see him.'

I take out a silver coin and hold it between my fingers. He reaches for it, but I keep it just beyond the ends of his fingers. He doesn't want to overbalance on his crutch trying to grab it. He's not planning to lose his dignity for twelve measly pence. 'So, did Admiral Digges try to stop smuggling here?' I ask.

'Of course he did. Navy man. Harsh with smugglers, he was. But not as clever as he thought. And he didn't know the coast as well as some of us.'

'So others smuggle here too?'

'You'll have to ask them,' he says. 'But you won't get the brandy cheaper elsewhere. We all charge the same.'

'You lost the leg at sea?' I ask.

Just for a moment I expect him to deny having lost a leg at all, just in case the knowledge of his past helps me in any way.

'Serving under Digges,' he says eventually. 'Fighting against the Dutch. Back in '53. Not that he ever recognised any of his seamen – not once we were on dry land. There's me and James Tutepenny in this town served him and served him well. Especially Tutepenny, who was with him much longer. But we might as well have signed up and served with the Devil for all the difference it made. Actually, we should have both gone over to the Dutch while we could – better commanders, better pay, better food. They recruited all the way along this coast during the last war. Lots signed up with them. But I'd lost my leg well before that – you need at least two legs or the Dutch won't even look at you. So, to cut a long story short, we both ended up back in Eastwold, with Bloody Digges also home and interfering in everything that's happening. If you can't let one of your old crew – a man who lost his best limb for you – do a bit of smuggling, it's a pretty poor world.'

'Indeed it is,' I say. 'So, if I was looking for a man who might have wished to murder Admiral Digges, where should I go?'

Benefice shows no more surprise than the vicar did at the suggestion that Digges may not have drowned accidentally.

'Go anywhere you like. The whole town would have murdered him if they had the chance on a foggy evening.'

'Including you?'

'Yes, of course including me. But as it happens, I didn't. And if I had, you'd never get a witness round here to say he saw me do it. Now, do you want that brandy or not? My leg aches with all this standing.'

'Me too,' I say.

Benefice looks at me suspiciously.

'Leg wound,' I say. 'It still troubles me after I've been travelling or in wet weather.'

'You got it at sea?'

'No,' I say.

He sneers at a landsman's wound and hobbles into the back room to fetch a bottle. He returns, faster than I might have expected, with a black bottle, sealed with a dirty rag.

I hand him the Shilling. 'It's French brandy, I take it?'

'Who told you that?'

'So, it's not?'

'It's a bit like French brandy.'

'Really?'

'No, not really. Do you still want it?' He pockets the coin to be safe.

'Keep the Shilling,' I say. 'When you get good French brandy at sixpence a bottle – or if you hear anything that I might find useful – let me know.'

He grins and nods.

Then I add: 'Who found the admiral's boat, by the way?'

'I did,' says Benefice. 'I was out one morning and spotted it beached not far from here. Cast up on the shore by the tide as far as I could tell. Six inches of water at the bottom of the boat, but the Admiral nowhere to be seen. Got help relaunching it, but I reckon I could have done it even with one leg. Nicely built, that boat is. Sailed it back down the coast. Handles nice too. Very nice. Mister Digby gave me ten Shillings for returning it. You got any problems with that?'

'No,' I say. 'Compared with others here, I have surprisingly few problems of any kind.'

* * *

'They all smuggle,' says Digby. 'Every one of them. Except perhaps Larter, now he's a Member of Parliament. Oh, and the vicar – he's getting too old. I suppose as magistrate I should do something about it. What do you think?'

'You could ask them to smuggle real French brandy,' I say. 'And to charge less. A Shilling is expensive for a bottle of something that may poison you.'

Digby nods and smiles with relief. I think that there are few of his duties as a Justice that he really enjoys. I can't imagine him sentencing anyone to more than an easily affordable fine.

'So Benefice fought under your father, Mister Digges?' Aminta asks.

'Yes. And Tutepenny. In the old days this town would have supplied hundreds of sailors for the fleet. But I think the two you name are now the only men of this town to have served the King – or Parliament – at sea.'

'Benefice seemed to believe that past service entitled him to smuggle whatever took his fancy,' I say. 'I doubt that your father approved.'

Digby pulls a face. Perhaps he is more aware than he lets on that the Admiral was not universally popular.

'Well, as I say, it is one of the town's more profitable sources of revenue, and there is a ready market inland of here – even as far as Bury St Edmunds and Thetford. Of course, elections now bring in a certain amount of money.'

'Is Benefice an elector? I suppose he would have voted in the Navy's interest if he is.'

Digby looks uncomfortable. 'Oh yes, he's an elector, but I doubt he would have voted for my father for any sum.'

'Benefice had a curse put on him,' says Silvia.

We turn to her. She has been sitting there almost without our noticing her. Thin, pale, silent.

'Benefice put a curse on the Admiral?' I ask.

'No,' she says. 'He *had* a curse put on him. Benefice wouldn't have the power to do it himself.'

'Who does?'

'Mother Catch.'

'She is a witch?' I ask.

'Some say that,' she says. 'Most people here go to her for one thing or another.'

'And is she related to Edward Catch, the former church-warden?' I ask.

'He was her father,' says Digby. He is not happy that Silvia has told me that the churchwarden's family is engaged openly in witchcraft. Perhaps it suggests further laxity on his part. But I too am reluctant to persecute reputed witches.

'The vicar refused to bury him in the churchyard,' I say. 'Was that because of his daughter?'

'I think not,' says Digby. 'Witchcraft would not have troubled Wraith in any way. Quite the reverse.'

'I'll go and speak to Mother Catch,' I say. 'She sounds like the sort of person who may know what's going on in the town. And it may be that Benefice was even less honest with me than I thought.'

'I can come with you,' says Digby.

'No, it would be better if I go alone,' I say.

'Of course,' he says, somewhat reluctantly. 'I would not attempt to interfere with what you have to do – not in any way. You must act completely as you see fit. But I can promise you that you are wasting your time there.'

Chapter 5

In a pleasant airy dwelling

By alone, I meant with nobody else, but Aminta has another interpretation of my words.

'You may be good at interviewing Dutch spies at sword point, but I fear you might not know how to speak to Mother Catch. Your usual bluster would not do.'

'I do not bluster,' I say.

'Yes, you do.'

'No, I don't.'

'You would lose your temper.'

'I would not.'

'You are losing it now.'

'That is very true.'

'Which is why you need me as a calming influence.'

'You believe you are a calming influence?'

'I shudder to think what you would be like now if I were not here.'

'I understood you had a great deal to talk to Silvia about.

You wished to compare husbands and their uncouth Republican ways. I had thought that was not a good idea, but I have changed my mind. It would be instructive and soothing for you both.'

'I fear not, my dear John. Digby seems in no way Republican. In fact, in most ways he appears perfectly satisfactory. Silvia has already moulded him as much as he can be moulded, whereas I still have a great way to go with you.'

'I had rather hoped you had finished.'

'Sadly not. I think this must be Mother Catch's house. How pretty it is! Are those anemones and hellebores growing by the porch?'

Aminta is right. This witch's house looks much like any other, only more comfortable and with more flowers in the garden.

'Yes,' I say. 'I think that's hellebore. Very nice. Well, since you have no more pressing engagements elsewhere, let us knock and introduce ourselves.'

The interior of the house is light and airy. The window glass is clean. The cat, sunning itself on a settle, seems to be just a cat – though cats give little away.

'I had heard that you had arrived here,' says Mother Catch, ushering us into cushioned chairs by the fire. 'From Solomon Larter rather than one of my familiars. My familiars are an idle lot. Cats these days would rather sun themselves in the window than carry messages to Satan. The ghosts of the cats of King James's time must despise them.'

She smiles. We all turn to the cat, who stares us down, then slowly closes its eyes.

Mother Catch is a small neat woman, dressed in a plain grey gown with a little lace at the neck and cuffs. Her hair is enclosed in a spotless linen hood. Everything about her speaks of a modest, decent prosperity.

'I am investigating the death of Admiral Digges,' I say.

'Not a nice man,' says Mother Catch. 'I have no wish to speak ill of the dead, but many people here would've preferred it if he had not returned from the sea. I don't think he would have been happy anywhere, but especially not here. I also don't think he was in Eastwold by choice. He was made to come.'

'Really?' I say, though the vicar has told me much the same thing.

'The Duke of York had tired of his incompetence. As a captain, his rashness was commendable. He had only one ship to lose. As an admiral it was less helpful, and ships are not cheap, even if the King has sailors to spare. But that is merely what I am told by those more acquainted with the Court than I am. Do you know the Court, Sir John?'

'No more than I have to. My wife is easier there than I am. There is more of a tradition of it in her family than in my own.'

'Yes, I can see that might be the case. Can I offer you both tea? We have it now in Suffolk just as the fashionable do in London. When I first moved to this house, some years ago now, I would have offered my visitors small beer. Now people serve tea and coffee and even chocolate to please their guests. What changes we have all seen since that terrible man Oliver died! I should reassure you that what I am offering is only tea – ordinary tea – not some witches' brew. I assume that, as a magistrate, you would not approve of such things.'

'I don't believe in witchcraft,' I say. 'Nor I think does your local Justice of the Peace.'

'How very modern of you both. Some still do, though. They occasionally seek my help.'

'And you give it to them? asks Aminta.

'I have remedies against colds and agues. And bruises and broken bones.'

'And if you are asked to curse somebody?' I ask.

'Yes, of course. I'd do that. People are often much happier for knowing an enemy of theirs has been cursed. And it's very little effort. It would be unkind to refuse. Is there somebody you'd like me to curse for you, my dear? My prices are very reasonable.'

I wonder whether to propose Lord Arlington to her as a suitable recipient of a mild curse. A boil on his neck, perhaps. She's right – I think that would make me happier.

'No,' I say. 'Not at present. So, it is true then that Ezekiel Benefice asked you to curse Admiral Digges?'

'I couldn't possibly tell you that. If somebody asks me to curse a neighbour, they don't want to spend the next month worrying that I'll reveal their little secret. There would be no point in that at all. But you ask me to confirm whether it is true, suggesting that somebody has said such a thing to you? If so, that person was acting most improperly. Oh dear. I see that in trying to reassure somebody I have betrayed a confidence. But perhaps it no longer matters. After all, the Admiral is now dead. You think he was murdered, don't you, Sir John?'

'Yes, I'm beginning to think that – though not by witchcraft.'

'And you are determined to find out who killed him?'

'If he was murdered, then the perpetrator must be found and punished. That goes without saying.'

'And it hasn't occurred to you that the person who killed him may have had good reason to do so?'

'Most people who murder think they do so for a good reason. I still intend to identify them if I can.'

'That is a very bad idea indeed. You should stop now. Ask no more questions – not of me nor of Benefice nor of anyone. Stop while it is safe. Stop before going on means that you have a difficult decision to make.'

'Thank you,' I say. 'I'm sure that is good advice. I only wish I could follow it. I was very sorry, by the way, to hear of your father's death. My most sincere condolences to you.'

She nods.

'It was a fever?' I ask.

'They are common here in winter. My remedies bring comfort but in the end some people do die. Indeed, everyone dies eventually. There's a limit to what even the most unlawful witchcraft can achieve.'

'I hope you don't mind my asking, but why did the vicar not bury him in the churchyard? Was it because he believed you to be a witch? If so, I can speak to Mister Digges and ask him to intercede—'

She shakes her head. 'No, it is nothing to do with that. I attend church and take the sacrament. In any case, the vicar intends that he too should be buried outside the churchyard.'

'Really?' I ask. 'The vicar? He does not wish to be buried in hallowed ground?'

'This is a troubled place, Sir John. It is a dead town. Can you not feel that? Have you not seen the bones that litter the beach? It is a dead town that cries to be buried and forgotten. My advice to you is that you should go home as soon as you can. You have come from the world of the living. Unlike me, you can still escape back to it. Eastwold will soon have vanished beneath the waves. And the quicker that happens the better for everyone here.'

We walk back in the warm sunshine along the top of the cliffs, the low, dark-green heather brushing my woollen stockings and Aminta's skirt. Contrary to what Mother Catch has told us, everything seems remarkably alive. Below us, the blue water is calm. It is almost unnaturally still. The sea is waiting for something.

'So what are we to make of that?' says Aminta. 'Mother Catch clearly realised that it was Silvia who told us about Benefice and his request. So, Silvia must have been to visit Mother Catch as well. And whatever her problem was, Mother Catch sought to offer her reassurance.'

'Did Silvia also ask her to curse the Admiral?' I ask.

'I doubt that the subject of Benefice cursing senior naval officers simply came up by chance during a conversation about the weather. Mother Catch probably reassured Silvia that she was not alone in having problems with her father-in-law.'

'I wonder if Digby is aware of that,' I say. 'His wife calling down maledictions on his father.'

'Wives don't need to tell their husbands everything,' says Aminta.

'No,' I say. 'I suppose not.'

From my Lady Grey's most excellent poem
The Election

The Age of Silver, so we're told
Came in the wake of that of Gold,
And nowadays we have instead
An epoch that was cast in lead.
Gone heroes of that finer age,
Now lesser players strut the stage!
While towns were once prepared to pay
To send the best Westminster's way,
They now would do no more than scoff: 'It
Would suit us best to make a profit.'
And so they set about to see
Who'd gift each one of them a fee
To vote him into Parliament –
T'would pay for ale, t'would pay the rent.
So anyone with coin would serve 'em.
Got fools and rogues? They did deserve 'em!

Chapter 6

By an open window

The day is warming up. The breeze through the casement is gentle and blossom-scented.

'He's mad of course,' says Digby. 'Eastwold is all Wraith knows, apart from his time at Cambridge. This is his world, and it is being eaten away by the sea, a few yards every year. Soon even the churchyard he hoped to be buried in will be gone.'

'Mother Catch says that Wraith does not plan to be buried there at all. He will be buried with Edward Catch beyond the walls.'

'That seems a wise and practical course of action,' says Digby. 'Or his bones would be down on the sands before his flesh had rotted. Not that he has much flesh about him. He is as close to a walking skeleton as I have ever seen. A ghoul of a priest for a dead town.'

'That is a horrible thing to say about your father's friend,' says Silvia without looking up from her sewing.

'His former friend. They were less close of late than before.'

'It is still unpleasant. And I wish that you wouldn't.'

'It is still true,' says Digby cheerfully. 'And, though my education may have been deficient in other ways, I was brought up to speak the truth. Of course, the tombs inside the church will also fall one by one to the beach. Perhaps we should try to rescue some of them? My wife tells me that many of them are things of great beauty. There is a knight and his lady, in Purbeck marble, from the time of Agincourt, his ungloved hand holding hers for eternity. Quite touching really. And my mother is buried there, of course. Is that my job or the vicar's, do you think, to dismantle the tombs and monuments and move them elsewhere? I fear George Wraith will do little but wring his skeleton hands.'

The criticism is also fair enough, but sounds equally harsh coming from the normally indulgent Digby.

'You have had a disagreement with him?' I ask.

'No, not especially.'

'He says you no longer come to church.'

'I may have been a little negligent. I have been busy with the estate and my other duties. Should I fine myself for non-attendance perhaps?'

'Only if you have worshipped elsewhere as a Quaker or Catholic. I myself have never fined anyone for simply lying abed on a Sunday morning. It is a pleasant thing to do.'

'But you do fine the Quakers?'

'I have only one in my own parish. He often goes off to a neighbouring village on Sunday mornings. I have never thought to enquire what he does there. If it is to meet and pray quietly with other Quakers, I should be obliged to punish him severely. But I tell myself that he goes only to get drunk, utter foul oaths and play skittles, all of which is quite legal and has the King's full approval.'

Digby nods.

'People rarely complain that their justices of the peace are insufficiently officious,' I say. 'And His Majesty disapproves of at least half of the laws he has to pass to please Parliament.'

He nods again. 'Then I shall follow your wise counsel and be lenient on myself. But you would not expect me to condone other crimes – smuggling, for example?'

'Your father was intent on stopping smuggling?' I say.

'Yes, most certainly.'

'Even by those whom he formerly commanded?' asks Aminta. 'I mean Benefice and his friend . . .'

'Especially those he had commanded, Lady Grey. He'd have given no quarter to Benefice or James Tutepenny if he'd caught them. My father would have had the pair of them hanged without a second thought. He believed in discipline, you see. Discipline and the rule of law. He expected everyone to obey him in every respect, and woe betide those who did not and brought shame on him in the process. Have you seen the epitaph he placed on my mother's monument?'

'I haven't yet been inside the church,' I say. 'What does it say?'

But before Digby can answer we hear a horse's shoes ringing on the road outside, then a commotion at the front door.

'Whoever can that be?' asks Silvia. 'We are expecting nobody, and chance visitors are rare on this coast.'

We wait to see who the serving man will announce to us, but the new arrival bursts through the door on his own account and smiles at us, expecting a warm welcome, for that is what he knows he deserves. He is short, round faced and well dressed in a new-looking black velvet coat and breeches. His periwig is long and flowing and undoubtedly London-made. He turns to me and Aminta, removes his hat and bows.

Then he carefully replaces it and grudgingly acknowledges Mister and Mistress Digges as the current owners of the room we happen to be in.

'Well,' he says, brushing some almost-dry mud off his breeches and onto the carpet. 'I'm glad to find you all together so that we may proceed with matters as rapidly as we can. Then perhaps you would like to call for dinner, Mistress Digges. I have travelled a long way this morning and wish to eat as soon as possible. Afterwards, we must do whatever is necessary to get me elected as Member of Parliament, so that I may return promptly to London. I have no wish to remain in my new constituency for longer than I have to. It is most inconvenient that I have had to come here at all, Mister Digges. I do of course offer you my most sincere condolences, but I have to point out that your father's death is a great trouble to the King and to his brother the Duke. A great trouble, I say. I shall expect a report from you, Sir John, as soon as Mistress Digges has found me a goodly chamber in which I can put my bags. They are in the hallway with your footman, madam, awaiting your instructions.'

'Good day, Mister Pepys,' I say. 'And what do you wish me to report on?'

'Your progress. Does Arlington tell you nothing?'

'Only what I need to know. Usually, not even that.'

'Then I shall repair the holes in your understanding,' says Pepys. 'The day is warm. Shall we take a turn in the garden? If you will excuse us, Lady Grey? Mister and Mistress Digges? Thank you. Thank you, all so very much. Lead on, Sir John. You will know the way round my constituency better than I do. At least, for the moment.'

Chapter 7

In an apple orchard

'I am pleased that you were able to accept my Lord's commission, Sir John,' says Samuel Pepys as we walk through the rows of blossoming apple trees, the damp grass leaving drops of water on my clean shoes and, less inconveniently, on Pepys's dirty riding boots. But Pepys wishes to be no closer to the house than this when discussing our business.

'But it's not a commission from Arlington,' I say. 'I was asked to do this by the Sheriff of Suffolk.'

'And it did not occur to you to ask yourself why you were being asked to travel across two counties almost, when so many near-idle Suffolk magistrates were available?'

'Aminta did say that was odd.'

'And I have always admired your wife's insight into matters of state, Sir John. Often so much better than your own. We needed to ensure that Admiral Digges' death was investigated by somebody we could trust. I consulted your master Lord Arlington—'

'He is no longer my master, if he ever was. I worked for him from time to time, when my legal duties permitted. He paid me a fee for each job, when he remembered to do so. I was never his servant in any sense.'

Pepys shakes his head. These are nice distinctions that we have no time for.

'As I say, Sir John, I consulted your master, Lord Arlington. We came to the conclusion that we needed somebody who was honest, intelligent, trustworthy and reliable. As you will imagine, we were unable to come up with many candidates at the Court of His Gracious Majesty King Charles the Second. But Arlington thinks highly of you – and I of course, knowing you so well, immediately concurred that you were the perfect choice.'

He smiles as if I should be grateful.

'Thank you,' I say. 'I am, as always, delighted to be of service to His Majesty. But the job is hopefully a simple one.'

'Of course. Simple but delicate. When we first heard of Digges' death, we were greatly concerned. Soon, Parliament will be asked to vote additional funds for building capital ships for the Navy. Parliament is reluctant to spend money that it doesn't have – or rather won't have unless we greatly increase taxation – an increase that Members have assured their constituents they will oppose at all costs. We need as many Members as we can gather together who have either been elected as creatures of the Admiralty or are willing to renege on any inconvenient undertakings to their voters in exchange for knighthoods or vague promises of the King's favour. The election of Digges as a Navy man was vital.'

'But you will now stand in his place?'

'Yes. I was reluctant to put myself to the trouble and expense, but there is nobody else of sufficient ability.'

'And when will the election be held?'

'In five days' time – next Tuesday. The writs have already been issued. If no other candidate had declared himself then Cavendish would have been elected without further ado. He is a Cavalier of the old school. He wants the King to give as much money and favour as possible to distressed supporters of His Majesty's late father, King Charles the Martyr. Why? What possible use can such people be to the present King, now everyone is a Royalist again? But we do need as many ships as we can muster – new ships, not worm-eaten hulks from the '30s and '40s. The truth is that Cavendish cares nothing for the country's safety and prosperity. We could not have counted on him in any way.'

'You have five days, then, to persuade the electors that the proceeds of taxation would be best spent on frigates rather than rewarding ancient Cavaliers for past services.'

'That should not be difficult. But in order to stand – or at least in order to have a vote myself – I must have a residence here. I shall apparently need to purchase a dwelling within the town – anywhere inside the ancient walls; that the house is currently under the sea is no impediment. It does not have to be watertight.'

'Then, you having declared yourself a candidate, everyone votes?'

'Yes, at the Guildhall.'

'Even though it is also now under the sea?'

'The charter specifies that elections must take place there. The Mayor rows or sails out to a spot above the Guildhall. The voters then row out to cast their votes. Finally, the successful candidate must, by tradition, be chaired from the Guildhall.'

'In another boat?'

'I sincerely hope so. I have no plans to swim ashore.'

'Does the charter say where bribes are to be paid?' I ask.

Pepys decides to treat my question as if it might have been a serious one. 'That is a matter of custom and practice, not of law, on which I must still question young Digges. I am hoping to have to pay no more than sixty Pounds in all.'

'That would be about five Pounds for each burgess?'

'About that. It is a considerable sum of money for a poor man such as myself.'

I suspect that sixty Pounds is about the price of his lace cravat. I also suspect that his constituents may demand a little more cash from a be-wigged courtier they have never heard of. They clearly hated Digges, but he was at least one of them.

'Then all is well,' I say. 'But I still don't understand why I was asked to come here.'

'If Digges were found to have been murdered, that would create problems for us. There are so many grounds these days for challenging the results of an election, and one cannot be too careful. Just consider – the murderer might prove to be one of the burgesses. If so, he would forfeit his position and his vote. The election might have to be rerun after his trial. There might be further cunning objections from our enemies delaying the issue of new writs. It could take months or years before the elected Member could finally take his seat. And in that time, our ships might remain unbuilt. The Dutch arrange their affairs better, sir.'

'So that is why you need somebody to investigate the matter urgently? So that the election result – your election result – cannot be challenged?'

'Yes.'

'But the jury's verdict was accidental death. Surely that meets your requirements perfectly? The less you do, the better.

My investigation can make things worse for you, but not improve them.'

'I wish that were the case, Sir John. Shortly after the Admiral's death, we began to hear rumours. Rumours that the Coroner's verdict was not all it seemed.'

'In what way?'

'Nothing that you need to worry about.'

'No? It would at least be helpful to know who was spreading misinformation.'

'I am unfortunately not in a position to tell you that. The information was given in confidence. But though our informant acted with the greatest propriety, I can assure you that the rumours themselves are mere tittle-tattle: utterly base suggestions that the Coroner may have decided to cover things up. Not that there is anything to cover up, of course. But false news of that sort grows and grows unless it is checked. It might be used by our enemies – if not to overturn the result then perhaps to discredit our party in some other way. That must be thought of too. We have to be ready to scotch such lies, if they start to be unhelpful to the King.'

'It would have been good if the Sheriff had explained some of that. Or if you had written to me yourself.'

'We could not avoid involving the Sheriff. This is his domain. It would have looked odd and we wish to allay fears, not excite them. But Arlington would have told him no more than he trusted him with.'

'You or Arlington could still have written to me direct, nonetheless, explaining what was required.'

'It would have been most inappropriate to try to influence your deliberations in any way. Your investigation must be fair and independent.'

'So, without any interference on Arlington's part, I am to provide the definitive proof that the Coroner's verdict was the correct one, in spite of the damaging, and clearly persuasive, rumours about which you can tell me nothing?'

'Thank you. That would be very helpful.'

'And if I conclude that it was, after all, murder?'

'You would need to find the best way of dealing with it, so that it did not trouble the King.'

'You want me to help you cover up a murder?'

'Help me cover up a murder? Of course not. As a Member of Parliament it would be unfitting that I should do anything of the sort. You would need to take action entirely on your own authority, without involving anyone else – and certainly not me.'

'I can see why you thought it advisable to consult Lord Arlington. This is very much his area of expertise.'

'His experience in such affairs is invaluable. And this is a matter of the greatest importance. If you succeed, I am sure the King will show his usual generosity.'

Pepys does not say who might benefit from the King's potential generosity. Probably Arlington. Maybe Pepys himself. Certainly not me.

'I had thought that I had been called in merely because Digby Digges had a conflict of interest,' I say.

'So he has. If Admiral Digges was murdered, I could scarcely ask his own grieving son to cover the matter up, could I? I would not be so inconsiderate.'

'That shows great delicacy of feeling,' I say.

'I knew that you would understand,' says Pepys, patting my arm. 'Mister Digges has to be kept away from your investigation – at all costs. He cannot be expected to take the commendably detached and dispassionate approach that you will.'

'I am grateful,' I say, 'that you have expressed yourself more clearly than the Sheriff did. I shall do my best to keep Digby at arm's length, whatever his own wishes in the matter.'

Pepys frowns. 'His own wishes? I trust he has not already attempted to interfere with due process?'

'Only a little. He said that the town would wish me to avoid scandal. In particular Mister Digges seems afraid that his father-in-law, Jacob Cavendish, will be suspected, on the grounds that Digges deprived him of his house and was about to defeat him in the election.'

Pepys nods thoughtfully. 'And did Cavendish kill him?'

'I think not,' I say. 'At least, I have found no evidence so far.'

'A pity. Though vague accusations of murder would be unhelpful, proof that my opponent was a murderer would not be entirely unwelcome to me. It would save me a lot of money. Can evidence be gathered of his guilt?'

'No,' I say. 'Not if he is innocent.'

Pepys shakes his head. I am acting too much like a lawyer.

'Is it only young Digby who suspects it might be Jacob Cavendish?' he asks.

'I think so, but the town seems full of people who disliked the Admiral. Two of his former sailors live in Eastwold – Benefice and Tutepenny. They are burgesses of the town. Both resent his past treatment of them at sea and his later attempts to stop them smuggling second-rate spirits. One tried to have a curse put on him.'

'What did you say their names were?'

'Benefice and Tutepenny,' I repeat. 'You intend to speak to them?'

'Yes, of course. To solicit their votes, as burgesses, and pay them whatever I need to pay them. I must leave the question of their being murderers – or, rather, not being murderers – to you. Anyone else?'

'Based on my admittedly brief conversation with him, I think the vicar may be mad. But he had no reason to dislike the Admiral. Mistress Digges actually referred to him as the Admiral's good friend – at least in former times. I have also met the local witch – a very respectable and intelligent person, whose father was churchwarden. As a woman, she of course has no vote, unlike the illiterate fishermen and the mad vicar.'

'Could she have killed Digges?'

'I think not – by witchcraft or otherwise.'

'That too is a pity. If a woman killed him it could not invalidate the result.'

'I'm sorry to say I have no evidence against her.'

'Very well – accidental death it is then. That must be your conclusion. It is, when you think about it, much neater and less open to discussion.'

'I shall continue to speak to people, of course.'

'A thorough and independent investigation preceding your determination of accidental death is absolutely in order. Could you have spoken to everyone by tomorrow evening?'

'No.'

'But you could say in your report that you had? Nobody would know, after all.'

'No.'

'Then you will need to work as fast as you can. You really must have made up your mind that it is an accident – or, if it can be finessed, that Cavendish is the killer – by the time polling begins.' He looks at his pocket watch. 'I expect we shall be eating soon. Perhaps we should return to the house? We should rejoin Mister Digges and the ladies. I am looking forward to talking again to Lady Grey. She is a most talented writer. A beauty. A true wit. You are a fortunate man.'

I doubt that Aminta is looking forward to renewing her acquaintance with Pepys one little bit. He has always regarded women, all women, as quarry that needs only to be hunted down. Actresses, serving women, other men's wives – it is always open season for the chase. I am sure Aminta will say as little as possible to him, but will have fun at his expense when she and I are alone together.

'Of course,' I say. 'Your own wife is well, I trust?'

Pepys stops and turns to me. 'Have you not heard? No, of course, you live in Essex now. Elizabeth died, Sir John. She died at the end of last year. She was only twenty-nine. A fever. It was after our return from a tour of the Low Countries and France – a tour that I had long promised her, but put off. I thank God that we were finally able to spend those two months together, without the distraction of my work. She hung on for some weeks back in London – through the damp autumn months – some days better, more days worse. We tried every remedy that my doctor proposed – bleeding her, shaving her head, placing pigeons on her feet. I spared no expense. But it was all to no avail. And the Brooke House Committee worrying me the whole time for answers to their questions about naval procurement, and the Duke demanding that I attend upon him day and night at St James and Hampton Court.'

'I am so sorry,' I say. 'I didn't know. News travels slowly in the winter.'

'She is buried in our parish church – St Olave's. I have ensured that there is space for me to be buried beside her in the fullness of time. But I don't know what to do with her things . . . her lace collars, her slippers, the tapestry wool she bought in Brussels when we were there. So much wool that was to occupy her for so many happy and industrious months. She left no will. I don't know what to do with it all. I can't just throw it away because she might ...' He swallows hard and then for a long time he stands there, saying nothing at all, staring into the distance, blinking. I look to see what he is distracted by, but it is something that I shall never be able to see, though a long way off I think I can make out a shadow moving. He takes a handkerchief from his pocket and blows his nose on it. 'Dust,' he says. 'Dust from the road. Spring will soon be properly upon us, Sir John, and then the summer not far off. Will you take my arm? Shall we walk back to the house together? I should like that very much.'

I do not say that Aminta and I encountered very little dust on our way here. But perhaps we were lucky.

We walk back in silence.

'Do you know who might have a house to sell within the town walls?' asks Pepys.

'You mean under the sea?' says Digby, putting down his knife and fork and wiping his lips with a linen napkin. 'There are a number that have deeds extant and are purchasable. When my father bought the Priory, he realised that it did not give him the right to vote or serve on the council, since it was built outside the walls. He purchased a suitable freehold from Mayor Spratchett for, I think, forty Pounds. I believe Spratchett has others that he might be willing to part with at a similar price.'

'Forty Pounds, sir? For a mere fiction of a dwelling? Do you take me for a fool?'

Digby laughs, being in no way offended by this rebuke. 'It

is a bargain, Mister Pepys. I heard that he was asking sixty for another submarine property – admittedly a slightly larger one with more hearths, but that offers no great advantage when you cannot light a fire in any of them.'

'I shall speak to Mayor Spratchett and see what he will ask, as one gentleman performing a trifling favour for another.'

Digby nods encouragingly. 'The surviving deeds of all such houses are much valued now. They are an investment that will return ten or twenty per centum per annum in gifts from candidates. More if we continue to have by-elections. My father had already distributed considerable largesse before he died.'

'Can we depend on any of the votes that he bought?' asks Pepys.

'Not one, I would think. The payments were to buy support for him and him alone. Any goodwill purchased died with him.'

'How much had he spent?'

'Two or three hundred Pounds in all,' says Digby.

'Two or three hundred! I was expecting to pay sixty at the most.'

'Seats become more expensive with every election. A thousand may soon be seen as cheap. It is not just a matter of paying individual burgesses. It is customary to contribute to the building of a new wharf or for repairs to the church.'

'Can I cut you some more beef, Mister Pepys?' says Silvia. 'You look quite pale. I think you need feeding up.'

I look at Pepys. Yes, perhaps he has lost weight this winter. A little anyway. And aged two or three years.

'Thank you, Mistress Digges,' he says. 'You have a fine cook.'

'I prepared it myself,' she says.

'So talented and so beautiful,' says Pepys. 'Your husband is the luckiest of men.'

Silvia smiles at him. Perhaps she does not know Pepys's reputation. Or perhaps she does and doesn't care. Or, then again, maybe she sees something in him that still escapes me. Pepys is a changed man, but I do not know what he has changed into and intend to be wary until I do. I think Aminta also sees an alteration in him. She is more willing to talk to him than she usually is – about the theatre and the Court and books and music and the sea – the things that Pepys enjoys.

'Whose votes can we depend on, then?' Pepys asks, taking out a small notebook and a silver pen. 'Other than your own, of course.'

'Strictly speaking, nobody,' says Digby. 'Solomon Larter, the other member, is the town's man – not the Admiralty's. He's the Water Bailiff – one of the officers of the town – and he'd had a long dispute with my father over the clearance of drainage ditches – there were some sluices that both thought the other should deal with. He wouldn't have supported my father and I fear he won't support you either.'

Pepys purses his lips. He doesn't mind the Admiral upsetting people, but there is no point in losing votes over ditches.

'The vicar?' asks Pepys, pen still poised. 'Grey says he has a vote.'

'Of course,' says Digby. 'Vicars of St Peter's are also *ex officio* the town Chamberlain.'

'I assume that he is above accepting money for himself,' says Pepys, hopefully. 'But I could offer to buy some new silver for the church. A small chalice, for example. Or a spoon.'

'I agree he would take nothing for himself. He lives very simply. But St Peter's will soon be under water, along with all of Eastwold's other churches. And it must already have a great deal of plate rescued from those now beneath the sea.

Moreover, Wraith is not entirely in his right mind. You should rely on nothing he tells you or promises you. Nothing at all.'

Again I am surprised at the vehemence in Digby's tone, though fallings-out between the manor house and the vicarage are common enough. Perhaps he has recently become aware that the vicar did not hold his father in quite the affection he had believed.

'I shall speak to him and see what I need to offer,' says Pepys, writing down the vicar's name. 'A favour, perhaps, if he does not require money – preferment to a royal chaplaincy for himself or a cousin. Everyone wants something. What about Benefice?'

'He is the Sergeant of the Mace,' says Digby. 'An ancient post of great dignity. He is a rogue and entirely open to the highest bidder.'

Pepys, somewhat optimistically, puts Benefice down as a likely supporter. 'Tutepenny?'

'The First Freeman of the town. As honest as the day is long, but poor. Again, you just need to offer him enough money. Very loyal to my father, of course, like all who served under him. Then there's William Peacock, the Town Clerk. He's a Republican. He did not like my father changing sides and serving the new king. I fear he saw my father as a traitor.'

'It is no treason to serve an anointed king,' says Pepys. 'Or not at present.'

'True,' says Digby. 'But if anyone is opposed to the election of a courtier, such as your good self, it will be Peacock. I do not think you will have his vote.'

Pepys looks at his notebook accusingly. There are still too few names in the left-hand column. 'Well, I don't need everyone's vote. Indeed, I plan to buy only as many as I require to be elected. Who else is there?'

'There's Elijah Spratchett – the Mayor.'

'Ah, the gentleman with many houses. I am losing track of these civic posts. How many officers does a non-existent town need?'

'A dozen or so are specified in the charter and in other documents that have come down to us. Some burgesses hold more than one post. Benefice is also Master of the Herring Boats and the Sealer of Leather.'

'Does that give him three votes?'

'No, just one. But it means he has two spare offices to sell if the price is right. You might like to become the Sealer of Leather yourself.'

'Is there any leather to seal?' asks Pepys.

'Not for the past hundred years, at least. But a small stipend, derived from funds accumulated long ago by a prosperous port, still attaches to each post. There is a trade in redundant offices, just as there is in non-existent houses. They might be seen as a type of annuity that also offers certain privileges. My father purchased the office of Recorder simply in order to attend council meetings, but it also returned him sixty Shillings a year.'

'And will Mayor Spratchett vote for me?' Pepys enquires.

'He will certainly offer to. He has already taken money from both my father and Cavendish. My father was not best pleased when he found out. He sought the Mayor out in the town's only inn and publicly berated him as a rogue and a liar. He said that once he was elected he would flog Spratchett all the way up the beach and all the way down again.'

'And what did Spratchett say to that?'

'He could scarcely deny being a rogue and a liar – not amongst people who knew him so well.'

'He said your father would need to come well-armed or he'd run him through the guts with a herring knife,' says Silvia. She has finished carving and now heaps Pepys's plate with slices of beef.

Digby gives a laugh, as if none of this should be taken too seriously. I feel quite sorry for him, being forced to come to terms with how many people disliked his father – Benefice, Solomon Larter, the vicar, Peacock, Spratchett. Did Catch warn Digby in some way as he breathed his last? Did he say the Admiral's life was in danger? Was that why Digby was so curious as to my opinion on whether dying men speak truthfully? But these are not matters that trouble Pepys.

'Who else is voting?' he demands.

'Your opponent, Jacob Cavendish, has a vote,' Digby continues briskly, 'but then so will you if you buy a house from Spratchett or another who wishes to sell, so the two of you cancel each other out. There's another Cavendish – Henry, a cousin. He's the town's Ale Founder.'

'Does he know anything about ale?'

'I assume he drinks it.'

'And he lives close by?'

'He now practises as a doctor in Lowestoft. It's about thirty miles away. But he has a house here too.'

'Below the tideline?'

'Of course.'

'I suppose he'll vote for Jacob?'

'Family loyalty will matter more to him than a few guineas,' Digby says. 'I doubt there is any point in trying to appeal to his sense of justice or reason.'

73

'He is a good man,' says Silvia, 'and a fair one, as you know very well, Digby.'

'Well, I would not advise spending a long day in the saddle, riding to Lowestoft and back, simply to ask for his vote.'

'Is that all?' Pepys asks, scribbling Henry's name in his book as one who might be persuadable.

'David Larter, the Coroner – the nephew of Solomon. He'll vote with his uncle, I think. No point in speaking to him either. And, as I said to Sir John, he's away at present.'

'I see. This is all less than satisfactory, Mister Digges. Any more voters?'

'Toby Dix and John Pettus. Fishermen. They work for Spratchett. Both own houses tottering at the top of the cliff. They hold no offices on the council. They have no papers proving ownership of the houses they occupy. If the houses fall, then they may lose their votes. But for the moment they are burgesses and are open to argument.'

'Good. I'll argue. I assume they are completely unlettered and have no idea what their votes are now worth. Yes? Excellent. Are there any more?'

'Just me,' says Digby.

Pepys adds up the names he has written in three columns. 'That's six potentially for me, four for Cavendish and three undecided,' he says.

I wonder which column Digby is really in. It may take more than Pepys's bluster to make Digby vote against his father-in-law.

'Allowing for your vote and mine, I'll need to bribe five burgesses to be sure of winning,' Pepys says. 'I know you say that your father had spent two hundred Pounds but that seems profligate and inefficient. We need to enlist to our cause those who will expect least. If we just bribe the fishermen then surely ten Pounds each should be enough? Or maybe five?'

'Most of the burgesses will be expecting close to a hundred,' says Digby. 'Certainly from a stranger like yourself. The fishermen may settle for fifty.'

'Fifty? Surely not? Will Jacob Cavendish pay that?'

'He's not an outsider. He may not have to. You won't know who is actually voting for you until we get to the polls, and you really cannot count on any votes at all unless you pay handsomely.'

'Except your own,' says Pepys.

'I have no plans to charge you,' says Digby. I note the ambiguity of this in a way that Pepys does not. I look at Silvia. She probably knows her husband's mind better than he does himself, but she's giving nothing away. Or not yet.

Pepys nods confidently. 'Benefice and Tutepenny are Navy men, when all's said and done. And Benefice has a small pension from the Admiralty in respect of the loss of a leg. They at least will vote with us as a matter of course?'

'You must ask them, Mister Pepys,' says Silvia. 'I am sure they have happy recollections of their days at sea, serving under my beloved father-in-law.'

We have finished eating. I am taking a turn with Aminta through the gardens. She too has a conversation that she wishes to have with me away from the house.

'I spoke to Silvia while you were with Pepys,' she says.

'I admire her,' I say. 'Many women would have baulked at the sudden arrival of a complete stranger, who demanded dinner and a bed as a right – not to mention stabling for his horse and her husband's vote.'

'It did not surprise her in any way. It is the sort of behaviour that she has come to expect from the men around her. At least, unlike Admiral Digges, Pepys did not arrive stinking of salt fish and threatening to flog everyone in the house before supper.'

'Pepys is a changed man,' I say. 'In some respects.'

'Indeed,' says Aminta. 'He still has the very highest regard for himself and his own abilities, and the lowest possible regard for everyone else. The highest compliment that he can offer a woman usually relates in some way to her utility to her husband. But he feels guilty for his wife's death – not just that she died of some fever contracted on the travels that he had proposed to her, nor contrition over the other women that he bedded constantly during her lifetime. I think he feels that she died of his neglect – that he had devoted too much time to work and too little to her. If he'd just watched her more closely – I mean in the way he watches over his money – she wouldn't have slipped away from him. He's planning to be buried beside her – not immediately but in the fullness of time. He'll make it up to her over the course of eternity.'

'You think so?'

'Yes and, having watched them over dinner, I think Silvia does too. She's clearly quite taken to him. He has the arrogance and lack of consideration that she's used to in men, but with a sophistication that she has never previously known. And she's sorry for him as a widower. She knows that, in his own very special way, Sam Pepys did love his wife above anything else.'

'You may need to guard her from her folly.'

'Or you might like to warn Pepys off.'

'Pepys won't listen to me.'

'And Silvia is very much her own woman. Ah well, that

may just have to run its course then. And she can face down men when she wants to. Admiral Digges did his best to terrorise her, from what she told me. I think he saw reducing his daughter-in-law to a nervous wreck as something of a challenge. But he didn't manage it.'

'Good for her,' I say.

'She was pleased to see him dead, obviously.'

'Hence asking Mother Catch to curse him.'

'I mean she could have had another twenty or thirty years of being berated by a greasy, smelly, bad-tempered ruffian who did little but drink rum and shout at the servants. And Digby was no use. Everything his father said was law to him. He never tried to stand up for her – or himself – in any way.'

'But Silvia hangs on Digby's every word,' I say.

'It's a trick we women have, my dear husband. Don't believe everything you see – or are told. When Pepys arrived, Digby looked at his wife to gauge what his reaction should be. Then Silvia gave instructions to the footmen. Silvia knows what she's doing and what is going on.'

'And what does she think is going on?'

'She told me, in great confidence, that she is certain the Admiral was murdered,' says Aminta.

'The vicar seemed to think so too, but lacked evidence. Did she have any?'

'The evening he died, the Admiral had received a note during the day – Silvia thinks it asked him to meet up with somebody.'

'Digby mentioned no note to us.'

'No, he didn't, did he? He just said that his father had a fancy to sail his boat. He seems less observant than his wife in so many ways.'

'Who delivered the note?'

'Again, Silvia doesn't know. She merely saw the Admiral reading it. Then he announced, somewhat improbably, that he planned to go out for a sail. It was not a day for sailing for pleasure – it was cold, wet and the afternoon already well advanced.'

'What did she do about it?' I ask.

'She told Digby, who seemed surprised and unsure what action to take. Far from being grateful, he seemed, if anything, annoyed that she had spied on his father. He eventually said that he would follow the Admiral, at a cautious distance, to the beach. But he did not leave at once even then. It was ten minutes later that Silvia heard the door close behind him as he set off.'

'A further departure from Digby's narrative. He said nothing to us about following his father, less still that he was slow to depart. He simply said that he went down to the beach when they became concerned, but could find nobody there.'

'Well, they are both agreed on that last point. He came back empty handed. Digby is very kind and well meaning, but not a man of action. Perhaps he delayed, as Silvia says, and lost his chance? Perhaps the Admiral deliberately gave him the slip? Silvia told me Digby came back after an hour or two, soaking wet with the rain, saying that he had searched everywhere but had seen nobody on the beach. Silvia asked him if his father's boat was still there. He said he hadn't thought to look.'

'There are inconsistencies in the two accounts, that is clear,' I say. 'But I rather think Digby may have just been trying to save his face in his abbreviated version of the tale for the Coroner. He didn't want to admit his wife had rightly feared for his father's safety, in a way that he hadn't, and that he had then been completely ineffective.'

'That may be so, but if Silvia is right about the note, and I have no reason to disbelieve her, then somebody must have lured the Admiral to the beach and killed him.'

'Digby is beginning to realise that not everyone loved the Admiral, but he is still reluctant to admit, to himself most of all, that anyone could actually wish to harm his father. Silvia is clearly under no such illusions. So who did the Admiral really go to meet? Benefice? Jacob Cavendish? But Silvia surely wouldn't have mentioned the note if she thought it was from her father?'

'Silvia said that she didn't know who it was from. Perhaps that hasn't occurred to her.'

'But what if Digby conversely knew it was Jacob Cavendish and isn't saying? It would explain why he was so concerned that his father-in-law would be accused, if he knew there was a lot more against him than appeared at first sight. It would also explain why Digby would not have wanted me to know about the note.'

'Silvia may be inadvertently leading her father to the gallows,' says Aminta.

'Perhaps, after all, it is Digby who is showing wisdom. Mother Catch said that I might not like what I discovered. But let's not forget Benefice. What if the Admiral was going to try to intercept some smugglers – what if the note was from an informer? That's at least as likely as a meeting with Jacob Cavendish, isn't it?'

'I did suggest that. Silvia said it wasn't a night for smuggling. Cloudy, but still too much moonlight. You want to bring in your ship, hull and sails stained black, as invisibly as you can.'

'Did the Admiral go armed?' I ask. 'I doubt he would have faced smugglers without a sword.'

'Neither narrative mentions one. But Digby, as we've said, was so late setting out that he wouldn't have seen what the Admiral had with him.'

'Silvia said Elijah Spratchett had offered to gut the Admiral with a herring knife. If it was a meeting with him, the Admiral would also have gone armed.'

'A challenge like that certainly needed answering,' says Aminta. 'So perhaps he and Spratchett exchanged two badly written and ungrammatical notes and arranged to meet on the beach? They fought and the Admiral was stabbed.'

'But he wasn't stabbed,' I say.

'Yes, he was. Silvia said so.'

'The Coroner ruled he was drowned. It looks increasingly like a murder, but I thought that much at least was agreed.'

'Drowning is what the jury decided on the basis of the evidence they were allowed to have,' says Aminta. 'The Admiral's body was dragged from the sea. But the Coroner was apparently well aware he'd been stabbed.'

'So, David Larter, the nephew of Solomon Larter, the town's other Member of Parliament, decided to conceal that very relevant fact?' I say.

'And Digges and Solomon Larter had quarrelled over the ditches.'

'Indeed,' I say. 'That may not be a coincidence. Our list of suspects grows longer and longer. Does Digby know his father was stabbed?'

'Not yet. Silvia found out only recently. She told me she hasn't decided what it would be best to do.'

'Did she give evidence at the inquest?'

'Since her husband was available, the Coroner did not consider it necessary.'

'She's very well informed, anyway.'

'Better than her husband, certainly.'

'She tells you a great deal more than she tells me.'

'I think she sees me as a sister. We do, after all, have so much in common – stolen estates, obstinate Republican husbands. And she does not have a great deal of confidence in men.'

'But where did she learn all this?'

'She wouldn't say.'

'In the morning, I must go and see whether David Larter has returned from his travels. I am beginning to understand what it is that I'm supposed to be covering up.'

From my Lady Grey's most excellent poem
The Election

No sooner was the Admiral buried,
Within the very parish where he'd
Hoped to celebrate a vict'ry,
Hailed by all the borough's gentry,
Than came a Clerk, sent by the Navy,
Who loved to dip his bread in gravy.
In every contract he was willing,
From each Royal Pound to take a Shilling.
Most loyal was he to his great Patron!
Likewise from every maid and matron
He sought to win a small percentage,
And make the lady drop her drawbridge.
Though he might feign to make his look cold
He'd have each burgess there a cuckold!

Chapter 8

At the house by the cliff

David Larter's house must once have been most desirable, on the landward edge of the town, with the town wall forming one boundary of its garden and orchard. It is large and built of red brick. The chimneys are heavy and ornate – patterned with diamonds and grooves and fretwork, each one slightly different from its brother, as chimneys were when they were rare and most households permitted domestic smoke to escape through a hole in the thatch. The porch is solid, designed to protect a visitor from storms while a servant travelled from the far end of the house to open the door to them. But the same front door is already perilously close to the cliff edge. Moreover, most of the orchard, on the seaward side of the residence, has gone. An apple tree hangs at a drunken angle over the precipice, its thick roots desperately scrabbling to keep a grip in the sandy soil. The tree promises to have much blossom but will, I think, never have ripe fruit again.

Larter opens the door himself. There is no doubt that he is back.

He is a few years older than I am and there is already some grey in his short hair. He is dressed in sober black, not having a Cavalier wife. He has a quiet authority about him. Whatever he told a jury, they'd believe him.

'I'm John Grey,' I say. 'The magistrate sent to investigate Admiral Digges' death. You are, I am told, the Coroner.'

This does not seem to please him. 'We have a magistrate, Sir John,' he says. 'We didn't need one from London.'

'Essex,' I say. 'It's Essex you don't need one from.'

'You'd better come in. I've no idea when that bit of path you're standing on will fall into the sea. It would be a shame to lose you when you've travelled so far and for no purpose.'

Little light penetrates the small, leaded windows of Larter's sitting room. It is hung with old tapestries, faded, in spite of the lack of sun, into many shades of brown and muted reds. The space is broad and generous but the ceiling is too low for today's tastes. The floor is orange tile. In happier times, Larter children must have played here, while a fire burned in the great brick hearth. Today it is bare of logs, and the room is full of chilly shadows. The solid oak furniture, much worn and polished, has also witnessed many generations of Larters. The dressers, tables and heavy, carved chairs seem uneasy, as if still hoping for better days but, at the same time, vaguely aware of the grinding of the waves at the base of the cliff.

'The house is the oldest still surviving within the walls,' says David Larter. 'It's been mine since my father died almost twenty years ago, but I'll be the last of the family to live here. All of this will be gone by next year. It could be gone by tomorrow. Only the salt water out there knows when it will come for me. The sea advances by jerks – twenty yards one year, almost nothing the next. It plays cat and mouse with us. Just when you think it has lost interest and will leave you alone, it pounces. Even when I was a child, the whole orchard was still ours and, further down a road that no longer exists, two houses with their gardens lay between us and the shore. I can still see it all, if I close my eyes. Now I can look out of my study window and there is nothing but cold, smiling water. And boats. I see boats too. Once they brought the finest goods the world could offer. Now we land herring by day and bad brandy by night.'

'You continue to elect officers of the town, even though there is little left of it,' I say. 'Ale founders with no knowledge of ale making. Leather sealers who have no leather to seal. Is your post also one named in the charter?'

'You think that my post of Coroner is also a sinecure for which I am unqualified? Benefice knows nothing about leather making, I'll grant you that. And it's anyone's guess what his duties might be as Master of the Herring Boats – I can't see Spratchett taking orders from a one-legged innkeeper. But most of the office holders are well enough qualified. My uncle as Water Bailiff, for example. He understands farming and drainage. There are sluices and dykes that must be maintained if the cornfields round here are not to flood. He was right to pursue Digges for not keeping his ditches clear. And Peacock is a competent Town Clerk, well versed in the history and the recondite customs of the town, as you'll see when the election is held. As for my own appointment, it is made by the Sheriff, not the town. I studied at Cambridge and know more law than most Coroners do these days. The office of Coroner has fallen into disrepair everywhere, I grant you that. We're no longer the most important royal officer in the district, as we were when the town was granted its charter. Any gentleman or tenant farmer with a volume of *The Compleat Justice* in his coat pocket is considered competent to do the job. I've also studied medicine at Leiden and served as a ship's surgeon, though fortunately not under Digges. Show me somebody's corpse and I'll make a pretty good attempt at telling you why he's no longer alive. Give me a sharp knife, and I'll have his liver and lights in a copper bowl to confirm my theories.'

'And you say Digges drowned?' I ask.

'I do, sir.'

'Others tell me that he had been stabbed.'

Some Coroners might take offence at being called a liar by a superfluous magistrate from Essex, but Larter simply smiles indulgently.

'Stabbed? Yes. With a large knife, I'd say. A broad cut but not deep. The fishermen who found him didn't notice it. The Admiral had been in the sea slightly too long. There was no blood staining his clothes. But I observed the slit in his waistcoat and in his shirt beneath. His body had already been placed in the crypt when I inspected it. I drew the attention of the vicar to the wound, as a curiosity.'

'So why did you report it to the Sheriff as a drowning?'

'Because that was what the jury quite rightly decided. Digges died of an excess of water in his lungs, not the small wound in his chest. The knife hadn't done much more than break the skin. He'd been in a fight and he'd not done too well. But he died somewhat later. I mentioned it, of course, to the jury. I think I said that there was a lesion of no great depth that had failed to penetrate the ventral cavity.'

'They understood that?'

'I assume so. Nobody queried it.'

'That is, if I may say so, a little disingenuous.'

'But perfectly legal.'

'Digby Digges should have known the cause of his father's death.'

'He does. The cause was too much of water, as Master Shakespeare called it – not the stabbing.'

'But the wound changes the circumstances of the death considerably. He'd been in a fight. When you stab a man in the chest, you're usually planning to kill him. The wound you describe considerably increases the chances that this was murder, by whatever means, and if that is the case then Digby – and others – would have wanted the perpetrator punished.'

'You know that, do you? You know that there is somebody in this town who would have wanted to seek out and punish the man who stabbed and then drowned Sir Robert Digges?'

'Digby at least had great respect for his father.'

'Admiral Digges was a harsh commander, Sir John, a harsh master to his servants, a harsh neighbour, a harsh parent . . . and a harsh parent-in-law. As I say, I've trained as a surgeon as well as a lawyer. And since I'm the only surgeon within many miles of here, I've been called on to treat members of that family. I know exactly how harsh.'

'Who have you treated? And for what?'

'I can't tell you that, Sir John. I may be no more than a ship's surgeon with a fancy Cambridge degree, but I'll still take my patients' secrets to the grave. Nevertheless I repeat: nobody in this town had reason to love him.'

'Including your uncle?'

'You'll have to ask him. I'm sure that whoever killed Digges did so with good intentions. I allowed the jury to have all of the information that I had. That is the limit of my responsibilities.'

'Somebody here disagrees.'

'Yes, I'd assumed that some fool had taken up their quill to express their dissent.'

'Who might that be?'

'Anyone here who can hold a pen and hold a grudge. The late wars still cast a shadow over the town. There are scores still unsettled after a quarter of a century.'

'Who was at the inquest?'

'Most of the town. Look, Sir John, I think this is a more interesting question for you than for me. The inquest is done and there was nothing wrong with the jury's verdict. A bad man has been sent to his death. Do you really want to send a good one after him? I would suggest that you report back to your masters that they have my word that the Admiral drowned. Somebody clearly wants to cause trouble, but nobody, either here or in London, is really going to thank you for opening the door to unlawful killing – Lord Arlington least of all.'

'It isn't that simple.'

'Really? Why should you worry how he died?'

'It's like your patients,' I say. 'You have a duty of care to them. Once a man is murdered he becomes my client, whether he likes it or not, and he stays my client until I've got him justice. Even a man like Digges. Even you, Mister Larter, if it ever comes to that.'

'Be careful as you leave, Sir John. The path outside is crumbling. You could easily slip. And it's an inconveniently long way down to the beach.'

* * *

Elijah Spratchett's house is an act of pure defiance. It must be only ten years old and it stands no more chance than the other houses within the old town walls of surviving the sea's encroachment. But, while it lasts, it may be the most comfortable house in Eastwold. It is, perhaps, what Admiral Digges would have built if he had been allowed to do so. It is constructed of brick, because there is no building stone other than flint within miles. But it has modern sash windows, tall and large enough to admit as much light as you could wish. The door is flanked by classical pillars, hewn from oolite in another part of the country, which might have graced a villa in ancient Rome or Athens. This does not look back to the dark and superstitious years before the present century. It smiles on the bright future and the triumph of the arts and sciences over ignorance. At least, it will do that until the sea sends it crashing onto the beach in a cloud of red dust.

'I congratulate you on your house, Mister Spratchett,' I say. 'It would not disgrace any city in the land.'

'Good enough for a poor fisherman,' he says. His smile shows the loss of a tooth or two. His glossy black periwig contrasts, not entirely happily, with the leathery face and unshaven chin. His dark green coat is just a little too good for gutting herring in, even without the lace shirt cuffs that reach halfway to his broken fingernails. He is friendly enough as we sit in his comfortable parlour with a clear view of the salt water, but I wouldn't wish to cross him without good cause. And if I did, I wouldn't turn my back on him for a decade or two afterwards.

'You get your living from the sea?' I ask.

'I've several boats, Sir John. But I don't sail them myself unless I have to. Not any more. Dix, Pettus, Bottulph, Dowsing, Cooper and one or two others, depending on the season – they work for me. They land the fish and dry it in the sheds. I sell it to merchants in London or to the Navy.'

'You sell to Pepys?'

'He wouldn't get his hands dirty inspecting smoked herring in my sheds. I sell to Sir Denis Gauden, the Navy victualler, and Gauden sells to Pepys. There's enough profit in a humble herring to keep us all happy, including Pepys, if you understand me. These are fat and prosperous times under good King Charles.'

'And the men you employ?' I ask. 'Is there enough to make them fat too?'

'They get paid the usual rate when the weather is good enough to go out. Nothing when they don't. What more could they expect? I may be Mayor, Sir John, but I don't command the winds.'

He smiles, as if there was a possibility that I did think that.

'I know of Dix and Pettus,' I say. 'They are burgesses. I don't know the other three you named.'

'They live outside the walls and have little enough money without buying a house under the water. Dix and Pettus may not be able to vote in the election after this one – not if the sea takes their houses. There must be proof that a house within the walls existed at one time, and they will have none. They're better at preserving fish than papers.'

'Then they will wish to make as much money as they can this time,' I say.

'I expect so. They would in principle want to take the gold of the highest bidder.'

'In principle?'

'I expect that they will, as a matter of courtesy, consult me as to which candidate would serve Eastwold best. And, as a matter of courtesy, I'll tell them what to do. And if they do it, they might keep their jobs and gain a few guineas besides.'

'And which way will you make them vote? Pepys or Cavendish?'

'That may depend on what Pepys and Cavendish offer me. And the good of the nation, of course.'

'Of course,' I say.

Mister Pepys may have to revise the three columns in his notebook.

'Would you have voted for Digges, if he was still standing?' I ask.

Spratchett tugs at his false curls. I am not sure he is comfortable with the new fashion, and they frankly give the impression that he is pretending to be something that he is not. 'I had not made up my mind,' he says.

'You had taken Digges' money.'

'Yes.'

'And Cavendish's.'

'Yes.'

'Is that not dishonest?'

'The true dishonesty lies in buying votes – not in taking a fool's money. Since I'd have voted for one of them, I was at least half-way honest. That's more than either of them would have been.'

'Digges confronted you at the inn, didn't he?'

'I gave as good as I got.'

'You said you'd kill him.'

'I said I'd stick a knife in his guts. He might have survived. You can never tell with knife wounds.'

'And he was stabbed.'

Spratchett's open smile fades slowly. 'I heard he was drowned. That was what the Coroner's court decided.'

'And stabbed,' I say.

'Who says?'

'The Coroner.'

'It wasn't mentioned at the inquest.'

'Apparently it was, but most people missed it.'

He shrugs. 'It wasn't me that stabbed him, anyway. If David Larter says it was, he's a liar. They're all liars in that family. Always have been. Does he say I did it?'

'No. But, as you point out, he's a liar.'

'Anyone else say I did it?'

'No.'

'Well then. Everybody hated Digges.'

'It's generally known you threatened to knife him, and in front of witnesses.'

He laughs. 'Generally known, is it? That's a shame.' He takes a gold watch out of his pocket, checks it in a leisurely manner, then snaps the case shut again. 'You'll still need witnesses in court. And, whoever did it, you won't get any. Not in Eastwold.'

I nod. He's right. I'll need witnesses in court. Even here, in a town where the vicar is mad, skulls litter the beach and churchwardens go to Hell, I'll need witnesses in court.

Chapter 9

At the Priory

I am not the last to return to the Priory. Pepys is still out in the town. Aminta is also abroad on some errand with Silvia Digges. But Digby is home and sitting in the garden, bare headed. His blond periwig reclines aimlessly on the bench, the flowing curls almost reaching the ground. On this bleak east coast, the year hesitates on the brink of spring. There is a scent of primroses and daffodils.

'Have you been able to conclude your enquiries?' Digby asks, running his fingers through his own short hair. 'It must be inconvenient for you to be away from your estates at this time of year, when there is so much to be done. If it were me, I should want to return post haste, lest, come September, I regretted my negligence of my crops in March.'

'I have a very good steward,' I say. 'He understands the tasks that have to be completed better than I do – though I hope I am learning fast. Another few days will do no harm.'

'But what is there for you to discover here? My father unwisely took his boat out and drowned. Can we not conclude this business? It is distressing for Silvia and for the household generally. And we already know all there is to be known.'

'I've been speaking to Mayor Spratchett.'

'What of it?'

'He and your father were not well disposed towards each other.'

'Of course they weren't. I've told you: Spratchett took both my father's money and my father-in-law's money, selling the same vote twice over. My father was not one to overlook accounting errors of that sort.'

'Spratchett said, in reply, that he would stab your father.'

'I think Silvia told you that. It was an idle threat.'

'He was stabbed.'

I watch Digby's reaction.

'But how . . .?' Digby's normally ruddy face has become distinctly pale. I am sorry to have to break this news to him in this way, but I have no choice if I am to continue my work here without constant polite evasion and sidestepping.

'How did that happen?' I say. 'I think that your father went to the beach, not to sail but to confront somebody – and I'm beginning to think that person may have been Spratchett. Do you know if your father took his sword?'

'I . . . I haven't seen it since he died. I suppose he must have done.'

'You didn't think to look for it, after his death?'

Digby blinks once or twice. But, since Silvia says that he didn't even look for his father's boat, it is unlikely he would have troubled himself over a sword.

'Since he drowned . . . I mean, I thought he drowned . . .

why should I have done?' he asks eventually. 'What relevance might it have had?'

'I think he and Spratchett may have met to fight it out. Spratchett stabbed him – perhaps before he could even draw his sword, because I can't believe that your father would not have beaten him in a fair fight. The Admiral, weakened by the shock or loss of blood, was overcome by Spratchett and drowned. Spratchett arranged for one or other of his men to take your father's boat a little up the coast and leave it there. At some point on that trip, your father's body was dumped at sea. From what you say, the boat, small though it was, could have accommodated one of the fishermen and your father's body. It would be easily done.'

Digby shakes his head in obstinate disbelief. 'But the Coroner's jury said that he had been drowned.'

'He was. But somebody tried to stab him first. David Larter chose to refer to the stabbing in terms that the jury failed to understand.'

'Why?'

Well, that's a very important question. To save a good man, apparently. But how good exactly would David Larter regard Spratchett as being? Not very, I think.

'You did not realise that was what Mister Larter had said?' I ask.

'No, not at all. Larter might have been speaking Dutch for much of the inquest.' He gives a self-conscious laugh. The education provided by his aunt and uncle may have left him with a high regard for the truth, but I think it included more religion than anatomy.

'Well, we must consider the facts in the light of what we now know. Spratchett had a dispute with your father. He had men to assist him in taking your father's boat up the coast and leaving it there. He would also have had access to the sort of blade that was used and had actually threatened your father's life at least once. He is also the least trustworthy man I have met since I arrived here.'

'But that is not proof of guilt.'

'With your leave, I shall obtain it.'

Digby's face is in his hands. 'You are right. I had long suspected that my father was not well liked . . . or not as well liked as he deserved . . . but this . . . I am sorry, Sir John. I have been blind to what was happening around me. Yes, you must of course talk to whomever you wish. And I shall give you every assistance – or none, if you prefer. Silvia and I would be honoured if you stayed with us a little longer. Will it delay the election, do you think?'

'Only if I arrested the returning officer. I think somebody told me who that was – is it Spratchett as Mayor?'

'No, it's Peacock, the Town Clerk. Mayor Spratchett has no more than a ceremonial role, I think.'

'Perhaps that's as well,' I say.

'Does Spratchett know you suspect him?'

'Yes. I told him as much.'

'You will have made an enemy then.'

'I am not here to make friends.'

'Perhaps not, but your Mister Pepys is. Spratchett may feel you and Pepys are tarred with the same brush. And Spratchett controls the votes of Dix and Pettus. He also still owns several freeholds under the water.'

'Surely he can vote only once, however many houses he owns?'

'Yes, but he could gift the freeholds to others who currently have no vote. It requires only a deed of transfer. The Mayor almost has a majority in his own right, if he wishes. You may have cost your friend the election.'

'I am here to investigate your father's death. That is what I shall do. Who wins the seat is no concern of mine, whatever Pepys or Lord Arlington may wish.'

Digby grins. Not for the first time, it occurs to me that perhaps he doesn't want Samuel Pepys to be elected – that he would be quite happy if the vote went to his wife's father rather than a courtier he has never seen before. Well, I can understand that.

Then we see Pepys coming through the garden gate. He bustles up the path, puffed up with his own importance. I hope that he has had a good morning so far.

'I've spoken to Benefice,' Pepys says, 'and reminded him of his duty to His Majesty. Benefice felt that the loss of a leg fighting the Dutch reduced his debt to the Crown somewhat, but I made it clear to him that I could stop the small pension he is paid at any time. It is dispensed in respect of his being unable to pursue any trade at sea, whereas he is clearly an active and inveterate smuggler. I threatened to report that to the Admiralty. He did not like the truth when presented to him thus, but I hope I held up a mirror in which he might see himself the more clearly and think upon what course of action might be prudent.'

'That course being to vote for you?'

'I left him in little doubt, sir.'

'And Tutepenny?'

'I was unable to speak to him. He was most inconsiderately out fishing. Unlike Benefice, I know of nothing that might force him to give me his support at a reasonable price. Unless either of you do?'

'I have not yet met him,' I say.

Digby shakes his head sadly. 'I suppose he deserves whatever he can get out of the election. Though Tutepenny holds the post of Deputy Mayor, he is probably amongst the poorest of the burgesses. If his house falls into the sea, this may be his last election.'

'Let us hope that the waves spare his dwelling until Election Day,' says Pepys. 'If he is poor and unlettered, I think his vote is there to be purchased cheaply. I shall seek him out this afternoon and see how little I can get him to accept. Five Pounds will seem a fortune to him. I have also spoken to Pettus and Dix. Both seemed inclined to vote for me.'

'Unfortunately they are the creatures of the Mayor,' I say. 'They work on his boats and will need to declare for whichever candidate he tells them to, if they wish to continue to eat.'

'So, Spratchett has in effect three votes?' demands Pepys. He clearly feels this is excessive.

'Not only that, but he may be able to manufacture more electors,' I say, 'if he is prepared to lend his freeholds beneath the waves to others.'

'A well-known trick!' says Pepys suddenly. 'The lending out of freeholds so that the new proprietors arrive at the hustings with the ink wet on their deeds and no idea where their family estates might lie. We must make sure that there is none of that here – or at least that such people do not vote for Cavendish. I shall have to speak to Spratchett and remind him of the advantages to the town of a strong Admiralty connection – especially to one who wishes to supply the fleet with dried fish at a good price.'

'We may have to arrest him first,' I say.

'You mean Spratchett could have killed the Admiral?'

'I fear so.'

'Is there any proof?'

'Mister Digges is happy that I continue to try to obtain it.'

'But you don't have it yet?'

'No.'

Pepys's features relax into a warm smile. 'Of course, young Mister Digges will wish to ensure that justice is done, as we all do. But if that proof is difficult to obtain, as I fear it must be, then he can scarcely blame you if you fail to secure a conviction. And a long investigation, leading nowhere, would be most distressing for Mistress Digges, however inured Mister Digges may be to the prospect. Not to mention the waste of your time, Sir John. For which there is – perhaps I should have made myself clearer – no question of payment. We must think on all of these matters. What do you say, Mister Digges?'

Digges looks from one of us to the other. 'I have said to Sir John that he is welcome to stay here for as long as he needs. As the magistrate in Eastwold, I have no objections to his continuing to question people here. Quite the reverse – I welcome the help of a more experienced colleague and would like to learn from him. But what you say, Mister Pepys, about my wife is very true. She worshipped the Admiral. It would upset her greatly if she were told that he was murdered but that we were unable to bring the killer to justice. I could not allow that to happen. Better by far that she continues to believe that my father drowned accidentally. To accuse Spratchett then have him slide out of it for want of witnesses – that would be bad for everyone.'

'But . . .' I say. Of the three of us, I am probably the only one who is absolutely sure that Silvia already knows old Digges was murdered and doesn't much care. I am almost certain that, like Benefice, she asked Mother Catch to curse him. And I believe that it was Silvia that David Larter was obliged to treat for some injury, in spite of his reluctance to confirm it. Of course, people have always worshipped cruel and violent deities. But I don't think Silvia is one of them. She had no illusions about the Admiral.

'Well, there you are then,' says Pepys, fortunately unable to read my mind. He pats me on the arm. 'There is little point in your pursuing Spratchett. After all, who will give evidence against the Mayor? You might commit him to the county jail, but he would most certainly go free for want of proof, even if he lacks friends on the bench. It would cause trouble for everyone with no possible gain. It would be best, I think, if he does not even hear that you suspect him.'

'I've already told him that I do,' I say.

Pepys's reaction to this revelation is not unlike Digby's a few minutes earlier, in that he feels I have acted foolishly. This does not, however, amuse him. 'That was very ill advised, Sir John. I shall go and see Mister Spratchett this afternoon to discuss his intentions with regard to his various freeholds and whether he plans to lend them out in a useful way. While I am there, I shall reassure him that there is no question of further unfounded accusations. With your permission, of course, Sir John.'

'I cannot give any such undertaking.'

'I am not asking you to give an undertaking. I merely need to tell him things so that he will vote for me. What you do afterwards is your affair, so long as it doesn't invalidate my election.'

'I have no intention of lying to him in any way,' I say. 'David Larter, the Coroner, is certain that the Admiral was stabbed before he was drowned. Stabbed in the chest. Probably with a fisherman's knife.'

Pepys, strangely, shows no great surprise. 'A fisherman's knife, you say? Of which there must be many in a town like this one. 'Od's fish – to use His Majesty's favourite oath – it could be anyone from here. Or from any town or village along the coast. My advice to you, Sir John, is not to bother Spratchett further. I think you will find that that would be Lord Arlington's advice as well. Obviously, I would not seek to influence your deliberations, but I think it is as well that you know where your own interest lies.'

'Lord Arlington has ensured, in his usual roundabout way, that my commission comes from the Sheriff, not himself. The Sheriff wishes me to investigate and report to him. I shall therefore continue my work as I see fit. And without any reference to freeholds, above or below the low-water mark.'

'Of course, Sir John,' says Pepys. 'You must do entirely as you think appropriate, without interference from any quarter.' And he winks at me.

'I think you can at least now rule out Spratchett,' says Aminta. 'You say he was unaware that Digges had been stabbed?'

She has returned from her walk with Silvia Digges and we are now in the orchard and hopefully well beyond Pepys's hearing.

'That's what he said – or wanted me to believe. But let's not forget he threatened Digges in public.'

'A strong argument against it being him. He would have been most ill advised to kill Digges in exactly the way he promised to do.'

'Sometimes people do follow up their threats,' I say.

'But to what end? He'd already got Digges' money and wasn't planning to give it back. Digges had been left looking a fool. And his threat to publicly flog Spratchett was mere bluster. How could he have done so when the whole town, such as it is, would have rushed to Spratchett's aid? It was a fight that Spratchett had already won, and he knew it. What's more, if Spratchett had wanted to make his point even clearer, it sounds as if he could have ensured that Digges was soundly beaten at the election, simply by enfranchising everyone in sight. Why risk meeting him alone on the beach in what might have turned out to be a fair fight? Why risk killing him?'

'You are right,' I say. 'As ever.'

'Of course I am,' says Aminta. 'And, anyway, would David Larter be so concerned to protect Spratchett?'

'You think it more likely that he would cover up the crimes of his uncle?'

'I'd have thought so. On the other hand, almost anything might happen in this town,' says Aminta.

'What do you mean?' I say.

'There is a strangeness to it. Have you noticed how few children there are?'

'That's true, now you mention it. Few young people of either sex and almost no children.'

'Those with families have left. When a town has no future, you take your children elsewhere. For the most part, it's only the old who remain. And the evil. Everywhere you go, the past is only just beneath the surface, its fleshless fingers threatening to break through and seize the present.'

'Very poetic.'

'Thank you. I try to keep in practice.'

'What does Silvia think about it? She is neither old nor evil. She can finally look forward to the future with confidence.'

'She hates it here, she says. She feels its strangeness all the time.'

'And Digby?' I ask.

'He doesn't notice.'

'No,' I say. 'Very little troubles Digby. He's a lucky man. Let's hope he continues to be lucky.'

Chapter 10

We dine at a fashionable hour

We eat well in Suffolk. The kitchen of the Priory, under Silvia's gentle direction, has produced a chine of beef, a stew of lamb and some pickled sturgeon. A salad, grown precariously under glass and picked this morning, sits in a large bowl. Even Pepys is impressed. The sturgeon is much better than one he had recently in London.

'The pickle had gone stale,' he says, 'and when we served it up to Commissioner Pett, I saw many little worms creeping about it, which truly turned my stomach.'

'That must have been awkward,' I say. 'When you had such an important guest.'

'Oh, Pett ate it,' Pepys says. 'The worms didn't trouble him. And he is out of favour now anyway – a good dinner would have been wasted. But this sturgeon, Mistress Digges, is magnificent. I am fortunate to be acquainted with many women of grace and wit – Mistress Knipp of the Theatre Royal and my Lady Castlemaine to name but two – but I am certain neither could direct a kitchen as you do.'

My wife, who has no difficulty in combining writing plays and poetry with organising ordinary domestic tasks, and who thinks Lady Castlemaine is frankly a high-class trollop, raises her eyebrows at me, but Silvia blushes. I am increasingly aware that compliments of any sort are rare in this house. It's true that Digby draws our attention to Silvia's good taste, but he clearly doesn't think good taste is something to aspire to.

The maid servants drift in and out of the room, chatting to each other and sometimes bringing additional dishes or removing dirty plates. They appear to have been recruited by the late Admiral for their durability and poor marriage prospects rather than their efficiency, and I cannot see Digby sacking them, or anyone else, whatever their faults. The servants would do well, however, to note how Silvia is taking charge of things, now that the Admiral has departed. The Admiral may have felt that the work of the kitchen was beneath his notice, but she doesn't.

Then, without warning, the footman brings a visitor to us. He is a large man, in both height and breadth, red-faced and puffing from his walk to the Priory. I think he too may have recently eaten slightly too well and perhaps consumed a certain amount of ale. His suit is well cut, dark brown broadcloth. He wears a plain neck cloth, simply twisted and falling informally down his shirtfront. Unlike many of the residents of Eastwold, he is aware that, for the last seven or eight years, it has been fashionable to wear a periwig. Unlike Mayor Spratchett, he knows how to wear one without constantly fiddling with it. False hair falls about his shoulders in extravagant curls. He scans those seated round the table, trying to work out if any of us are important enough for him to think of removing his hat. He decides not.

'Still eating, Digges?' he says to Digby.

'We keep London hours for our mealtimes,' says Digby, apologetically. 'At least, when we have guests.'

The man takes his watch from his pocket and inspects it. 'Past two of the clock,' he says. 'I can remember when plain men ate their dinners at eleven and were beside their work benches again by twelve.'

'Mister Larter, may I introduce to you Sir John and Lady Grey, from Essex,' says Digby, sidestepping the question of whether any of us will be at our work benches in the near future. 'This, Sir John, is Mister Solomon Larter. He is our other – and only currently serving – Member of Parliament, and the uncle of our esteemed Coroner. Mister Larter, you'll already know Mister Pepys, Clerk of the Acts to the Navy Board?'

Larter draws himself to his full height and width, and looks at the Clerk of the Acts with distaste. 'Indeed. He comes to the House from time to time to hoodwink us into giving more money to the Navy.'

'I hoodwink nobody, sir,' says Pepys very stiffly. 'I explain to the House why it is essential that, if we are to have a Navy at all, then it needs to be properly equipped with ships in a good state of repair and enough sailors to man them. Spending a little on the Navy is to throw money away, no more, no less. It is to offer the Dutch some easy target practice for their own well-funded fleet. Fortunately the House has been wise enough to listen to me. And to ignore you, Mister Larter.'

'Unwise enough to be hoodwinked, you mean,' he says. 'We'll be putting a stop to your games, Pepys. You'll see soon enough. So will your master, the Duke.'

'I take it, Mister Larter, that you are not planning to vote for Mister Pepys?' says Aminta.

'There are enough courtiers in Parliament already, my Lady. We don't need more.'

'Fortunately, I am not counting on your vote in any way,' says Pepys. 'You may do with it as you choose, Mister Larter.'

Solomon Larter scowls at him, but the best retort he can manage is: 'I'd rather stuff it up my arse than give it to you.'

He is untroubled that nobody is greatly impressed with his ready wit. Solomon Larter is not much like his nephew. Both are confident enough, and neither cares much what I think, but there is none of David's learning here. I doubt that Solomon has read a book since he left school. He goes to Westminster to show them what a true-born Englishman looks like – bred for strength, irritability and dogged persistence.

'I wanted to talk to you about ditches,' he says to Digby. 'Unfinished business. Your father wouldn't keep them clear, drat him. Now he's dead, it's your job to do it, see? And I'll make you scrape them clean with your own fingernails if I have to. I'll show you on a map. You've got a map of your estate, I take it?'

'Of course.'

'Know where it is?'

Digby looks round the table. 'If you'll excuse me, I have to talk to Mister Larter. I think another course is on its way. I hope to join you before you finish it.'

In fact we finish the meal and Digby has still not returned. Silvia apologises for him. She is not happy. Whatever the Admiral's faults, he'd have told Larter to go to hell until his guests had been fed and watered. During the final course, she is particularly attentive to Pepys. If she were a Member of Parliament, she'd vote for a whole new fleet. No doubt about that.

Pepys departs, to speak to Spratchett and explain to him how he should cast his unnecessarily large number of votes. I leave Aminta and Silvia to discuss aspects of Puritanism and take a turn round the garden. Unfortunately, I'm very visibly seated on one of the benches when Solomon Larter finally quits the house, having doubtless told Digby what was what.

'Arlington has sent you, hasn't he?' he demands across the lawn that thankfully separates us.

'I am here at the request of your Sheriff,' I say. 'I don't work for Arlington.'

Larter waddles, uninvited, in my direction and stops a foot or so from me, his fat legs planted firmly on the damp grass. I remain seated, obliging him to bend his ample waist in order to thrust his face into mine, as he so clearly desires to do. 'Don't give me that, Grey. I hear you're his lapdog. Well, I'll tell you this just once, then you can clear off back to Essex. Admiral Digges drowned. It was an accident. Nobody here killed him. That's what my nephew says. And nobody wants the likes of you questioning my nephew's judgment. Have you got that plain in your head? Right? When I next look around myself, I don't want to see your face in my town.'

His nose is almost touching mine but I look him straight in the eye. I can put up with a certain amount of fishy breath. In Arlington's service I've had a lot worse than that.

'I can't promise,' I say. 'It depends on how long it takes.'

'What takes?' He straightens himself with a grunt. His back isn't up to this sort of interrogation, even if his breath is.

'Getting people to tell me who killed Admiral Digges.'

'You think he was murdered?'

'Yes.'

'You think anyone cares?'

'I've no idea whether anyone cares. But I believe a number of people know and sooner or later one of them will talk to me.'

He rubs his back. Merely by remaining seated I have caused him a certain amount of pain. This has not endeared me to him. 'Nobody's going to tell you anything, Grey. An Essex magistrate counts for nothing here.'

'Oh, I count for very little in Essex either. But I have no plans to leave with my questions unanswered. If you're right, then I fear you may have both my face and the rest of me around for some time.'

By way of retort, he clears his throat and spits yellow phlegm onto the grass at my feet. 'Tell Pepys, we don't want him here either.'

'I'm not your messenger, Mr Larter. I would suggest you write Pepys a note and leave it with one of the servants. Or I believe you might find him at Mister Spratchett's house, soliciting votes.'

'Well, he'll not have mine.'

'I don't think he'd want it after it had been up your arse.'

'Very amusing, Grey.'

'You'll vote for Cavendish then?' I say.

'Cavendish is a fool. His, and his brother's, opposition to Cromwell cost the lives of two good men here – better men than him. But rather Cavendish than Pepys. Rather Cavendish than Digges too, if that had been the choice. I wish you no luck, Sir John, in finding his killer. Whoever it was, he did the town a good turn.'

'I suppose,' I say to Aminta, 'that you're going to tell me that Solomon Larter couldn't be the murderer, because otherwise he wouldn't have told me that he approved of the killing.'

'No, I'm not going to do that,' she says. 'His case is very different from Spratchett's. Spratchett had already won his argument with Digges. He had nothing to gain by taking it further. Larter was going to have a hard battle to get Digges to do what he wanted. He's right. If the dykes and ditches are not maintained, then Eastwold faces flooding in every direction, not just from the sea. And there was a real danger Digges would be elected rather than Cavendish and prove a very difficult colleague at Westminster. Now, if things go his way, he can have Jacob Cavendish beside him in Parliament, voting against another war with the Dutch. And he has a more than pliant new landowner to push around. I'm sure Digby's already amiably agreed to everything Larter wanted. Both Spratchett and Larter are big enough and strong enough to have overcome Digges on the beach but, of the two, only Solomon Larter really had a good reason for killing him. And if David Larter wasn't covering up for his uncle, then I'm not sure what he was doing.'

'Our Coroner was certainly less than plain in his dealings with the jury. Somebody there must have understood him, though, because somebody thought it was worth spreading rumours in London that the Admiral was stabbed. The question remains, who? Time, I think, to try the ale at Benefice's inn. Wish me luck.'

Chapter 11

I sample Benefice's ale and it is almost good enough

'The hospitality at the Priory isn't to your liking then? First you're after my excellent French brandy – now it's my ale.'

Ezekiel Benefice puts his head on one side and watches me lift my tankard to my lips.

'The ale's always good on the Suffolk coast,' I say.

He shrugs. Like Ben Bowman back home in Clavershall West, he has no doubt that he brews the best in the Eastern Counties. His only surprise is that I recognise the fact. I'm the sole drinker this afternoon though. The other inhabitants of Eastwold are all engaged in fishing or net mending or smoking herring or covering up the murder of an Admiral.

'So, tell me about Solomon Larter,' I say. 'Is he a conscientious Member of Parliament?'

Benefice looks at me suspiciously, but he'd have probably done that whatever I'd asked him. 'What's it to you?'

'I'm just curious. There's an election going on and a certain amount of money changing hands. I'd like to know if you get good value here. Just in case I want to come and live in Eastwold myself.'

He laughs, though I cannot say whether it is at the idea of anyone moving to Eastwold or at the notion of an honest Member of Parliament.

'He's the same as the rest of them. You vote them in, then they go off to Westminster and forget you exist. He got his seat cheaply. We'll make Pepys pay well.'

'But Solomon Larter doesn't quite forget you all, does he? He's Water Bailiff here and he seems punctilious in carrying out his duties. He certainly wasn't going to let Digges neglect his ditches. That's his job, isn't it?'

I lift the tankard again, watching Benefice's face as I drink. The beer's not as good as Ben's. Nothing like. I hope I don't have to order another one.

'He chased Digges for his own sport, not mine,' says Benefice. 'Larter hated Digges. They'll have told you: Larter was a Royalist during the war, but Digges fought for Parliament as a General at Sea. Once Eastwold was firmly under Parliamentary control again, Digges was suddenly the big man in town, and he did everything he could to rub salt into Larter's wounds. Solomon Larter had been Mayor since before the war, but Digges and some others got Larter evicted from the council as a malignant supporter of the Stuarts.'

'Larter mentioned none of that to me,' I say.

'He hasn't forgotten, I promise you that.'

'So who became Mayor in his place?' I ask. 'It's Elijah Spratchett now. But I thought he was a Royalist too?'

'That's right. He is. It was William Peacock that Digges got appointed then. He's a corn chandler and Town Clerk.

A Puritan and a strong man for the Republic, even now. A strange peacock who always dresses in black and squawks extempore prayers. He stood down when King Charles was restored, of course. That was Digges' work too, since he was a Royalist himself by then. Larter could have been Mayor again but by then he didn't want it. There was a new Parliament and new opportunities. Decided he'd do better for himself at Westminster. So, Digges and Larter got Elijah Spratchett made Mayor. They were pretty thick in the old days, Larter and Spratchett – a pair of Royalist thugs on the make. Larter's got fatter in the meantime and Spratchett's lost a few teeth and found himself a periwig, but if you'd stood them side by side back then, apart from the reek of herring coming off Spratchett, you'd have hardly known the difference. Larter's come up in the world as Member of Parliament but, in spite of that brief alliance of the three of them against Peacock, he's never forgotten that it was Digges who originally got him thrown out as Mayor. That's why he got his teeth into him over the ditches. Digges might have bought the manor house but Solomon Larter would make sure he didn't enjoy owning it. And he planned that Digges shouldn't be elected to Parliament either. In spite of Larter's best efforts, it looked as if Digges had enough votes. Then, strangely, Digges died. Not that I'm saying I know who killed him.'

'What about David Larter?' I ask.

'Mister David? Nothing like his uncle. His father died during the war. He went to Cambridge at about the time they executed the old king, but when he returned he couldn't settle in Eastwold under Peacock and his friends. He went off to Holland and became a surgeon.'

'He said he was a ship's surgeon. Was that serving in Cromwell's navy?'

'In the Danish Navy, I think. Didn't want to help the republic, I suppose, after his father died fighting for the King – died most unnecessarily too. Still, Mister David did eventually come back, twelve or thirteen years ago, and took the job of Coroner. The sea's stolen his land, of course, and it will soon take his house, but he earns his living a bit as a surgeon and a bit as a lawyer and a bit as a Coroner. He won't have to take up smuggling – not that there are currently any vacancies in that line round here.'

'Is he a good surgeon?'

'If I had to have my other leg cut off, I wouldn't go to anyone else.'

I drain my tankard and push half a crown across the table towards Benefice. He stares at the silver coin, the King's head with XXX beside it denoting thirty pence. XII is probably the largest numeral he sees on a regular basis. 'I don't have change for that,' he says.

'Then don't give me any,' I say. 'I've enjoyed our conversation, Mister Benefice, and, as it happens, my purse is rather heavy.'

'Well, I'm always happy to help with a problem like that, Sir John.'

'Are you? Tell me then, were you at the inquest into Admiral Digges' death?'

'Yes. It was here at the inn.'

'Who else was there?'

'Who else? Almost everybody in the town, I think.'

'Somebody who was at the inquest – somebody who understood what David Larter meant – wrote to London to say that the inquest had been improperly conducted. That

Digges had been stabbed as well as drowned. Who here enjoys writing letters?'

'Does it matter?'

'I think it may. David Larter's verdict of accidental death may have let somebody off the hook very nicely.'

Benefice shakes his head. 'David Larter's a decent man. A proper gentleman. He doesn't tell lies. Not for anyone.'

'Not for his uncle? As a ship's surgeon he must have noticed that blood was thicker than water.'

'I didn't say Solomon Larter killed him.'

'You said the Admiral's death would have suited him.'

'It would have suited a lot of people.'

'Pepys threatened to take your pension away, didn't he?' I say.

'Could he do that?' asks Benefice.

'Yes,' I say. 'A man like Pepys, rich and comfortable in his high office and wearing a lace cravat that costs more than you earn in a year – he could take away the pittance that the King pays for the loss of your leg. He'd do it without a second thought – not because he hates you, but because, other than as the holder of a vote, you're of no interest to him at all. That's how the world works.'

Benefice swallows. He's seen enough of the world to know it doesn't work to his advantage.

'I might be able to stop him doing that, of course, but equally I might not. So, if somebody with a heavy purse offered you a chance to make a few more Shillings, I'd take it, if I were you. If you hear anything interesting – something more interesting than you've told me so far – let me know. I'm not hard to find.'

'That's true,' he says. 'You're not hard to find.'

Chapter 12

I visit a fellow Puritan but am found very much wanting

Peacock's business premises are on the edge of town, just inside the old town wall. It could be some years before the sea reaches him. The red-brick residence merges imperceptibly into his spacious storehouse. If you own a farm near here, then Peacock is the man you sell your corn to. If you want flour, this is where you buy it. Once, there must have been many corn chandlers in town, but, like Benefice and the vicar, he now has the monopoly of whatever remains in his line of business.

The man against whom Digges, Larter and Spratchett briefly allied ten years ago is much what I expected. A thin individual, dressed in waistcoat and breeches of very serviceable plain back serge, topped with a wide-brimmed, black hat, decorated with a simple black silk band. His nose is proud and aquiline, but he really needs a better face to go with it – or at least a mouth that lacks a permanent sneer of contempt. This is what you look like when you live on small beer and righteousness for slightly too long.

'You must be John Grey,' he says to me.

'That's true enough,' I say. 'I have little choice in the matter.'

He squints at me. 'I had heard rumour that you were a Puritan,' he says. 'One of us.'

'Then perhaps you have been speaking to my wife. As you may see from my velvet coat and lace neck cloth, however, I am a loyal member of the Church of England.'

'Then your church will soon be in the sea,' he says with satisfaction. 'And the graven images therein and the tawdry coloured glass in the windows will lie on the seashore, shattered by the Lord's right hand.'

'And your own church?' I ask.

'My church is wherever godly, pious folk gather. My church, sir, is everywhere.'

'Having a church that is everywhere must be very convenient for you,' I say. 'The very shortest of walks on a Sunday morning.'

Peacock does not smile. I think he laughs rarely and then only when he contemplates sinners in Hell.

'What can I do for you, John Grey?' he asks.

'If you know that my wife believes I'm a Puritan, then you will probably also know that I am looking into the death of Admiral Digges. The murder of Admiral Digges, I should say.'

He nods. 'Good.'

'You approve of what I am doing then?'

'Why not?'

'You are the first here to say so.'

'God's will must be done.'

'You'd like to see the killer of a fellow Republican punished?'

'Digges used to be a Republican. He's been a Royalist for ten years now. He turned his coat very quickly when young Charles Stuart came in. One day he was one of the Republic's

Generals at Sea. The next he was one of the King's water spaniels.'

He'd spit, if Puritans spat, but I don't think they do.

'Plenty of us had to become one of those,' I say. 'You can't serve a republic that no longer exists. Not unless you intend to hang as a traitor. Most of us had other plans for the rest of our lives.'

'It's one thing accepting that the Stuarts are back – holding your tongue and not speaking out against a profane monarch and his foul-mouthed, lecherous hangers-on. It's another entirely to work for them and do their every bidding.'

I suspect Digges would have been unpleasant under any regime, however godly. But Peacock knew him better than I did.

'But he was formerly your friend? In Cromwell's day?'

'We all make mistakes in our youth.'

'You weren't planning to vote for him, then?' I ask.

'I hadn't decided what I was going to do. I still haven't. What sort of man is Pepys?'

'A loyal follower of the King, and the King's imitator as far as he can afford or dare. He works hard and has made himself rich. He has no conscience in the sense that you would understand it, but occasionally he is driven to do the right thing out of cowardice. Like me, he was a Republican in the days when everyone was a Republican. Does that help in any way?'

'Perhaps I shall vote for nobody. There is nothing to make me vote for Cavendish. He and his brother, Isaac, led the town into the folly of opposing Parliament and caused the death of two of our men – good men even if they were Royalists. Jacob Cavendish is too proud to work as the rest of us work. His is an aimless, unprofitable life, growing roses and dreaming of regaining his ancestors' lands. Well, I am pleased to say that God is taking back that land, inch by inch, with every tide. Thou didst blow with thy wind, the sea covered them: they sank as lead in the mighty waters. Who is like unto thee, O Lord, among the gods? Who is like thee, glorious in holiness, fearful in praises, doing wonders?'

'Exodus?' I ask.

'You do at least know your Bible, then?'

'No, just a lucky guess. Of course, God also seems to be taking the houses of many people who have led relatively blameless lives. And sparing the fortunate sinners who chance to live a mile or two inland.'

'That is close to blasphemy, John Grey. God hears every word you speak.'

'My hopes of heaven depend on God being rather like the King – amiable and ready to forgive anything within reason.'

'The Bible suggests nothing of the sort.'

'Then our vicar in Clavershall West must have misled us quite badly. He believes God and the King are on very good terms. If you love one, you should love the other. Where were you on the night that the Admiral was murdered, Mister Peacock?'

Peacock, thinking this was a purely theological debate, stares at me, his mouth open, a well-considered rebuke undelivered.

'What?' he says.

'Where were you, Mister Peacock? Where were you when the foul-mouthed water spaniel met his well-deserved end?'

'You can hardly imagine I killed him!'

'I can imagine all sorts of things, but it would help me if I didn't have to guess where you were that evening.'

'I was at prayer.'

'All evening?'

'Of course not. But I was here at home when the Admiral was killed.'

'Any witnesses?'

'God.'

'We can of course swear him in if necessary. Anyone else?'

He decides to stop drawing my attention to blasphemy. He doesn't have that much time to spare. 'No,' he says. 'My wife is dead. No servants live at my house. I was alone. But this is a ridiculous accusation!'

'But you disliked Admiral Digges? You thought him a turn-coat? A traitor to the Good Old Cause? Unfit to be a Member of Parliament?'

'All of those things. And a great deal more. But I didn't kill him.'

'He was responsible for putting Spratchett in as Mayor in your place?'

'Yes. Him and that scoundrel Solomon Larter.'

'So, you'd have stopped at nothing to prevent Digges taking his seat in Westminster, alongside that scoundrel Solomon Larter – your two enemies enthroned together?'

'This is an insult,' he says. 'I still have friends at Court. You will not get away with this.'

'Powerful friends who could bring me down?'

'Yes.'

'That's helpful to know. So, we have established that there would have been nothing to prevent your leaving the house, unobserved by any except the angels, and sneaking down to the beach. There you could have met with Admiral Digges. You might have argued and fought with him. Then you let God drag the sinner down into the waters, as he dragged

Pharaoh's army in the bit of the Bible that we agreed was probably Exodus.'

'That's ridiculous. I wouldn't have written—'

'You wouldn't have written to London if you had been the murderer?'

'I didn't say that.'

'No, you stopped yourself just in time, but it's a good point. Mister Pepys refused to tell me, but I think it was you who wrote to London and I think you accused Solomon Larter. Most people here would like to see Digges' killer go free. So the informant had to be somebody who hated one of his fellow burgesses more than he hated Digges. That narrowed things down a lot. Oh, and they also had to be able to write and preferably to know one or two influential people at Court, as you have just said you do. In your days as Mayor, you would have known all sorts of people who were then close to Cromwell but are now close to the King – so many people changed sides, didn't they? I'd worked out most of that already, but I still wasn't sure who had enough malice in them to do such a thing until I met you. Then I was.'

'Very clever, Sir John. I congratulate you.'

Peacock really does need to learn not to sneer when delivering a well-earned compliment.

'I suppose you'd like it if Larter had killed Digges – one Royalist dog eating another?'

Peacock says nothing, but he clearly thinks that would be a good plan.

'Or did you have some proof to go with your accusation?' I ask.

'His nephew misled the jury to cover up for him.'

'That's not proof.'

'Solomon Larter and Robert Digges may have conspired together to have me expelled from my office as Mayor, but they fell out again pretty quickly after that. They've been fighting over what's left of this place ever since. You've heard about their dispute over the ditches? Larter would have been as sick as a cat if Digges had been elected. And he would have been elected. It's not difficult to see why Larter stabbed him.'

'That still isn't proof.'

'It's obvious to anyone with any sense.'

'Don't hold out too much hope of getting a jury with any sense, Mister Peacock. You could be sorely disappointed. In the meantime, you won't mind my mentioning your accusation to Mister Larter and asking him to respond to it?'

'My letter was written in confidence. Absolute confidence. I must insist that the assurances I have received are respected.'

'I am working for the Sheriff, and I don't believe he has given any assurances to anyone. But perhaps for the moment I need say nothing to Solomon Larter about your secret denunciation of him – the one that might still get him hanged. I probably won't need mention it at all, not if I get some proper evidence. Everyone comes here to sell their corn or buy their flour, don't they? Ask your many customers what they know. Then come and see me at the Priory. It's always good to speak to a fellow Puritan. Next time we'll talk about Leviticus. A bit dry compared with Exodus, but I expect that means you'll like it better.'

I walk back along the beach with the cliffs above me and much brick and tile beneath my feet. It is low tide, and the damp sands stretch out almost as far as the eye can see. The water is a blue line, far away. An old fisherman is mending his nets in a leisurely manner, enjoying the sun. He is dressed in an ancient doublet, perhaps twenty years old, predating the current fashion for long coats and waistcoats. His grey hair is tied back neatly. His face and his leather boots are much the same colour. The boots are solid and serviceable. Nobody wants to spend hours in a boat with wet feet.

'Good morning. I'm John Grey,' I say.

He puts out a large rough hand and grips the one I have offered him. 'James Tutepenny,' he says.

'I'd hoped to meet you,' I say.

'Well, sir, now you have.'

'You served under Admiral Digges, Mister Tutepenny?'

'Indeed, sir, I did. With Benefice, until he carelessly lost a leg at Scheveningen and had to find work ashore. I remained in the Republic's then the King's service until the Admiralty started paying off ships after the King's return. That's how I met Mister Pepys.'

'You know him?'

'Oh yes. I know him. He was responsible for dismissing us and giving us whatever money we were entitled to. Unfortunately the King was short of funds then, as he usually is, and so we were paid in tickets rather than cash – you know the system, sir? We each received a piece of paper promising money at the later date, when the King could find his way to doing it. Every one of us went off and sold the paper of course for whatever we could get for it – not much, as it turned out. But we needed to eat and so did our families, and beef and bread are available only for ready money. Mister Pepys was very apologetic, of course. Very sorry indeed that he had no silver coins in his box. He looks quite prosperous now, doesn't he? I suppose he must have found some from somewhere. I'm very pleased for him.'

'It is a question of priorities,' I say.

'I never said it wasn't, sir.' Tutepenny eyes the repair he has just made to the net and pulls a thread tight.

'Will you vote for him in the election?'

'I like Mister Jacob better, but they say that Pepys will pay more. I may as well get back some of those Shillings I was owed.'

'That is your only concern?'

'When you're in a small boat, with the rain lashing down and the wind blowing half a gale, it makes very little difference to you who is sitting comfortably on a padded bench in Westminster Hall. But half a crown in your pocket is half a crown in your pocket, whether it's Sunday or Wednesday or Candlemas.'

'Pepys thinks he can get you cheap,' I say. 'I'd ask for a hundred and settle for fifty if you have to. He'll pay it.'

'Shillings?'

'Pounds.'

'Thank you, sir. That's very helpful.'

'Would you have voted for Digges if he was still alive?'

'We'd have seen less of him here if we sent him to London. But I wouldn't have minded seeing Mister Jacob put one over on him.'

'Really?'

'I suppose you'd have to be quite old now to remember it, but the Cavendishes weren't bad landlords, when they did own everything round here. But none of them had much sense. Their stewards robbed them. They went off to the wars and got themselves killed, completely free of charge. Each generation poorer than the last. The fines from Parliament were simply the final straw. Same with most of the Cavalier families who lost their land round here – they'd have lost it sooner or later anyway. But Mister Jacob and Mister Isaac didn't like having to sell to Digges for next to nothing, because nobody wanted to buy big houses then – or not half-demolished ones. Mister Jacob's last hope was to become a Member of Parliament to see if he could fight alongside the others to get compensation from the King. But he knew Digges was outbidding him. Mister Jacob must have realised he'd probably just thrown away what money he had left. Of course, when Digges died, the field was suddenly clear for him . . . until that Pepys man turned up. Sorry, sir – but perhaps you know all that. And you're a busy man, I think. I'm talking too much and wasting your time.'

'Not at all,' I say. 'That is a very clear explanation. Digges' death was quite convenient for Cavendish, then?'

He pulls another thread tight and snaps it off.

'Convenient? Maybe. But I can't see Mister Jacob lifting his hand against anybody. Not for anything. He'd had enough of killing,' says Tutepenny. 'Rather like me.'

'Of course,' I say.

I look up at the cliff. I think some more of it fell last night. We are beneath the churchyard here and the end of a coffin is now protruding from high up on the cliff. In another few weeks, the coffin will be splintered over the beach and the bones will litter the sand.

'John Pettus's wife,' says Tutepenny, following my gaze. 'She was buried in that grave twelve years ago – about the same time as Venetia Digges was buried in the church. Of course, the church won't last much longer. They'll all be down here on the beach soon enough, rich and poor. It's just a matter of time.'

'Mad though he is, the vicar shouldn't leave that coffin hanging over the beach. Pettus is still alive. He shouldn't have to watch his wife's bones fall to the ground one by one. It must be possible to disinter the coffin from above and move it. I'll find the vicar and speak to him.'

'You'll find him at the church, this time of day. He usually goes there to pray. Same prayer over and over. But I suppose it's all much of a muchness to God.'

'I expect so,' I say, reaching for my purse. Tutepenny deserves some reward for the information he's given me. He shakes his head.

'Keep your money, sir. I'll be getting fifty Pounds from Mister Pepys soon, thanks to your advice. I shall be a wealthy man. Richer than Jacob Cavendish, anyway.'

I push the heavy oak door open. There is an earthy, damp smell to the interior of the church, in contrast to the dry, sandy heat outside. It is like entering a tomb, though one with a door through which you may leave again.

Coming in, from the spring sunshine, I have to wait a moment and let my eyes get accustomed to the shadowy half-light. The nave stretches away to my right, long and low. The walls are covered with memorials to past inhabitants of the parish, Venetia Digges' somewhere amongst them. Close to the altar is a large monument topped with two recumbent figures, perhaps the one that Digby was worrying might be his responsibility to save. Even from here, it is clear that moving it will be a difficult task.

I hear Wraith before I see him. A sort of low buzz, rising and falling, like a swarm of despairing bees. 'Lamb of God, who takes away the sins of the world, have mercy on us. Lamb of God, who takes away the sins of the world, have mercy on us.'

I cough and his voice stops abruptly. I see him rise slowly from the pew in which he has been slumped and turn towards me. He looks uncertainly, trying to make out my face with the afternoon sun behind me.

'I am sorry to trouble you, Vicar,' I say. 'I was down on the beach and it is clear that the late Mistress Pettus is about to join the rubble on the sands below the church. I thought you should know.'

'Yes, of course. Another section of the cliff has fallen. I have often watched a hand or a leg appear out of the sand above me and drop, bone by bone, over the weeks and months. Pettus's father went like that last year. His wife will be next. Families choose to be buried together. A great mistake here, if an ancestor was buried on the seaward side of the graveyard. But it will all go eventually.'

'The coffin in question could still be saved.'

Wraith's expression is amused but forgiving. 'Do you really think I have nothing better to do than dig up my parishioners, Sir John? And where would you have me put them? In the field next to the church? And, when the sea comes for that, am I to move them again?'

'You can't move everyone, clearly, but I thought that you might want to do so for Pettus. The disintegration of the coffin will not be a pleasant thing for him to have to watch. It would be a charitable act.'

'Pleasant? What right has he to expect life to be pleasant? This isn't the Garden of Eden, Sir John. It's Suffolk.'

'Perhaps I could arrange for some of the fishermen to do it? You would not need to assist in any way, but I should like to have your permission.'

The indulgent smile fades from Wraith's lips. 'You ask

permission to commit sacrilege in my churchyard? Certainly not, Sir John. Mistress Pettus was entrusted to the Lord and the Lord will look after her until Judgment Day, when the last trumpet shall sound and we shall all be made whole, wherever our bones may lie. If He chooses to change her purely temporary resting place, through the agency of His sea, then that is His affair. But I shall not interfere in any way. Nor will you and your fishermen.'

'Perhaps you will at least consider my request,' I say. 'On reflection you may feel that burying her where she is was in no way pre-ordained and that it should be all the same to God if He had to raise her in another place. It would be a kindness to Pettus if you were able to agree it.'

Wraith shakes his head. He isn't planning to reflect. But perhaps I don't need his approval – just a few willing helpers.

I turn back towards the door, but one of the newer memorials catches my eye. It is Venetia Digges'. Somebody said that it was worth reading. And so it is. It records her name and the date of her birth and of her death. There is also a short verse from the Bible, doubtless chosen with care:

And of Jezebel also spake the LORD, saying, The dogs shall eat Jezebel by the wall of Jezreel.

I wonder what the youthful Digby made of that, whenever his puzzled glance strayed from his prayer book on a Sunday morning. It's surprising that anyone in this town is wholly in his right mind. But perhaps nobody is.

I walk to the door and open it. It creaks protestingly on its hinges, as if in pain. As I step through, into the March sunlight, I hear the vicar's voice again: 'Lamb of God, who takes away the sins of the world, have mercy on us. Lamb of God, who takes away the sins of the world, have mercy on us. Lamb of God ...'

Chapter 13

We have supper

Aminta and I are changing our clothes prior to supper – that is to say Aminta has just, with the aid of Silvia Digges' maid, changed from her day dress into another rather grander one. I am in my waistcoat, my best coat having been taken to another part of the house by a footman to be brushed clean of sand. We are finally free of any of the Digges' servants.

'Well,' I say, 'I think I have put the fear of God into one of those I saw today and offered another a glimpse of the riches that might be his if only his memory was better. I have baited my hooks and cast my lines. We must now wait patiently and see if we get fish on either of them. Did you have a profitable afternoon?'

'I think so. I visited Mother Catch again,' says Aminta.

'Our very respectable witch?'

'The same. Silvia wanted to see her to buy some medicines. I went along. It seemed polite to do so. You see, there is

something very odd about Mother Catch's domestic arrange-
ments. Did that not strike you?'

'It's a very pleasant house.'

'Where, as she told us, she has lived for some time,' says
Aminta. 'While her father inhabited a one-room hovel by
the church.'

'I believe it was referred to as a cottage.'

'Lacking any chimney except a hole in the roof.'

'So how did that happen?' I say.

'Well, my visit gave me the opportunity to enquire. About
ten years ago, it would seem, Mother Catch's aunt, her father's
sister, died and left her the house in her will.'

'The aunt did not leave it to her brother Edward, in spite of
the fact that he clearly had need of it?' I ask. 'She preferred to
leave it to the brother's daughter?'

'It would seem so,' says Aminta. 'Thereafter relations between
father and daughter were somewhat distant. Edward Catch is
not the luckiest of men. His own sister knew something about
him that caused her to disown him in her will. Then, a month
or so ago, the vicar refused to bury him in holy ground. And
only our kind host, Digby, it would appear, was willing to be
with Catch in his last hours.'

'Yes, it's odd that the daughter wasn't there. Her house is no
more than ten minutes' walk away. Whatever Catch had done,
nobody would have blamed her for visiting a dying father.'

'She said she was not sent for.'

'Then Catch continued to hold a grudge? He was unwilling
to be reconciled to his daughter, even on his deathbed?' I ask.

'We must assume so.'

'But this terrible thing – the unforgivable act that Catch
had committed – Digby was prepared to ignore it?'

'The local magistrate clearly has more Christian charity than the vicar,' says Aminta. 'That much is clear.'

There is a knock on the door. My coat has been returned, brushed clean. I am now fit once again to enter polite society.

'I had a very satisfactory conversation with Spratchett,' says Pepys, putting down his glass. 'This is excellent wine, by the way, Mistress Digges. One of the finest I have ever drunk. I congratulate you on your cellar.'

'It's one of the New French Clarets,' says Digby. 'I ordered it myself from London.'

'Ah, did you?' says Pepys. He had not intended to please Digby and is sorry he has wasted a perfectly good compliment. 'Perhaps on reflection it is not as fine as Mister Pontac's Haut Brion, but still, it is very pleasant. Yes, a pleasant little wine, to be sure. Where was I? Of course, Spratchett. I think I have persuaded him to let me have his three votes – at a slightly higher price than I would have liked, but, with the others I have spoken to, it should be sufficient. I also managed to find Tutepenny. I was obliged to offer him fifty Pounds. He would not do it for less. He tried to demand one hundred. These fishermen drive a hard bargain, Sir John. But Tutepenny is a man of some skill and intelligence.'

'Yes,' I say. 'I thought so too.'

'I also saw Wraith on my way back here,' Pepys continues. 'Strictly between ourselves, Sir John, I do not believe he is in his right mind – not at all. He listened in silence to my very reasonable arguments in favour of my candidature then, without a by-your-leave, started to berate me on the subject of a Mistress Pettus, who appeared to be a parishioner of his. What is Mistress Pettus to me? I said. Does she have a vote?

It transpired that she is John Pettus's wife and that she died years ago. The vicar is worried that somebody will try to move her coffin – I could not quite understand why they would wish to do so – Wraith was far from transparent. So, I simply told him that if anyone attempted it, they would have me to deal with. I hope that was sufficient to convince him that I was the right candidate for Eastwold. If so, it's cheaper than a silver chalice and easier than a royal chaplaincy. I must go and see Peacock next, I suppose. As a Puritan, he cannot possibly wish to vote for that fool Cavendish, with all due respect to your father, Mistress Digges.'

Silvia nods and smiles. She will of course be voting for nobody herself.

'I spoke to Peacock,' I say. 'He does not intend to vote.'

'Really? Well, thank you for attempting to win him to our side. I'm sure you did your best. I had thought that he might be a difficult person to deal with . . . But, no matter. That at least saves me a journey and fifty Pounds. With Peacock thus out of the reckoning, I cannot see that Jacob Cavendish has more than four votes: two Cavendishes and two Larters. With us round this table, Wraith, Benefice, Tutepenny and the three votes controlled by Spratchett, that makes eight for me. I am beginning to regret bribing Tutepenny. I clearly do not need him.'

'Are you assuming that because Spratchett has taken your money he will vote for you? He might still support Mistress Digges' father. That would give you five, including Tutepenny, and Cavendish seven.'

'I do not think he would play false with me, sir,' says Pepys, with slightly more confidence than is justified by Spratchett's past record.

'I am sure that you are a good judge of character,' I say.

I do not add that I am not certain that Digby's vote can be taken for granted either. Silvia may still prefer her father to become the new Member of Parliament and has more influence with Digby than Pepys is willing to admit to himself. Calling Jacob Cavendish a fool may not have been Pepys's wisest move this evening.

'I trust you have no intention, Sir John, of making a public declaration that you suspect Spratchett of murder?' says Pepys. 'Of course, the votes of Dix and Pettus would be untainted, but I would wish Spratchett to be there to enforce the bargain, as I have paid him to do.'

'If anyone killed Admiral Digges,' I say, 'I think it is more likely to be Solomon Larter. His nephew seems to have done his best to ensure that a verdict of accidental death was arrived at. The Coroner's careful circumlocution makes more sense if his aim was to cover up the deeds of somebody close to him. But, for all that the inhabitants of Eastwold wish to accuse each other, there is a great lack of hard evidence.'

I look Pepys in the eye. Does he realise that, after my visit today, I now know that Peacock was Larter's secret accuser? If so, he gives nothing away.

'You have found no evidence? That is a thousand pities,' he says. 'Convenient though Larter's guilt would be, I would not wish to proceed against anyone without sufficient proof. The Duke wishes the election to pass with as little fuss as possible. In which case, have you spoken to everyone you need to speak to?'

'I still have a few people to question here. I also wonder if I should go to Lowestoft and speak to Henry Cavendish.'

'As I told Mr Pepys,' Digby interjects, 'it is a long way. In your carriage it might take all day – indeed, you might not get there at all if the road is flooded. And in any case, Henry would have nothing he could tell you. He has not been to Eastwold for some months.'

'But Sir John could ride there on your own horse, Digby?' Silvia asks her husband.

'I cannot spare him,' says Digby. 'I cannot spare him even for an hour. I have to inspect the drains that Larter was complaining about. There are many drains and the fields are flooded. It cannot be done on foot. I should sink up to my knees. I would like to help you, Sir John, but it simply cannot be done.'

I suspect Digby does not want to risk lending a perfectly good horse to a stranger who may return him in a state in which he cannot be ridden again for a week. Our own driver is similarly solicitous about the wellbeing of our carriage horses, which are not used to the saddle.

'Well, perhaps after you have finished inspecting the drains,' I say. 'It would be helpful, but perhaps not essential, to speak to him. You mentioned Mistress Pettus's grave, Mister Pepys. I think the vicar may not have explained things well. Her coffin is about to tumble from the graveyard to the beach. It would be more seemly to gather her remains together and reinter them before they fall. It would be a kindness to Pettus, since he and the other fishermen mend their nets there. He cannot fail to notice the constant shower of family bones.'

Pepys shakes his head. 'I have given the vicar my word on the matter. And Pettus's vote seems safe enough anyway. Between what I have paid him and what I have paid Spratchett, his vote is already dear enough.'

'In that case,' I say, 'I will not look to you for help. But I still think that the coffin should be raised as soon as possible, don't you, Mister Digges?'

Digby looks at me. 'Mistress Pettus's body?'

'Yes, you remember, surely? She died at about the same time as your late mother. I'm certain you would not allow your mother's remains to be swept away in that manner.'

'I cannot permit you to do as you ask ... not if the vicar has already forbidden it.'

'Surely you are in a position to overrule him? I mean as a magistrate. There must be grounds for forcing his hand. It is a matter of public decency. We just need to sit down together and study the relevant legislation—'

'I would not seek to overrule the vicar concerning his own churchyard,' says Digby. 'In that one place, at least, the law of God must trump any legislation in Westminster.'

Silvia is frowning. But she knows her husband will not oppose anyone if he doesn't have to.

'Then I shall not imply to the vicar that I have the support of either of you – not if it would embarrass you in any way. I can still get together a group of fishermen regardless—'

'No,' says Digby.

'But surely—'

'No, Sir John. You may be carrying out an investigation into my father's death, but for all that I am still the only resident magistrate here in Eastwold and all other matters of law must be referred to me. I forbid you to interfere with any of the graves. And I shall deal promptly and firmly with any fisherman who tries to assist you. Even if your own privileged position allows you to escape the consequences of your foolish actions, I shall take action against them. The laws against witchcraft prohibit the digging up of bodies, and the penalties are severe.'

'It was certainly not my intention to allow Pettus and his colleagues to end up in court as necromancers. When the time comes, I hope that Mistress Pettus's bones will at least be collected from the beach and given decent burial elsewhere. If there is any question of cost, I shall of course pay.'

Digby opens his mouth but at that moment two footmen arrive with the next course. And the process of serving supper prevents any further discussion of corpses.

'Well,' says Aminta, when we are back in our room. 'I hadn't expected Digby to stand up to you like that. Either he has found a new sense of courage, or he is very afraid of the vicar.'

'Too afraid even to go to church?' I ask.

'He tells us his absence is merely temporary,' says Aminta. 'And there are as many reasons not to go to church as there are to go.'

'There's something very odd about the relationship between those two, don't you think? Sometimes they seem to be so distant as to be sworn enemies, sometimes they seem to be working hand in glove.'

'There's something very odd about Eastwold,' says Aminta. 'If you told me that the Devil walked here every night, it wouldn't surprise me in the slightest.'

From a long way off, we can hear the waves crashing against the shore, each rush of water pushing the land back a little further. And perhaps I am being too fanciful, but somewhere in the distance I could swear that I hear the deep tolling of a large bell.

From my Lady Grey's most excellent poem
The Election

Thus does our clerk, none think it odd,
Retread the path the Admiral trod
And those that took the Admiral's gold,
Now have a few more coins to hold.
A Guinea here, a promise there,
To make the burgesses declare
Their firm support for all things naval,
In place of help for men who gave all
When Charles the Martyr lately called 'em.
(And then the roundheads cruelly mauled 'em,
Took their lives and took their houses
Beggared all their sons and spouses.)
'If kings forget old loyalty,'
Quoth they, 'Then so, we think, may we.'

Chapter 14

I have breakfast with a loyal supporter of the late, martyred King

It is another cloudless morning. The sun shines and there is a breeze that will not displease the fishermen, their sails cracking then billowing as their small boats work their way out to sea. I look along the beach from my high vantage point, shielding my eyes from the sun with my right hand. The more distant cliffs are half hidden by spray, which rises as the sea strikes home and lingers in the early morning air, like a cloud of tiny diamonds. Another high tide. Another chance for the saltwater to nibble away at the town. I turn and press on, past fronts of houses that no longer possess backs, navigating roads that often end in a vertiginous drop to the beach. It is fortunate that, like Digby, I do not believe in ghosts, or I would see anguished faces in every ruined window and start at the crash of every wave on the beach below.

I have told Digby, with prudent economy, that I intend to walk along the cliff this bright spring morning. For some reason I have not told him that my walk will end at his father-in-law's house. Perhaps I had not told myself when I set out. This may be an awkward discussion.

Jacob lives in a small cottage to the north of Eastwold and a little inland, though his nominal residence, the one that gives him the right to vote, lies some twenty feet beneath the sea at high tide. Last year the front garden of the cottage was clearly planted with vegetables, because the forlorn remains of cabbages and tomatoes are evident. Everywhere, new plants are now robustly and independently pushing up through the dead ones, but there is no evidence of any strategy for this year's campaign. Jacob has other concerns.

He answers the door himself when I knock. I am taken aback by his lined face and the strands of grey hair peeping out from under his soft velvet cap. Such stories as I have heard of him date back to the Civil War and to his youth. There is little of the bold Cavalier on show now. His smile, to me as a stranger, is mild and conciliatory. I can see why Tutepenny thought that this was not a man who would raise his hand against another, whatever the cause. The knee-length blue coat and waistcoat are faded and stained. The brave display of lace at his throat is ragged and would not pass muster at Whitehall Palace. But there is still a steel glint in his grey eyes. He intends to treat me kindly, whether I like it or not.

'Ah, Sir John,' he says. 'I was warned that you might visit. Have you eaten yet? Or are you one of those who still regards breakfast as suitable only for women, children and invalids?'

'Like Mister Pepys,' I say, 'I usually content myself with a draft of small beer in the morning.'

'Well, today you may join me in some smoked herring, or

not, as you choose. When I was campaigning for the King, I could never be sure when my next meal might be coming. I ate whenever I could, and the early morning was a time when Cromwell's cavalry rarely troubled us. One of the blessings of these days of peace and plenty, Sir John, is that I can now eat when I wish. But I have not forsaken my habit of breakfast.'

I nod. When working for Arlington, I missed a great number of meals. And politely declining food into which one of my country's enemies had introduced poison has saved my life on several occasions. Of course, in spite of the welcome, I cannot be certain that the fish I am being offered now is safe either.

We are served by Cavendish's maid, whom I doubt he can afford, and like my mother in the impoverished years of my childhood, he may owe his servants many months' or years' pay.

'I assume you want to know whether I killed Robert Digges?' says Cavendish.

'Why do you say that?'

'If you don't want to know, then I've really no idea what you're doing here. It must have occurred to you that I was a likely murderer. Digges took my ancestral home in a most underhand way and he was my rival for the vacant seat. And he was a roundhead cur of the sort that I fought for four years to exterminate. Why shouldn't I have killed him?'

These were precisely the reasons that Digby quoted to me as making his father-in-law an obvious suspect. It is good of Cavendish to sum them up so neatly.

'So, did you?' I ask.

'No. I really thought I would beat him in the election, and all the rest was such a long time ago. The older you get, the more grudges weigh you down. Would you like another herring?'

I allow him to add more fish to my plate. If the food is poisoned, I'm dead already.

'Where were you when the Admiral was killed?'

'Here. Depending on the exact hour he died, I may have already been in bed. I lead a very dull existence, Sir John. There is a limit to how much excitement a man is allowed over his entire life. I used up my allocation between 1642 and 1645. Indeed, I probably used most of it during a single charge with Prince Rupert's cavalry at Edgehill. Rupert's strategy, you see, was always to try to win a battle quickly and single-handed. He thought that if the infantry couldn't keep up with him that was their bad luck. What he never realised was that it was his bad luck too. You're not old enough to have fought in the war?'

'No, not by a long way, though service with Lord Arlington has added a good ten years to my age and provided me with a number of mementos, including an old wound in my leg that still troubles me and a more visible scar on my face that does not.'

'I wasn't going to mention that.'

'People don't. They consider it impolite to tell me I must have cut my cheek badly. And the story of how I got it is very prosaic. Inattention at the wrong point in a fight. For weeks at a time I now forget that it is even there, except when shaving. If you were with Rupert during the war, then you may know my father-in-law, Sir Felix Clifford?'

'Yes, of course. He usually made Rupert's conduct look prudent and considered. Can he really still be alive?'

'Very much so. He lives with us now and is probably making the most of Aminta's absence to reduce the stocks of wine in my cellars to manageable levels.'

'A whole generation of country gentlemen lived all of their

useful days and expended much of their inherited wealth over a meagre four years. We have since had a quarter of a century to contemplate our folly.'

'The King won't make any reparations to those who were fined,' I say. 'He's ensured that the Church and the big landowners who had whole estates confiscated by Cromwell have been compensated. As for the small fry, they may have fought for his father, but they also lost the war. If they wanted to avoid ruin, they should have won it. It was entirely their mistake. What money the King has, after Pepys has taken what he needs for the Navy and Lady Castlemaine has gambled away most of the rest, scarcely keeps him in clean linen. He'd need to raise new taxes, and new taxes were the mistake his father made.'

'We can make him see sense.'

'He does see sense. That's why you'll get nothing.'

'One of us should have supported Parliament,' says Cavendish. 'Me or Isaac. Many families arranged things thus. Whichever side won, they would have somebody in the winning camp. But we both fought for the King.'

'Was your brother also with Rupert?'

'Artillery – more static and more thoughtful. An artillery duel can be won by the better mathematician. He worked out after the war that we could no longer afford to live in the Priory – not after our loans to the King and the repeated payment of fines to Parliament. We should have been grateful to Digges for taking it off our hands at any price. I'm not, of course, but I should be.'

'So, Isaac wasn't in any way rash?'

'Not at all.'

'But he killed Venetia Digges in a fit of rage? That's the

story, isn't it? He wanted them to escape together. It was his last chance. He believed – wrongly – that her husband was due home at any moment. She refused to go with him. He killed her. Nobody has ever come up with a better motive for the crime, have they?'

'That's why I'm sure he didn't do it,' says Jacob. 'Nothing could have been less like him. Digges was a brute, as you will have already found out. Venetia's life with him was deeply unpleasant. But Isaac, whatever else he did, would not have run off with her. He had no money. He knew that he'd be taking her to a life of penury. And Digges was away more often than not, so it wasn't all bad. And she could never have taken young Digby with them. The idea they might have run away together was nonsense.'

'So why did he flee?'

'Because she was dead – by accident or suicide – and he knew he'd be accused. Even if he wasn't arrested by the magistrate, then Digges, as you say, was expected back the next day and would have made up his own mind what to do about things.'

'You say accident or suicide, but isn't it equally likely that Digges came back early and caught them together?'

'No, that's simply not possible. I said that Digges was due to arrive the following day – as near as you can predict these things – but he was miles away that evening. His fleet had been stationed just off the Dutch coast, near Texel. He'd sent word he was returning, and most of his fleet arrived in Chatham as expected, but his own flagship was delayed by bad weather and a broken rudder. He became separated from the others for a while. When his wife drowned, he was still in hot pursuit of the rest of his fleet, who probably hoped he'd sunk. He didn't reach the Medway until two days after Venetia died.

Then he was kept in London, reporting back to the Duke of York, and explaining why he'd been the only one to lose his way. He wasn't noted for his navigational skills. It's all well documented at the Admiralty. There was supposed to be some sort of commission of enquiry into his competence, though I think he slid out of it with the aid of his friends. It was over a week later that he finally arrived here – too late even for his wife's funeral. He immediately swore vengeance on Isaac and indeed the whole of my family. But that was all he could do.'

'Would Isaac have been afraid of Robert Digges?'

'Isaac was never afraid of anything. But either Digges would have killed him or he'd have killed Digges in self-defence. Neither eventuality was desirable. And Isaac was a gunner, not a cavalryman. He'd have made his calculations very carefully. I know that my brother would never have killed Venetia Digges, whatever the jury thought or was made to think. I don't know where he went, but I'm sure he is dead now. Had he lived, he would have found a way to contact me, and he never did. No, Isaac was too rational and reasonable to kill in a jealous rage.'

'So Venetia's death was accident then?' I ask.

'I actually believe suicide is most likely. I think she and Isaac discussed their situation calmly on the beach. It became clear to her that my brother wouldn't take her away. He went off and left her standing there. She couldn't face going back to being Digges' wife. She drowned herself. When Isaac heard she'd been found dead, he slipped quietly away. I don't doubt that he felt some guilt, of course – I would have done, if I'd led her on.'

'Why did the Coroner not consider this possibility?'

'Because the Coroner, then as now, was David Larter.'

'He has a high opinion of himself, but he seems a fair man. I can't see why he would wish to see your brother hang.'

'Jonathan Larter, David's father, was one of the two men killed during the siege of Eastwold. David never forgave the Cavendishes – any of us. That ruling was how he got his revenge – in my opinion, anyway. I'm surprised he hasn't tried to get me hanged for the Admiral's murder now. You may think something is buried in the past but sooner or later, like the coffins that fall from the cliffs here, old rivalries and jealousies poke their way up again.'

'I wasn't at either inquest, but I think you may be blaming him unfairly. He definitely isn't trying to blame you, this time anyway. Could he be covering up for his uncle though?'

'I've no idea. But that's the trouble with Eastwold. After you've been here for a while you start looking for problems where there aren't any. When there is strangeness all around you, you start to believe that anything might be possible.'

I stand. 'Thank you for breakfast,' I say. 'I must try it again one day.'

'Feel free to call round when you do. Don't worry – I'm not after your vote.'

'I don't have one. But are you sure you should stand against Pepys?'

'Perfectly sure.'

'I don't want you to waste the money that remains to you fighting a lost cause.'

'Why should you care?'

'I probably don't. Not that much. But it's the advice I'd give to my father-in-law, if he ever felt inclined to stand for Parliament.'

'I know what I'm doing,' he says. 'I've thought it through.

Rupert taught me that charging headlong into battle isn't always the best policy.'

'Sir Felix always tells me the exact same thing,' I say. 'It must have been a hard-earned lesson, but it's good to know that the war wasn't a complete waste of everyone's time.'

'Back again for some of the best ale in the Eastern Counties?'

'I've been eating salt fish for breakfast,' I say.

'What do you usually eat?' asks Benefice.

'Nothing.'

'Very wise.' He leans forward on his crutch and pushes a battered pewter tankard towards me. He straightens himself again and allows me time to drink. 'So, what's the real reason for your coming here?'

'Why do you ask?'

'Because I doubt that you ever go anywhere for just a drink.'

'I'm looking for problems where there aren't any,' I say.

'You've come to the right place then. If you're going to ask me again who killed the Admiral, though, then the answer is still that I don't know – or care. Not even for a few more Shillings. And if Pepys wants to take my pension away, then that's what he'll have to do.'

I shake my head. 'If he tries to do it, I'll go to Lord Arlington and ask him to get it restored. I'll have to lick my Lord's shoes, but it will amuse him to grant me that small favour, after he's enjoyed making me sweat for a day or two.'

'Thank you,' says Benefice. 'But I've told you I've still no information for you. You're gentry, so you won't be doing me any favours because you like the look of my face.'

'It's more whether I like the look of Pepys's face, to be honest. I'm still hoping my Shillings aren't wasted and you'll remember something you've temporarily forgotten. In the meantime, though, what do you know about Mary Pettus's death?'

He pauses and considers. 'That would have been about the time that Venetia Digges died. Fever, as I remember. Like Catch. It's not uncommon. What has that got to do with Admiral Digges' murder?'

'Quite possibly nothing at all, but her coffin is about to fall to the beach.'

He looks out of the window that faces the sea while he considers this. 'It happens all the time. There are always one or two coffins hanging up there, as the churchyard gets eaten away. There are always bones on the beach.'

'I want to exhume the coffin and move it to a safer place. The vicar says no.'

Benefice considers this carefully. 'Does he? How close to the edge is the coffin?'

'You can already see the end of it sticking out of the cliff.'

'Too dangerous, then,' he says with a quick shake of the head. 'That'll be the reason. You couldn't ask a man to dig there – right where the cliff is about to give way.'

'So, there's no way of extracting the body?'

'We did it once, years ago. But that was just close to the edge, not hanging over it.'

'I'll pay, of course. It's not only the vicar who is opposed though. Mister Digges is threatening to prosecute anyone who tries, so I may also have to refund whatever fines Digges imposes.'

'It's not a question of payment. They'd do it for nothing, if I asked them. But I wouldn't want to send them to their deaths, and nor should you. I think you may be asking too much, Sir John, even if you do save my pension.' He turns slowly, stabbing his crutch against the floorboards at each movement.

'In that case, what do you know about Cavendish and Venetia Digges?' I ask.

He looks at me, mid-revolution, half over his shoulder. 'Nobody knows for sure. She was badly treated by Digges and left alone for months on end. Digges was a foul-mouth oaf. Cavendish was a gentleman, a romantic hero, ruined by fighting for a lost cause.'

'Why did she marry Digges then?'

'Her first husband was killed in the war. She was left a penniless widow. Digges was better than that. And even Digges was young and good-looking once.'

'And everyone in the village knew about her and Cavendish?'

'I'd say everyone except the Admiral.'

'And she never decided to run away with Isaac Cavendish?'

'Isaac? Oh, I see. I thought you meant Jacob. Yes, later she was attached to Isaac – just before he vanished. But not to begin with. To begin with it was Jacob. It caused a lot of bad feeling all round. Jacob and Isaac – they weren't exactly on good terms. I doubt that the brothers would have ever spoken to each other again. If Isaac had lived, that is.'

Chapter 15

We meet more of the Digges family

I return to the Priory to discover that I am late for an event that I did not know I was invited to. We are to dine with Digby's uncle and aunt, a little way out of Eastwold. Digby and Silvia have already departed. Pepys has elected to travel with Digby.

'Or should I say with Silvia?' says Aminta as we drive in leisurely pursuit in our own carriage, jolting along the rough Suffolk lanes. 'I fear that may be the case. Pepys has been following her all morning like an ancient and rather shameless hound with his nose into something he likes.'

'Does Silvia object?' I ask.

'Not a bit, unfortunately. She in turn seems like an indulgent mistress, always feeding her dog some tasty little morsel that is probably very bad for it, then looking very pleased with herself. I have warned her as much as is decent in a conversation between two respectable married ladies. I even alluded to certain practices of Pepys's that should have brought a blush to her cheeks and mine.'

'And did they?'

'I fear not. But, in fairness to myself, I have now been married twice. And though Silvia has only been married once, she has had the chance to observe closely two males of the Digges family, so perhaps there is little about men that now surprises her. She saw nothing untoward about Pepys's behaviour, even when I was being quite explicit. Do most men behave like that?'

'I have no idea what Pepys does,' I say.

'Shall I describe it to you in greater detail?'

'I would greatly prefer it if you did not. How do you know anyway?'

'The actresses with whom I am acquainted have withheld very little from me in that respect. He asks them very directly for what he needs. I suppose when you are short of time, and have a wife waiting at home or the King waiting at Westminster, it's best to avoid any misunderstandings that he might later regret.'

'I suppose it is,' I say. 'Were you aware that Venetia Digges had been encouraging both Isaac and Jacob Cavendish?'

'Silvia said something of the sort. Venetia was a frequent visitor to her house when she was young. She can remember conversations about it between her father and mother, though they meant little to her at the time. Now they mean slightly more.'

'And so Digby knows too?'

'About his father-in-law? I doubt that very much. The liaison between Isaac and his mother is painful enough. Jacob would be one Cavendish too many in the family history. His mother's love life must have been almost as complicated as—'

'My mother's?'

'No, not quite that complicated. Still, we really do have a great deal in common with Digby and Silvia, don't we?'

'A little, perhaps. But Silvia hasn't told Digby how complex things were?'

'Just as Digby is careful to protect Silvia from harm, I think she would wish to avoid causing him distress. Or indeed causing Jacob distress. As you say, Jacob is now Digby's father-in-law. There are things that it is good for Digby to know and things that it is not.'

'Pepys also being one of the things that is not?'

'I do hope so. Your friend Samuel is at least discreet. And he has the happy knack of not fathering children. Perhaps no harm will come of it.'

'He's not my friend.'

'He thinks you're his friend.'

'I shall undeceive him.'

'No, I may need you to be his friend if things get difficult – I mean if Silvia starts to believe any of the things that Pepys is saying to her. A man listens to his friend's good advice.'

'I'm not going to give him advice,' I say. 'Good or bad.'

'That's what you think at the moment. You may be surprised what you think in a few days' time. I'll let you know.'

Of course, Aminta is right. A few days can change things a great deal.

We have travelled some way to a modest little farmhouse. Five miles or all the way back to the previous century, as you please. The floors are stone and strewn with rushes. Plates here are still made of wood rather than pewter or silver. Many of the windows, other than those in the main room, lack glass, the deficiency being made good with wooden shutters. In the winter, the choice of darkness or cold must be ever-present. This is where Digby grew up, when his father was away at sea. The darkness. Or the cold. It must have helped form his view of the world in all manner of ways.

Both Alexander and Barbara Digges are plainly dressed in faded black wool and very clean white linen. Their faces are gaunt. Their hair is grey. I imagine that they pray a lot, but I'm not sure what they pray for. I think they pray mainly against things.

'You are welcome, Sir John and Lady Grey, and you, Mister Pepys, to our humble home,' says Alexander.

'It seems very comfortable,' says Aminta.

Barbara Digges says nothing. Perhaps she was aiming for godliness rather than comfort. Comfort is probably sinful. A soft feather cushion can drag you halfway to hell.

'It is some distance from the town,' I say, by way of mitigation.

'We prefer it thus,' says Alexander.

Elseways they would be in danger from the temptations of Eastwold – the inn, perhaps, or the church. One or the other.

'It is a pleasant country,' says Pepys. 'My family have owned land and farmed in Huntingdon and Cambridgeshire.'

'We have never been to either,' says Barbara. 'Nor shall we ever go there.' The enticements across the border are clearly worse even than those of Eastwold.

'You did not attend Cambridge University?' I ask Alexander.

'A waste of money,' he says.

'I am determined that our children – that is to say our sons – will go there,' says Silvia.

'Really?' Barbara looks at Digby for instant denial.

'Well ... there are arguments on both sides ... that or

perhaps the Navy . . . we have not decided anything . . . not for certain . . .' says Digby.

'Your wife seems to have done,' says Alexander. 'So, I expect that is what will happen. You are fortunate that you have more money than you need – if your father has not already given it to the voters of Eastwold.'

'Fortunately not. Or only a little,' says Digby.

'You have found the will?' asks Alexander.

'Yes,' says Digby.

'But you thought fit not to tell us what it contained?'

'It did not concern you, Aunt,' says Silvia.

'Not in any way?' Alexander asks.

'Not in any way at all, I'm afraid. He left his estate in its entirety to Digby and me, except for a few small bequests. There was one to the vicar, who declined it, and another to Edward Catch, who sadly did not live to claim it, and finally one to James Tutepenny. Oh, and he asked forgiveness for his sins and commended his soul to God, an act of which you will doubtless approve. There was nothing else of note in the document.'

'A bequest to the vicar personally, not to the church?' asks Barbara.

'The will was made some years ago and the Admiral and the vicar were formerly good friends,' says Silvia. 'And in any case, the church is about to fall into the sea. There would be little point in buying a new pyx or repairing the roof.'

'Who is Tutepenny?'

'A sailor who served under my father-in-law for many years. I am not sure that Digby has even yet told him that he has been left the money.'

'Yes, I must do so,' says Digby quickly. 'I am failing in my duties as an executor.'

'And the churchwarden?' asks Barbara. 'What possible reason could he have for giving him money?'

'Edward Catch undeniably needed it,' says Silvia.

'My brother-in-law was a fool,' says Barbara. 'First these senseless bequests and then the expense of standing for Parliament. Pure vanity.'

'He could afford both. You need not fear that Digby and I have been left impoverished and a burden on the parish.'

'But nothing to his own brother?' asks Barbara. 'Nothing at all?'

Silvia smiles sympathetically. 'I fear not, Aunt,' she says.

'And we brought up his son,' says Barbara. 'Brought him up to fear God.'

'For which I am eternally grateful,' says Digby.

'On the contrary, you seem to have forgotten everything that we taught you,' says Barbara. 'Even if we can't always be there to see how you are backsliding, remember that God is. Wherever you are, whatever you are doing, God is watching. He sees not only your outward actions but also the inward state of your soul. He sees you attending a church with an altar rail and vestments and incense – all three abominations unto the Lord. He sees you bowing, like a romish puppet, at every mention of the name of Jesus. He sees you eating meat on a Friday. He sees you marrying into a Royalist family.'

Silvia's smile remains sympathetic. She is not about to condemn her husband's judgment in marrying her, but in many other respects she clearly agrees with Barbara. There is something lacking in the amiable Digby.

'Everyone is a Royalist now,' says Aminta. 'My husband says so all the time, though only to avoid discussing the amount of time he was a Republican. The King has undertaken to forget who supported his father and who did not – a wise decision for a man who is not always very wise and doesn't like making decisions. But even so, it is considered impolite to remind him now of your past allegiances, implying you require either rewarding or forgiveness.'

'Don't speak to me of that man,' says Barbara. 'Do you know what his Court is like? Since you are a respectable married woman, I hope you do not.'

'If I did not know the Court intimately, then I should not be able to write plays satirising it,' says Aminta.

There is a long silence following this remark, which Aminta does not try to break. Indeed, I think she may be enjoying it. I doubt that I shall be invited here again, with my Court-frequenting, play-writing satirist of a wife, but it is quite a long journey over rough roads anyway.

'If we have all finished eating,' says Alexander, 'then perhaps we should repair to the garden.'

Digby stands.

'After we have said suitable prayers of thanks,' says Barbara.

Digby sits again.

Alexander prays extempore for some ten minutes, taking in each of his guests and their sins in some detail. Fortunately he doesn't seem to know about most of mine. I look at Aminta to see if the prayers have been effective. No, she still seems to be a playwright.

Alexander adds his hopes that God should assist me in my mission to bring his brother's killer out into the light of day. That's thoughtful of him, but he has to realise that it still doesn't rule him out as a suspect. He surveys us all in silence for a moment then says: 'Amen.'

'Amen,' says Pepys, with apparent sincerity, though he

clearly has doubts that God would really go against Arlington's instructions to cover things up in the interests of the Admiralty.

'Amen,' says Digby, who is already standing again, deceived by the cunning pause in Alexander's orisons.

'Amen,' says Aminta sweetly. I can see that Alexander has unwittingly set himself up as a character in her next play. She has already committed much of his prayer to memory for later parody.

'Amen,' says Silvia. She stifles a yawn, perhaps not quite as well as she wished, or perhaps exactly as she intended.

Those of us who are not already standing awkwardly now stand and we all troop out into the sunshine, shaking off the holy chill of Alexander and Barbara Digges' dining room.

Silvia immediately takes Barbara affectionately by the arm and steers her off down the path for a cosy chat. Barbara clearly does not wish to go but can find no way of politely refusing her guest. As a sharp-edged piece of irony, it is the equal of anything I have seen in one of Aminta's plays. Pepys is in earnest conversation with Digby, almost certainly about the election, though they must have had plenty of time to discuss it in the coach coming here. Perhaps Pepys's mind was elsewhere.

Alexander nods in the direction of his departing wife and her companion.

'I warned Robert not to let his son marry that knowing minx,' he says. 'Pretty enough, if that's what you value in a wife. And clever. Too clever. But that family was never any good. You can respect the poor – some of them anyway – if they have truly lacked the opportunities to make money. But a family born into great wealth that then dissipates it over two generations. God does not forgive that sort of profligacy. There is no place in heaven for the spendthrift.'

'Many Royalist families felt that they had little choice but to make loans to the King,' I say. 'In most cases that King, or one of his ancestors, was the source of their wealth in the first place. They were merely paying a long-standing debt. It would have been shameful to refuse.'

'The Cavendishes mismanaged their land even before the war.'

I think of Tutepenny's analysis of the reasons for the loss of Royalists' estates. Had he been born into a different family, and not had to spend quite so much time gutting herring, he might have done quite well for himself.

'My mother always regarded ignorance of the mechanics of agriculture as proof of gentility,' I say. 'The only reason that she did not ruin herself by handing money over to the King was that she was already deeply in debt. She would have needed to borrow from the servants but, since she had ceased to pay them some time before, that too was impossible. Of course the servants would have given her their last penny if she'd asked. You don't have to deserve loyalty in order to get it unquestioningly. Or my mother didn't.'

'Your mother's family also ruined itself through their neglect of their duty?'

'That, and high treason. They did both. I forget how many of my ancestors were beheaded for choosing the wrong side – I mean my West ancestors – the Greys on the whole usually declined to commit themselves one way or the other, which was wise. They survived the wars of York and Lancaster, the Pilgrimage of Grace, Queen Mary, Queen Elizabeth and the Gunpowder Plot without any loss of life or property. But the Wests believed in letting people know exactly what they thought of them. As for me . . . I fear I am more of a Grey than a West.'

Or am I? My mother was vague over critical parts of my ancestry. She died with the question of how much of a Grey I am still only partly answered. And, now I consider the matter, I have told Lord Arlington what I think of him more often than was perhaps advisable.

'The Diggeses have always been simple yeomen,' says Alexander. 'And that is what we should have remained. Wealth is a glittering snare that traps and does not release the victim. I am pleased that my brother saw fit to leave us nothing in his will. It was a benison. He knew that we have no love of gold or silver – we store up riches in heaven, not on earth.'

'Your wife is of the same opinion?' I ask.

'She resents Robert's ingratitude – for the sake of his own soul, rather than any gain on our part. It is good that a man should pay his debts.'

'To his brother and his sister-in-law, if not to his King,' I say.

Alexander opens his mouth, then closes it again.

'Was your brother's view of Silvia much the same as yours?' I ask. 'You say you warned him against the marriage, but it went ahead all the same. I doubt that Digby would have wed against his father's will.'

'No? Digby is more stubborn than he looks. When he gets an idea into his head, nothing will change his mind. The Devil is in that one, Sir John. It always was, much though we tried to beat it out of him with rod and strap. As for Robert – he eventually saw through Silvia Cavendish well enough. He admonished her faults when her husband neglected to do so. He chastened her when God required her to be chastened.'

'And how did she respond to that?' I ask politely. 'With humility and gratitude?'

'With her usual sly cunning.' He looks again in the direction that Silvia led his reluctant wife. 'She doesn't argue back. She doesn't beg on her knees for forgiveness. She simply smiles with lowered eyes and persists in her folly. But I pray for her. I pray that she will find the path of truth and righteousness. I pray that she will submit herself to Digby's rule and become his true companion in managing their estate in a prudent and godly manner. As Barbara is mine.'

'Do you farm much land here?' I ask.

'A hundred or so acres,' says Alexander. 'But it is poor land. Marshy. It makes us little money.'

'A great blessing, then,' I say.

'A blessing indeed,' he replies. And for a moment, I cannot say why, he stands there grinding his teeth.

There is some competition not to accommodate Pepys on the drive back to Eastwold. Our respective coaches sit under the trees, some twenty or thirty yards apart – close enough that from our seats we can hear every word spoken over by the shafts of Digby's coach while the horses are being attached.

'I am sure that Sir John and Lady Grey would welcome your going with them in their carriage,' says Digby. 'It is unfair that we should have the pleasure your company on both journeys.'

'We still have much to discuss concerning the election,' says Pepys, placing his foot on the step.

'I think that we have already said all we need to say,' says Digby, an outstretched leg blocking Pepys's way in.

'But there is the question of the procedure on the day. That is to be thought on.'

'You will need to consult Spratchett or Peacock. I have never voted before. I am as ignorant as you of the customs. If that is all, then business need not keep you from the enjoyment of the company of Sir John – and his good lady.'

I can see the stubbornness of which Alexander complained. Beneath Digby's obliging exterior, the glances towards his wife for approval and reassurance, there is a grim determination to get his way. Pepys is not to be allowed to enter the carriage.

'Very well,' says Pepys suavely, never one to argue a case that he knows is lost. 'It will of course give me great pleasure to accompany my old friend, Sir John.'

'Digby has finally noticed Pepys's attention to his wife,' Aminta whispers to me. 'I think Sam has had his last ride in that carriage. Sadly that means he must ride in ours or walk.'

'I think that he would have had difficulty in achieving much with the wife in the other coach, when the husband was present,' I say.

'My actress friends tell me otherwise. They say he has a way with his hands that really is quite remarkable and can have come only with diligent practice.'

'Then Silvia has had a lucky escape,' I say.

'My fear is that she may not think so.'

'Well, well,' says Pepys, climbing up into our coach, 'it would seem that we are to travel back together.'

'Not with the Diggeses?' asks Aminta. 'I thought you might have preferred it.'

'Ah, no . . . they proposed that I should join them – begged me, almost – but I politely declined.'

'Mistress Digges' loss is my gain,' says Aminta. She spreads her skirts so that the only place Pepys can sit is next to me.

* * *

We reach the Priory first and are able to watch as Digby and Silvia emerge from their carriage and enter the house without speaking a word to each other or to us.

Aminta looks at me. I shrug. Pepys thanks us both profusely and goes into the house to prepare, he says, his address to the voters of Eastwold. Our carriage disappears round a corner towards the stables with much clattering of wheels and harness and the ringing of horseshoes on cobblestones.

'The Diggeses are not the best of friends,' says Aminta.

'Because Digby deprived Silvia of Pepys's company?'

'Because Digby made a fuss in public that everyone will have noticed.'

'Everyone?'

'Well, the two of us most certainly did. I doubt if Pepys missed it. And Digby's aunt and uncle listen to everything in case they need to report somebody to God.'

'I feel sorry for God,' I say. 'He has to put up with a lot of complaints and backbiting by some fairly unpleasant people. Where did you go to after dinner? I noticed that you did not join Barbara and Silvia in their walk. I had an interesting conversation with Alexander, by the way. Digby's upbringing sounded harsher than I had been led to believe – frequent beatings for obstinacy and disobedience. Alexander seemed to confirm that Silvia had suffered at the Admiral's hand, though only when God permitted it.'

'Well, I am pleased that you noticed my absence, even though you and Alexander were getting on so well. I thought that I would talk to the servants. A small amount of sympathy and genteel condescension can yield a surprising amount of information.'

'And?'

'And Alexander and Barbara Digges are deeply in debt.

The farm is unprofitable and the last two harvests have been poor. Alexander has borrowed heavily from his co-religionist Mister Peacock and is unable to repay even the interest, let alone the principal. There are fears that Peacock will foreclose and insist on possession of the farm, which he would like and may have always plotted to seize. Alexander and Barbara had been pinning their hopes a great deal on a loan – or better still, a legacy – from Admiral Digges. His death must have raised their hopes very considerably only for them to be cruelly dashed. Such a shame. Of course, now we know a little more about the way they treated Digby it is unlikely that a loan will come from that direction – still less so if Silvia has anything to do with it. But there is a rumour that the estate is entailed and would pass automatically to Alexander if Digby dies without male heir.'

'Is that true, or just wishful thinking on Alexander's part?'

'I suspect it is just Alexander clutching at straws. Of course, if it were true, then Silvia risks being ejected from her home if Digby dies and she remains childless or makes the mistake of just having girls. Though she seems to have regained possession of her ancestral home, her position may be more precarious than we thought.'

'Of course, Alexander and Barbara might let her remain there, in some lowly and servile capacity, out of their abundant charity,' I say.

'I wonder if our servants are as well informed as Alexander's,' says Aminta.

'I must remember not to get into debt,' I say.

'Or we could just treat the servants with the respect due to them,' says Aminta.

'Yes,' I say. 'We could always try that.'

Chapter 16

An act of worship

'The maids tell me that we should attend morning service,' says Aminta.

'That is good advice, both spiritually and legally,' I say. 'The Act of Uniformity passed in the first regnal year of Queen Elizabeth establishes quite clearly a duty on all of us to attend church on Sunday at the risk of a fine of one Shilling – though I believe Digby is no stricter in enforcing fines for non-attendance than I am. But why are the servants so concerned with ensuring observance? They did not strike me as being especially religious. Largely content and reasonably well paid, but not religious. And, though they are charged with ensuring their employers' breeches and petticoats are in good order, they have no responsibility for their souls.'

'Indeed, I think they are happy for us to go to Hell or not, as we prefer. But they look as ever to the largesse that we shall distribute before we leave. They want us to be content with the service received and not feel that we have missed a good thing through their failure to inform us of it. They are expecting an interesting sermon. George Wraith has had a vision, apparently.'

'A vision of dearth or plenty?'

'I can't imagine Wraith having a pleasant vision. Or, if he did, he'd keep it quiet. No, it must be something really bad if he wishes to share it with us.'

'I suppose so,' I say. 'How do the servants know such things?'

'Servants know everything. If you are good to them, they will tell you some of it.'

'Then I shall inform Digby that we plan to observe the Act of Uniformity of 1558, as amended by subsequent Acts of Parliament and Royal Proclamations.'

'But not until after breakfast,' says Aminta. 'You and Pepys may of course have a draught of small beer if it pleases you.'

'Small beer? No, I'll have some smoked herring if it's on offer,' I say. 'I suspect that Wraith's sermon will not be short and dinner may be late.'

Digby, perhaps stung by earlier accusations of recusancy, has readily agreed that we should all go to Matins this morning – family, servants, guests. Thus we are now walking along the cliff top, Digby and Silvia leading, Pepys bobbing half a pace behind them, Aminta and I arm in arm, and then various Digges domestics, in strict order of precedence, the Steward first and the knives-and-boots boy at the very back, scuffing his heels and picking his nose. The day is warm, the sea calm and the sky untroubled. There are bright yellow blooms on the gorse bushes. Whatever disaster the vicar is about to predict, it must be still some hours away. We have time to pray it won't happen.

The church is fuller than I expected, but perhaps word of the sermon has spread. Solomon Larter MP and his wife are in the left-hand front pew, together with Mayor Spratchett and the Lady Mayoress. I recognise Benefice and Tutepenny, placed by authority in the second row on account of their respective high offices. Several other fishermen and their families are behind them. There are in fact one or two children in the congregation, dressed reluctantly in Sunday clothes originally purchased for older siblings and reflecting the buttoned-up style of dress of the Republic. Pepys nods gravely to Dix and Pettus. The others, Dowsing, Cooper and Bottulph (all non-voters and of no interest to Pepys), are pointed out to me by Digby and acknowledged with a smile. Mother Catch, looking very much unlike a witch but still somehow apart from the rest, sits behind the families. At the very back of the church is Jacob Cavendish, bolt upright. Close by, David Larter lounges, legs stretched before him, like one who does not expect the next hour to be profitable in any way. Also at the back, but at some distance from Larter and Cavendish, Peacock sits, sneering, in his black suit of clothes. To show his disapproval of popery, he has kept his hat on. The building almost hums with expectation. They clearly know that today is a day to be in church, with or without a hat. They just don't yet know exactly why.

We take our places at the front of the church, to the right of the town's senior dignitaries. Nobody else, not even the Mayor, would presume to sit in these pews. This must have been where the Cavendishes sat in times past; now it is the rightful property of the Diggeses, who have succeeded in moving closer to heaven by three or four rows. Pepys, by means of several feints and a final nimble sidestep, inserts himself next to Silvia. Aminta bravely sits on the other side of Pepys, to act as a critic and censor of his behaviour rather than for the pleasure of his company. Suddenly the congregation, which had been maintaining a low and reverential buzz of conversation, is silent. In a billowing white surplice calculated to give Peacock apoplexy, Wraith has swept into the church. We rise to greet him. The Sabbath entertainment has begun.

We say our confession, sing a psalm, pray . . . but it is the sermon that we have come to hear. Finally George Wraith ascends into the pulpit and surveys his congregation from his accustomed vantage point. Whatever he says, it's going to be good.

He coughs once, though the church could not be quieter, and begins. 'And God saw that the wickedness of man was great in the earth. And it repented the Lord that he had made man on the earth, and it grieved him at his heart. And the Lord said, I will destroy man whom I have created from the face of the earth; both man, and beast, and the creeping thing, and the fowls of the air; for it repenteth me that I have made them.'

Wraith pauses and wipes a small speck of spittle from his lips with the back of his bony hand. Just outside, only yards away, we can hear the savage hiss of waves striking the seashore. They strike and retreat like some giant, ever hungry serpent.

'My friends, my very dear friends, the Bible tells us that God saw that the people He had created were wicked, just as you are yourselves. God therefore resolved to destroy them – and not only the people, but the blackbirds and the wrens and the deer and the rabbits, even the spiders and the weevils and the fleas that now nestle in your filthy, shit-caked underclothing. In His great wisdom and mercy, He decided to destroy everything that moved. He spared only Noah and his family and bade him gather together two of every kind of creature and put them into a large boat. How did Noah do that? I have no idea. He lived in Palestine whereas, as you know, there are certain animals that dwell only in the distant icy North or in the jungles of Sumatra or in the Americas, far across the Atlantic Ocean, a place of which Noah can have had no possible knowledge. How did he assemble them all? How did he know that he had left none out? Was he obliged to limit all creatures to just two? If so, how did he eliminate the surplus fleas and lice? How did he feed them all while he was building the ark, since each would have required a different sort of food, mostly completely unavailable to him in Palestine? I cannot say. How did he keep the bears from eating the deer while they were confined to the boat? I do not know. They were there for forty days and forty nights, or perhaps for a hundred and fifty days – the Bible is unclear on that point. But for forty or a hundred and fifty, whichever pleased God most, what did Noah do with the vast mass of dung and piss that must have accumulated in the hold? How did he prevent the birds flying away? Did he have to collect frogs and newts or did he leave them to swim along behind the ark? What about freshwater fish, which would have died when sweet and salt waters were mixed together, as they must have been? We do not need to trouble ourselves with such details. The Bible informs us that he did it. But Noah was able to do these things only because God had warned him. Now God has visited me in a dream and warned me of what is to come. He told me, my dear, sweet friends, of your own nauseating wickedness, though I was already aware in broad terms of what you were all doing and, strangely, I was less disgusted by what God told me than

I expected to be. He further informed me that he repented of creating this sandy coast, which does nothing except fill an otherwise untidy gap between Essex and Norfolk. He told me, in conclusion, that he intended to destroy Eastwold. I asked if he would kindly spare us if we sincerely repented, but he said, no, he'd already tried that with Noah and been disappointed with the results. So, there it is, my good friends. God gave me no instructions to build you an ark. You are all about to go to Hell. A great flood is coming that will sweep you all away – and me, too, since I also am a sinner. My sins are not the same as your sins – they are the sins of a refined and educated man – but I still shouldn't have done the things I have done. I know that now and, truly, if I am being honest with you all, I knew it at the time, so there it is. By next Sunday, Eastwold will have gone and you will all be in the eternal torment that you so richly deserve. We shall now sing Psalm 100 – O be joyful in the Lord, all ye lands.'

'The servants do not look unduly distressed,' I say to Aminta as we stand, along with the rest of the congregation, and prepare to leave the church. 'I am not sure that they plan to stop sinning, to the extent that their terms of employment permit it. What the vicar said was speculative rather than conclusive. It would be a strange world in which everyone's dreams proved to be an accurate prediction of what will happen.'

'They all know that the vicar is mad. It's probably not the first time that he has prophesied their destruction.'

'He could be right, though,' I say. 'I've been looking at the records at the Priory. The sea constantly nibbles, but every now and then it takes great bites. In March 1292, they lost three churches in one night. In October 1507, the market square, with all of the houses surrounding it, vanished during two days of storms. You don't need a vision of God in order to know that the same thing could happen at any time, and the spring, with its gales and high tides, is probably one of the more dangerous seasons.'

Those in the lesser pews know not to leave before the Lord of the Manor and his guests do, and we are amongst the first to reach the door, where Wraith stands smiling.

'A most interesting and informative sermon, Vicar,' I say. 'Thank you.'

'I'm glad you enjoyed it, Sir John. My last ever in this church, of course. I'm pleased that Mister Digges was present to hear it too.'

I look beyond him to where Pepys, Digby and Silvia are already out in the sunny churchyard.

'Yes,' I say. 'You said he would not come here again, but he has.'

'His body is here, but his soul is elsewhere. It waits trembling in the shadows for the Devil to take it.'

'And your soul?'

'Already lost, I fear,' he says cheerfully.

'How careless of you,' says Aminta.

Wraith considers this and nods. 'Yes,' he says. 'It would have been so easy to avoid it. So very easy.'

'His employer is merciful,' I say. 'He forgives the sinner.'

He shakes his head. I suppose he knows God much as I know Lord Arlington, and trusts him as little.

We pause idly amongst the tombstones, many leisurely Sunday hours still stretching before us. I leave Digby to talk to his neighbours and Pepys to seek whatever votes he can pick up, and wander over towards the cliff, where a new grave, heaped up with bare earth and as yet unmarked with a monument, sits perilously close to the edge.

'That will soon be in the sea, sir,' says a voice behind me.

I turn to see Tutepenny.

'Whose is it?'

'The Admiral's, sir.'

'A strange place to choose to bury him.'

'It was the vicar's decision,' says Tutepenny.

'I thought he and the Admiral were good friends?'

'Once perhaps, but lately they were somewhat distant,' says Tutepenny. 'Very few loved the Admiral, as you know, and the vicar hates most people. It was not to be expected that they would agree with each other.'

'You must have known the Admiral better than anyone in the town.'

'Yes, sir. Better even than his family, I'll wager, since he spent so much time at sea. He trusted me. Whenever he was rowed ashore, he always wanted me at the tiller, guiding the boat through the shoals.'

'And he was good to you in return?'

'That's not to be looked for, is it, sir? Not from those who don't need to treat you kindly.'

I think of those to whom I have given my loyalty over the years. 'No,' I say. 'It is not to be looked for.'

'And from the Admiral least of all,' says Tutepenny.

It occurs to me that Digby must still not have told Tutepenny of the legacy from his father, but the administration of wills can take time.

For a while we both stare out to sea, each with our own reflections on gratitude.

'And young Mister Digges . . . he didn't object to burying his father there?' I ask.

'No, sir, he did not. His mother is of course safe inside the church. Safe for the moment, at least.'

'Does the vicar have some sort of a hold over Mister Digges?'

'I don't know, sir. But Mister Digges allowed his father to be buried in a place that may not be here next week. I would not have permitted it myself for a member of my own family. Not for anything.'

'Has the vicar always been mad?' I ask.

'Oh no, sir, not at all. Odd perhaps, but not mad. I remember when he was more or less in his right mind.'

'So how did madness strike him?'

'It has done so bit by bit, as the sea destroys the town – imperceptibly much of the time, but with savage speed at others. I do recall when it started though. There's no doubt about that.'

'When?' I ask.

'It was . . .' Tutepenny pauses for so long I wonder if he hasn't fallen into a trance.

'It's no matter if you have forgotten,' I say.

'No, it isn't that. I'd just never quite realised . . . I hadn't made the connection before.' He looks over my shoulder as if checking whether we can be overheard by any of the congregation. 'The first time I thought he seemed really odd . . . it was my first time back in Eastwold after he'd buried Mary Pettus. Of course, that's when it was—'

I am about to ask more, but Digby is suddenly at my shoulder, urging me to return to the house as soon as I please. Dinner is, by long-standing custom, served early on Sunday.

* * *

'I saw you in discussion with Tutepenny,' says Pepys, 'but I could not quite hear what Tutepenny was saying to you. I hope he is not wavering in his support for me?'

We are back at the Priory and are now at the dinner table, though it is scarcely noon. Pepys's mind is, however, running two days ahead of the clock in the hall.

'The election? We did not touch on that,' I say. 'We spoke of other matters.'

'You were talking for a long time.'

'It did not seem relevant.'

'Not relevant? Really? It is essential, Sir John, that we lose no opportunity to ensure that the votes for our party remain firm.' He looks at me sternly then adds: 'Thank you', as Silvia Digges helps him to some roast beef. She simpers in a way that will certainly worry Aminta and that causes Digby to grip his knife so that his knuckles show white.

In the face of more immediate concerns, everyone has already forgotten the vicar's warning of inevitable doom. The encroaching sea, the futility of our building any sort of ark, the problem of keeping bears and deer together for forty days and forty nights – all have been put for the moment to one side. Aminta is more concerned with future sins than past ones. Pepys is more interested in the various permutations of votes that we may conceivably have to deal with than his forthcoming descent into Hell.

'I am sure,' I say, 'that you will have a clear majority.'

'I am not. I fear that Spratchett may have deceived me.'

'You mean he may have taken your money and Jacob Cavendish's? You surprise me, Mister Pepys.'

'Spratchett and Larter seemed to be very much friends in church today,' he says. 'They and their wives sat together in complete harmony. Spratchett avoided speaking to me afterwards. If he has betrayed me, then it is not just his own vote – I do not know how much to trust that I have the votes of Dix and Pettus in my pocket. That would make just four for me and seven for Cavendish, with only Wraith and Henry Cavendish as yet undeclared, though I hope Wraith is with me, knowing me to be sound in the matter of graves.'

'David Larter will not vote as a matter of course with his uncle – he has an independent mind. That could make five votes each, with Peacock not voting and with Henry Cavendish and Wraith uncertain. Of course, the Devil may carry Wraith off before he can cast his vote.'

'I think, Sir John, that this is not the time for frivolity,' says Pepys. 'I do not object to your joking about the vicar going to Hell. But my election is another matter entirely. Tutepenny said nothing of the intentions of his fellow fishermen, I assume – whether they will indeed follow Spratchett's instructions?'

'As I say, we did not speak of the election at all. Tutepenny is not the illiterate bumpkin that I was originally led to believe. Not at all. He spoke of your father, Mister Digges, and the trust the Admiral placed in him – that he would allow nobody else to steer the boat when he was taken ashore.'

'I did not know that. Every time, you say?'

'Apparently. I had understood, by the way, from our conversation at your uncle's house, that Tutepenny was left money in your father's will. He does not seem to be aware of it. I know you must be very busy, but I am sure that he would welcome being told, however small the bequest might be and however long it may take to pay it. He would remember your father more kindly for it.'

'Of course,' says Digby. 'I shall attend to the matter.'

'Thank you. Oh, and Tutepenny spoke of the vicar. He dates the vicar's madness from the death of Mary Pettus. It seemed to surprise him when he made the connection between the two things. Can that be so? What was she to the vicar?'

'Nothing at all,' says Digby. 'She was one of his parishioners. She came, I think, from Lowestoft. Henry Cavendish might know, living in the same town, but we cannot easily consult him. As we've said, he may or may not come and vote.'

'So why would her death affect the vicar so? And why would he be so opposed to moving her body now? Benefice thought that perhaps the vicar simply believed it was unsafe, but Wraith said nothing of the sort to me. I do not think that, if a few fishermen died trying to raise her coffin, it would really trouble Wraith very much. He believes after all that we are all to die before next Sunday.'

'I cannot explain his reasons,' says Digby. 'I am no theologian – far from it.'

'But you have supported the vicar's refusal. Surely that implies understanding on your part?'

'I did not say I understood his reasons. I merely feel that it is his area of authority. I have no wish for him to intrude upon mine. In return, I try to observe scrupulously his right to determine church matters. As my father did before me.'

So, is this just another example of Digby's subservience to his father – an inability to think for himself? Digby's kindness – to Catch, to his wife, to his servants – is clear, and his loyalty to the Admiral is touching. But I fear for somebody going through life with so few ideas of his own.

'Well, I shall speak to Tutepenny again,' I say. 'He seemed to know something. Something important. If we had been elsewhere, I think he might have told me more.'

'But you have already spoken to Tutepenny in the context of my father's death?' asks Digby.

'Yes.'

'So this is some speculation about Mary Pettus's burial?'

'I suppose so.'

'Which Tutepenny cannot have witnessed since he would then have been at sea with my father?'

'Yes – you are right that must be the case.'

Digby smiles, as if a happy thought has just occurred to him.

'I have said quite clearly, Sir John, that I would prefer your investigations to be completed as soon as you reasonably can. Another visit to Tutepenny – whom you cannot possibly regard as a suspect in my father's murder – is clearly not necessary. But you still seem determined to uncover some scandal relating to Mary Pettus. Very well! If I let you travel to Lowestoft, where she lived before she married and many people will have known her, will you finally admit that you have now done all you can?'

'With respect, Mister Digges, I do not need your permission to travel to Lowestoft or anywhere else in Suffolk. My commission from the Sheriff is sufficient. But I think that I am willing to forego a journey there. Lowestoft is, as you have said, a long way, you have no horse to lend me and I doubt that my carriage horses would tolerate a saddle even for part of it—'

'Take my horse, Sir John,' says Pepys suddenly. 'I should be honoured to lend him to you. And he needs the exercise. Like Mr Digges I think that we should do everything we can to speed your conclusions and allow you and Lady Grey to set out for London.'

I look from Pepys to Digby and back again. The formation of this alliance was very sudden and unexpected. Does Pepys want me out of the way?

'Very well,' I say. 'I am grateful, Mr Pepys, for your offer of transport. But I think the journey can wait until Tuesday, after I have spoken to Tutepenny again.'

'The weather is fair at present for your journey up the coast,' says Digby. 'Fine spells such as this are not to be counted on. Not at this time of year. But, as things are, you can be there and back in a day.'

'Tomorrow then,' I say. 'I shall by all means go tomorrow.'

'Good,' says Digby. 'Tutepenny, if you really must speak to him again, can wait his turn.'

'I could see him this afternoon.'

'Not on the Lord's Day, Sir John, if you please. It ill befits a Justice of the Peace, appointed to enforce the laws of the land, to be seen to work on a Sunday.'

Pepys nods, though like me I suspect he has had to work on many days of rest. Again Digby seems to feel obliged to take the vicar's part. And of course he is right. Today is the Sabbath and part of my duty is to enforce it. More to the point, with a long ride ahead of me tomorrow, it makes sense to rest my leg this afternoon rather than tramp the cliff tops and beaches trying to find Tutepenny.

Later I find myself briefly alone with Pepys.

'I think that went well,' he says.

'In what way?' I ask.

'Your journey to Lowestoft. Under cover of this nonsense about Mary Pettus, you can quietly meet with Henry Cavendish, without Jacob suspecting a thing, and persuade him to come down and vote for me. I think fifty Pounds for his agreeing to travel to Eastwold would be handsome.'

'I can pay Henry a visit while I'm there,' I say. 'But I cannot promise more than that.'

'Do your best,' he says. 'We need every vote we can get. The more I think about it, the less I trust Spratchett.'

'That is very wise of you,' I say.

Later still.

'So Pepys thinks you will win him another vote?' says Aminta.

'There is no harm in visiting Henry Cavendish. He may have useful information relating to the Admiral's death. He is a burgess of Eastwold and knows all of the other burgesses. And I may discover something interesting about Mistress Pettus.'

'It is a long way to go, perhaps for very little.'

'Yes. But I feel that if I do not get out of this strange town for a day, then I may go mad.'

'And me? Am I not permitted to go mad too?'

'You are made of sterner stuff. Anyway, one of us has to keep an eye on Silvia and Mister Pepys.'

'I think your ride to Lowestoft over muddy roads may be the less tiring task,' says Aminta.

From my Lady Grey's most excellent poem
The Election

For every man within the town
(At least for each who chanced to own
A house above or 'neath the sea)
The question now appeared to be:
Who'd quench the thirst within their throat
Best, in return for their prized vote?
The London clerk, it seems to most,
Has gold to spare, such is his boast.
The Cavalier, though mean and poor, bears
The loyalty of all their forebears,
Who would in time past bend the knee
To him in happy fealty.
And so each burgess swore an oath
To vote for one, or better both,
According to their inclination
(Dressed as the interests of the nation)
And thus was money pledged and passed
In ways that would have left aghast
The townsmen of that nobler age –
More honest? Yes, but much less sage!

Chapter 17

In Lowestoft

The ride has hurt my leg less than I feared. Perhaps it is the change in the weather. Or perhaps the wound that has troubled me for so long is finally healed. Not everything goes from bad to worse.

Lowestoft is a busy place compared with Eastwold. It is what Eastwold was fifty or a hundred years ago, when there was enough of it left for it to be a real town. The harbour is full of boats. There is constant bustle and noise in the streets. I can see why, if he doesn't mind the underlying smell of fish and tar, Henry Cavendish may prefer it. I think a doctor may be easier to find than a fisherman, so I decide that I will begin by fulfilling my promise to Pepys – and seeing what, if anything, Cavendish knows about the Admiral's death. The second person I speak to in the street gives me clear instructions for finding him. When I finally force my way through the narrow, cobbled lanes to his house, I find Doctor Cavendish hospitable but puzzled by the idea that he might be able to help me with a murder.

'I am very happy to tell you all I know,' he says. 'But I fear you have had a long journey for very little. I have not been to Eastwold for over a year.'

He is dressed in a white linen shirt with billowing sleeves, a long dark blue waistcoat and black breeches. There are large silver buckles on his shoes – the only ostentatious thing about him. He is not wearing a coat. He has just finished a consultation with a patient and the day is a warm one. Like me, he has not yet chosen to purchase a periwig, but as a professional man, with clients to impress, he will soon have to remedy that. Who would trust the skill of a physician who possessed no hair but his own?

His wife joins us, followed by a maid bearing a teapot. It is not only in Eastwold that London habits are being copied.

'I had heard that Admiral Digges had died, of course,' Henry Cavendish continues, 'and that a magistrate from Essex had been summoned to investigate the death. News from Eastwold always reaches us sooner or later – much too late in this case for me to attend the funeral, though I doubt that I would have done so anyway. Nobody liked the Admiral and I liked him less than most. I'm sorry I can't be more helpful than that.'

'How are Silvia and Digby?' asks his wife.

'Well,' I say, taking my teacup and sipping the hot, black liquid. 'Digby mourns the loss of his father, of course.' A warm drink is very welcome after a long ride. Soon they will be consuming tea everywhere.

'But Silvia is happier now the Admiral is gone?' she says.

'She seems happy enough,' I reply. 'I can't say whether she is more or less happy than before. My acquaintance with her is a recent one.'

'She was deeply unhappy in the past,' says Henry. 'The Admiral was a brute. He spared nobody in the family their allocated share of his tongue or his rod. If I practised in Eastwold, that one household could keep me well employed.'

'I'd heard the same from the man who does practise there as a surgeon, when he is not serving as Coroner. But surely Admiral Digges did not actually assault his daughter-in-law?' I ask.

'She fled here twice, once over muddy winter roads with only a light cloak to keep off the snow,' says Mistress Cavendish with a sorrowful shake of her head. 'The poor thing was more dead than alive when she arrived at our door.'

'I didn't know any of that. It was because of Admiral Digges' violence?'

'I suppose so,' says Henry Cavendish. 'Somebody had attacked her. She would never say who. She stayed until the bruising went down. Then she returned.'

'Could she not have fled to her father's house, which is no distance away, winter or summer?'

'Her father wouldn't have been a lot of use against Digges,' says Henry. 'Too decent to give somebody a good thrashing, except in the heat of battle. The Coroner you referred to – David Larter – he helped her. She'd have been a sight better off married to him than that useless lump Digby. I suppose she could have stayed with Larter, but it was best that she got well beyond the range of Digges' fist.'

'If she was safe here, why did she return to Eastwold?' I ask.

'She was a bit like the Admiral in one way,' says Henry. 'She never quite knew when she was beaten. She was willing to quit the fight for essential repairs. But, as soon as she could, she sailed back in, all guns blazing. She didn't have the Admiral's firepower, but her aim was accurate.'

'Would that have extended to killing him?' I ask.

'You don't think it was an accidental death?'

'No. Somebody tried to stab him, then drowned him.'

Henry Cavendish whistles between his teeth. 'Well, I wouldn't have blamed her. But why stab him when she could have poisoned him any day of the week? She supervised the cooking, and I doubt the servants would have cared if she came into the kitchen and added hemlock to his portion of stew.'

'She wouldn't have wanted the blame to fall on the servants,' says Mistress Cavendish.

'True,' says Henry. 'So, how would she have found the opportunity to stab him?'

'Perhaps, somehow, she lured the Admiral to the beach,' I say. 'We know he received a note just before he set out. The Admiral may not have been expecting to see her and certainly wouldn't have been expecting her to attack him with a knife. To that extent she had the advantage. She botched the stabbing but wounded him enough to be able to force him into the water and drown him.'

'That doesn't sound like Silvia,' says Mistress Cavendish. 'She'd have found a way that was more subtle and more certain. Anyway, I wouldn't have expected her to botch the stabbing. She's quite adept with a sharp knife.'

'It's easy enough to miss a moving target,' I say, 'however experienced you are.'

'I suppose it is,' says Henry. 'When I use a knife professionally, my target is as motionless as they can manage.'

'That is very wise of your target,' I say. I put my cup back on the table. 'Of course, it may not have been Silvia herself. It could have been a friend of hers. Where were you when the Admiral was killed, Doctor Cavendish?'

He laughs. 'I'm not sure I know exactly when that was. But I have many patients here, and the journey to Eastwold is, as you now know, a long one. My absence, even for an afternoon, would have been noticed, I can assure you. To have been away a whole day or a whole night would have been impossible. But do ask around town about my movements. I have no objection at all. There is, however, a much stronger reason why I wouldn't have done it. When I last heard from Silvia, she seems to have solved her problems.'

'Did she say how?' I ask.

'Not exactly,' says Henry.

'She'd spoken before of seeking the advice of a Mistress Catch,' says Mistress Cavendish. 'It may be that she was able to help in a way that the rest of us were not.'

'I know Mistress Catch,' I say.

'Good,' says Henry. 'Then she may be able to tell you more. Is that all? I still think you've come a long way for very little.'

'I'm not sure that's true. You've both been very helpful. But I do have two other errands here. First, Doctor Cavendish, did you ever know a Mary Pettus?'

'I don't think so. Why?'

'She came from here originally. She married a fisherman named John Pettus in Eastwold but died about twelve years ago.'

'Could she have been called Mary Butt before she married?' asks Mistress Cavendish. 'I think William Butt had a sister who lived in Eastwold. If so, then she must have left here almost twenty years ago, just before Henry and I married.'

'There's something odd about her death and burial,' I say.

'The oddness is connected with the Admiral's murder?' asks Mistress Cavendish.

'Yes. In some way that I don't understand.'

'Her brother, William, still lives down by the harbour,' she says. 'He's a grocer. You could speak to him.'

'I'll do that.'

'And the remaining thing?' asks Henry.

'I send you the compliments of Mister Samuel Pepys, Clerk of the Acts to the Navy Board, and request on his behalf that you tell me whether you plan to vote for him in the forthcoming election.'

'He's the Admiralty's candidate in place of Digges, then? I know the Pepyses. They're a good family from the next county, though I think Samuel is just a poor relation of the ones I know – or he used to be poor until he became Clerk of the Acts. Well, I'm not voting for Jacob, that poor excuse for a parent. Tell Pepys he has my vote. No charge.'

'I am empowered to offer you fifty Pounds.'

Henry laughs again, then shakes his head.

'My husband has a rather severe idea of what is and what is not gentlemanly conduct,' says Mistress Cavendish. 'Sadly, this excludes taking bribes. I tell him he is out of sympathy with the times.'

'So he is. But I shall inform Mister Pepys of his intentions,' I say.

Well, there's one person at least who won't consider my visit here a wasted one. Even without Spratchett, I think Pepys has his nose in front again.

The lanes by the quay are narrower even than the one in which Doctor Cavendish lives and practises. It is not difficult to find William Butt's shop. It appears to be well known and, when I finally reach it, prosperous and thriving. Mary Butt may have come down a little in the world when she went to Eastwold to become Mistress Pettus.

'I am sorry to hear of the state of my sister's grave,' he says. 'But, if the vicar will not allow her body to be moved, then there is nothing I can do.'

'I may yet be able to find a way to prevent her fall,' I say. 'In spite of the vicar. But can you think of a reason why Wraith should have taken against her in some way? Did you hear of any ill feeling between them?'

'My sister and Wraith? No, but he is well known even here for his oddness. Our own vicar visited him once. He said that Wraith was completely mad – not just a little odd, but raving, like some actor in the tragedies that were performed in King James's days.'

'He didn't feel he should report that to the authorities?'

'To the Bishop or to the Master of the Revels?' he asks.

'Either.'

'I think that our own vicar found it amusing rather than otherwise. And once people get a reputation for something, they try to play up to it, don't they? But you have come many miles to tell me all this.'

'I am investigating the death of Admiral Digges,' I say. 'I believe he was murdered.'

'Another name that is familiar to us here,' says Butt. 'There are former sailors in ports all the way along this coast who curse his memory. If anyone in Lowestoft knows who killed him, I doubt they will tell you. But how is that connected to my sister?'

'I wish I knew. And I am aware that nobody wants to give me the evidence that might hang the man who killed him.'

Butt nods. 'He was said to beat his wife, sir.'

'You disapprove?'

'A man has the right to chastise his wife, that is true. As a lawyer you know that. But such a man has no respect here, begging your pardon, sir. A man should rule his own household, but one who has to resort to beating his wife to get her to obey him is no man, sir. How is a husband to govern if he has no self-control? Those who beat their wives are treated to rough music here. We gather outside their house and give them a song.' He draws a deep breath and then sings, not entirely out of tune: 'There is a man in our town, Who often beats his wife, So if he does it any more, We'll put his nose right out before.' He pauses, pleased rather than otherwise with the general effect of the piece. 'And if that doesn't do the trick, sir, then we make him ride the pole backwards all the way down to the harbour and into the sea.'

'And if he can't swim?'

'We don't enquire too much about that, sir. Not in advance anyway.'

'I shall let my wife know of the customs in this part of Suffolk,' I say. 'She would find them instructive.'

'The Admiral spared neither man nor woman,' says Butt.

'No,' I say.

'Take poor Tutepenny, for example. You'll know James Tutepenny, sir? Like my sister, he formerly lived here, but later settled in Eastwold. He lives there still, I believe?'

'Yes, I have met him, but what did the Admiral do to him?'

'He had him almost flogged to death. Did you not know that?' says Butt.

'No,' I say. 'That was poor reward for Tutepenny's loyalty and the trust the Admiral placed in him.'

'It would have made no difference to the Admiral. Past service counted for nothing.'

'Then Tutepenny showed much forbearance in not murdering the Admiral before now.'

Butt looks at me, clearly wondering if he should have said what he has said. 'I don't mean that Tutepenny would have killed the Admiral. That was not my meaning at all.'

'Why not?' I say. 'It seems a very reasonable thing for him to do.'

'A reasonable thing for most people, but Tutepenny is a philosopher, sir, and a Christian. He is no murderer. I'll wager my life on it.'

'Tutepenny wanted to tell me something. I was distracted. I didn't stay to listen to him.'

'Something about the Admiral?'

'Yes. Or the flogging. Or about your sister. Or all three. Or something else. I don't really know. I'll ask him when I get back. Had I known how badly he had been treated . . .'

'Of course, sir. Is there anything else?'

'No,' I say. 'Thank you. It's been a long ride but, in the end, perhaps quite a profitable one. I at least know what I must do next.'

I return to Henry Cavendish's house where Pepys's horse is waiting in the stable, apparently well rested. My enquiries have taken less time than I thought. We can reach Eastwold before dark without doing much more than a gentle trot. My leg is starting to ache again.

'I hope you didn't have a wasted journey?' Digby enquires as I dismount, my leg muscles now throbbing in what I recognise as a dangerous manner. I shall scarcely be able to walk tomorrow.

'A little,' I say, circumspectly.

'Well, you must tell me what you have discovered – once you are recovered from your ride, of course. But your investigations are complete? You are ready to return to Essex?'

'I just need to talk to Tutepenny again,' I say.

'Ah,' says Digby. 'I fear that will not be possible. He was found dead this morning. David Larter says that he was run through with a sword. And I was about to pay him the bequest from my father that you so kindly reminded me of. Most unfortunate, but there it is. Tutepenny. Catch. The poor mad vicar. I fear that none of the legatees of my father's will have prospered.'

Chapter 18

Two magistrates discuss procedure

I have changed out of my mud-spattered clothes into the only other suit that I have brought with me and now face Digby across his sitting room. Today there is no sign of the weakness that I and others have noticed. But I do detect a trace of the stubbornness that his aunt felt would, in the fullness of time, send him down to Hell.

'I shall investigate Tutepenny's death,' says Digby. 'I do not doubt that he has been unlawfully killed – David Larter agrees. But you are here only to investigate the death of my father – not that of my mother and certainly not that of Tutepenny. If you attempt to do so then you considerably exceed your remit. I shall protest to the Sheriff that this cannot possibly have been his intention that you should take over every aspect of my work here.'

'But if Tutepenny knew something about your father's death . . .' I say. 'There was some information that he wanted to give me. Foolishly I did not realise how important it might be.'

'And you know it concerned my father?'

'Not for certain. But I am beginning to wonder if our conversation was overheard – that somebody might have wanted to prevent my talking to him again.'

'Almost the whole town was in the churchyard, having come for Wraith's sermon. I do not doubt that Tutepenny's killer was there. But it will take time to question everyone – time that you do not have.'

'But you agree Tutepenny was killed to stop him talking to me?'

'On the contrary. There is no evidence for that at all. You cry up your own affairs mightily, Sir John. You seem to think that the longer you stay here and the more pies you stick your fingers into, the better for everyone in this town. I must remind you that Tutepenny was not a witness to my father's death nor did he give you any useful information on either occasion that you spoke to him. Whatever trifling bit of gossip he had just recalled yesterday was most unlikely to add to what you knew: that although my father was less popular than I had believed, there is no evidence whatsoever that he was unlawfully killed. As for Tutepenny's murder, I positively forbid you to interfere with every new case that arises in the town, merely because it interests you. In conclusion, therefore, let me repeat: I assume you have now interviewed everyone you need to interview concerning the only matter that the Sheriff has entrusted to you? Yes?'

'Yes.'

'And have you yet found any shred of evidence, here or in Lowestoft, that it was not an accident? Clearly not.'

'There is still the stab wound,' I say.

'I admit that I initially found that persuasive. But it was a very slight one, according to David Larter.'

'That is true,' I say.

'It could be accidental.'

'Unlikely.'

'David Larter suggested that the wound might have been made when the fishermen cut my father's body free of the net.'

I wonder if that is in fact Digby's own suggestion to which Larter politely made no specific objection. Larter certainly never said anything of the sort to me. I can question him again in due course.

'It's possible,' I say. 'But the net would have been too valuable to cut, if they could have avoided doing so.'

'They could have afforded it if they'd stolen my father's snuffbox – an item that you have lamentably failed to recover.'

I had thought Digby was not seeking its return, but I agree that I might have made enquiries anyway. It is highly likely that the Admiral's finders have already sold that and anything else they found for a fraction of its value to some rascally tradesman up or down the coast.

'I suppose so.'

'Sir John, Mister Pepys informs me that it was always your plan to conceal the fact if you discovered my father was murdered.'

'He told you that?'

'Not in so many words, but he is inexplicably confident that your investigations will result in confirmation of the Coroner's verdict. He implied that you were the creature of Lord Arlington and would follow his instructions to the letter.'

'What you describe may be the intention of the Duke of York and indeed Lord Arlington. I assure you that it was not in any way my plan.'

'But you clearly knew what they wanted and you told me

nothing of their intentions. That was neither proper, bearing in mind that I am magistrate here, nor kind, bearing in mind that it is my much-loved father that we speak of. How would you like it if it were your father?'

'My father died some time ago in Brussels with his mistress. The circumstances were certainly unfortunate, but he lived and died very much as he wished. Please feel free to investigate his death if you have time and the inclination to travel to the Spanish Netherlands.'

'Your frivolity ill becomes you.'

'I'm sure you're right. The office of Justice of the Peace does not lend itself to frivolity of any sort. As for covering up any aspect of your father's death, I apologise for not warning you of the Duke's wishes, but as I said: it was not my plan. You must take the matter up with the Duke.'

'And if you had discovered the culprit, what would you have done?'

I consider this. What would I do, even now, if I found evidence that the killer was Silvia Digges? Would I have her hanged?

But, of course – isn't this what Digby has feared all along? That his wife has killed his father? He knew how badly the Admiral had treated her. He was aware that she had been to see Mother Catch. He knew that she had time to kill the Admiral on the beach, having perhaps sent her husband off in the wrong direction on the fateful evening. That is why Digby has tried to send me home at the first opportunity, to interfere as much as possible with my investigation and to bluster every time I started to get close to the truth. Of course, he also helpfully sent me to Lowestoft, which served to provide evidence that his wife had an excellent motive. But I did not tell him that I was to visit Henry Cavendish; and Pepys, who is capable of keeping his own secrets at least, will not have told him either. Time to break more bad news to Mister Digges.

'I think you mean: what would I do if the killer is your wife?' I say.

'That is a monstrous suggestion,' says Digby. 'You are a guest in my own house, Sir John, and you accuse my wife – your hostess – of killing my father? That is truly unworthy of you. I was reluctant to admit another magistrate to Eastwold, but I did so with what I hope was good grace. I believed you to be a decent and honourable man. I have welcomed you here and given you every possible assistance. Now you choose to insult me and my wife in our own home. Your investigations have come to nothing but still you blunder on. You are utterly incompetent. You have wasted my time and the Sheriff's. But you still propose to prolong this ridiculous charade and usurp my authority?'

I carefully consider all aspects of this wide-ranging reprimand.

'Yes,' I say. 'If you've no objection, that's what I'd like to do.'

'Mister Digges is most upset with you,' says Pepys smugly.

'I know that.'

'Mister Digges accuses you of being ungrateful and ill-mannered.'

'I undertook to investigate a death. I have never promised to be agreeable to anyone.'

'Mister Digges tells me that he wishes you to conclude your investigation immediately.'

'And do you share that view?'

'It would be unsurprising if I did, Sir John. Consider your progress. You have accused Mister Spratchett of murder, which I fear may have alienated him and his three votes. You have accused Mister Solomon Larter, whose guilt would have been helpful, but sadly been unable to provide proof. You have now accused Mistress Digges, which is most ungallant. Enough, Sir John, enough, I say! You have done your best, no doubt, but even you must be tired of an investigation that has produced so little of value to anyone. Time, I think, to write your report to the Sheriff. Nobody will blame you for confirming what the Coroner has already ruled to be the truth.'

'I haven't *yet* found any proof. I still hope to do so, even though I am not sure what I shall do when I find it.'

'But from whence do you suppose that such evidence might come? It must be clear to you by now that nobody cares who killed the Admiral.'

'Peacock cared enough to write to London with the information that the Coroner's verdict was suspect.'

'Ah, you have discovered that?'

'Yes. I think you might have told me. Peacock hoped of course that it was Solomon Larter.'

'But, as you say, there is no evidence. It was thus scarcely worth mentioning to you.'

'I disagree. It might have saved me valuable time had I known what Peacock had told you.'

'And what would you have done with the time thus saved? Besmirch the good name of everyone in the town?'

'I shall do whatever I need to do. You are aware of the maxim: *Fiat justitia ruat caelum*?'

'Indeed. We must do justice even though the heavens fall. And you might add: *Justitia nemini neganda est*. Nobody, not even Admiral Digges, should be denied justice. But there is no legal maxim that imposes on you a duty of continuing searching for a killer when the task is beyond any reasonable man.'

'I have never claimed to be reasonable.'

'What if it was Tutepenny?' says Pepys suddenly. 'Digges had him flogged. And he's dead now, so his vote is of no consequence.'

'Flogged? So, you already knew that?' I ask.

'I had heard it said,' says Pepys. 'Nothing more.'

'You didn't tell me that either,' I say. 'At least, you didn't until his vote no longer mattered. Then you did.'

'An oversight on my part. I apologise unreservedly. Nevertheless, you must concede it was an excellent motive.'

'I suppose so. What I don't understand is why, after living in the town together so long, Tutepenny would have suddenly decided to kill him. If he didn't want him to become Member of Parliament, he had only to vote for Cavendish and persuade his fellow fishermen to do the same.'

'Does it matter, if his guilt serves our purpose?'

'Your purpose, Mister Pepys,' I say. 'Not mine.'

'The election takes place tomorrow at two o'clock,' says Pepys. 'I can give you until then to absolve everyone still living who might vote for me from the slightest suspicion. I have pointed out to you the many advantages of Tutepenny being the killer. Your master, Lord Arlington, would do the same if he were here.'

'I do not doubt that,' I say. 'But I've always felt that it was better to hang the actual killer, even if there was somebody closer to hand. I am sorry you have lost one voter with Tutepenny's death, so I do at least undertake not to lose you another one unless it is absolutely necessary. But I have good news as well as bad. Henry Cavendish intends to vote for you – mainly because of the respect he holds for Lord Sandwich and the rest of your family. I offered him money and he declined it. So I think that, even without Tutepenny, you and Jacob Cavendish have a parity of votes – five each.'

Pepys smiles. 'I have six,' he says. 'I have purchased an additional freehold on your behalf. You now have a vote, Sir John, which tomorrow you will cast for me. You simply need to countersign the transfer. After the election you will convey it back to me for resale. You will be pleased to know that I shall lose very little once the sale is made. I think that we are home and dry.'

'And, as a voter, shall I receive my fifty golden guineas along with the others?' I ask.

Pepys stares at me open-mouthed. 'You intend to charge me for a small favour, such as one gentleman would readily perform, gratis, for another? We have been friends for a long time, you and I. I have done you many good turns over the years.'

'No you haven't.'

'Well, I would remind you that we were at the same college at Cambridge University—'

'I jest, Mister Pepys. I jest. And I congratulate you on your forthcoming victory. Can I give you one piece of advice, though?'

'Certainly, Sir John. All advice from one as wise and experienced as you is very welcome.'

'I do hope so. My advice, Mister Pepys, is to keep your grubby hands off Silvia Digges, much though you would like to get them on her. We've had two killings already in Eastwold. I don't want to find that Digby Digges has murdered you and that I have a further crime to cover up on Lord Arlington's behalf. One is more than enough.'

'I don't know what you mean.'

'Yes, you do.'

'Very well. I understand why you might have formed a false impression in that regard. Your fears are utterly misplaced, but I shall do my very best to ensure that Mister Digges does not gain an equally false idea of my intentions. Does that satisfy you?'

'Perfect,' I say. 'That will do very nicely indeed.'

I expect that the atmosphere will be tense at supper and that conversation with Digby will be difficult after our discussion of his wife's guilt, but in fact he directs most of his chatter at me and Aminta. Having failed to get rid of me, I think he is now anxious to make me his friend – somebody who would never consider pressing formal charges against a member of his family. It is Pepys with whom he seems discontented. Hopefully my warning to the Clerk of the Acts will have come in time to prevent an outbreak of armed warfare. Pepys certainly shows admirable caution in his dealings with Silvia. We are all polite to each other and retire early to our respective chambers.

'Digby's bluster when you accused his wife of murder was quite sweet, when you think about it,' says Aminta. 'He cares for her very much. And I hope she cares for him.'

'Digby has failed her badly – failed to defend her when she most needed it. Henry Cavendish said in effect that it was a shame she hadn't married David Larter.'

'Was that ever a possibility?' asks Aminta.

I consider this. 'David Larter is quite protective towards her,' I say. 'I can't say whether it goes deeper than that or why it should. Henry Cavendish also said that Mother Catch had been helpful in Silvia's gaining some sort of ascendancy over the Admiral. But Silvia does not believe in witchcraft any more than we do. She is one of the more rational people in this town.'

'There's a lot more to Silvia than meets the eye,' says Aminta. 'Or at least your eye. Take her hair, for example.'

'What of it? It's sort of frizzed out at the sides, isn't it?'

'You mean, my dear husband, that the sides of her hair are curled and brushed out in a mass of small ringlets, contrasting with the flat centre parting on top of her head. You will have also observed, because these things can scarcely have escaped your notice, the long back hair, which is drawn over the shoulder in very becoming ringlets.'

'If you say so. I don't usually analyse hair. I agree it's quite pretty.'

'It is the latest French fashion. And I know that only because a friend of mine in Paris wrote to me describing it. All of the ladies of the English Court will be wearing their hair thus by the end of the summer. But Silvia is some months ahead of them.'

'And that makes her a less likely murderer?'

'If I'd taken the trouble to have my hair dressed so fashionably, I would think twice about ruining it just to kill somebody.'

'Really?'

'No, not really. But she is very much her own woman with interests that go well beyond what remains of this small fishing town. If you could be bothered to ask her, you'd find that she has intelligent views on many things that Digby has probably never even heard of. As I say, I hope she still loves Digby, in spite of everything, but in so many ways she deserves better and I think that Digby knows it.'

'You think that it is important that a husband respects his wife's intelligence?'

'And takes her to London to buy dresses.'

'We shall go to London just as soon as I have finished here,' I say. 'Does Silvia's hair bring us any closer to being able to decide who the murderer is?'

'I fear not. Like you, I just hope that it wasn't Silvia. I agree that she had good reason and an excellent opportunity, but there is no proof – nothing that could count against her in court.'

I nod. 'When you think about it, the biggest argument against Silvia being the murderer is the same as with all of the others being the murderer. I can see why they would want to kill him, and I can see how they might have done it, but I can't see why any of them would choose to do it *now*. Their disputes with Digges were in the past – or they had better ways of getting revenge. Pepys may still know more than he is telling me, of course. He withheld both the source of the complaint to London and the fact that Tutepenny had been flogged at the Admiral's command.'

'I am not sure why his duplicity surprises you in any way.'

I nod. 'That reminds me: I warned Pepys about his conduct,' I say. 'Hopefully he'll now keep his distance from Silvia.'

'They were in the garden together just before supper,' says Aminta. 'I think your warning may not have struck home in the way you believe it has.'

'What was Pepys doing?'

'It was what he was inducing Silvia to do that was of interest. He just stood there while she did it.'

'I hope it was a secluded part of the garden,' I say.

'Well, I saw them.'

'Let's hope Digby didn't,' I say.

'He was quite cold to Pepys during supper.'

'The election is tomorrow,' I say. 'Pepys can't stay much beyond the vote. He'll need to get back to his masters in London. If I can stop Digby killing him in the meantime, then I shall.'

'Don't worry if you can't,' says Aminta. 'Or not on my account anyway.'

Chapter 19

Contrary to any promises I may have made, I do investigate another death

I am beginning to like breakfast. I would have spent some time over it but for two things. First, I have to speak to people about Tutepenny's killing. And second, somebody has sent me a gift. It sits in front of me now on the sackcloth in which it was wrapped and left at the front door of the Priory for the servants to find and deliver to me. It is gleaming white, slightly worn and smoothed of any rough edges. It is a skull. Examining it more closely, I detect a few grains of sand clinging to the interior cavity. It may have come from the beach.

'A warning of some sort,' says Digby. He is not entirely displeased. He thinks I should heed it and conclude my activities here as soon as may be.

'The sender could have made their intentions clearer,' I say.

Digby pulls a face. He thinks not. 'It portends death,' he says. 'I would have thought that was clear enough.'

'But for whom?'

'It was addressed to you, Sir John. You, and nobody else.'

'In divination, the obvious meaning is not always the true one. The death that this foretells may be somebody else's. Or, as in dreams, the true outcome may be the reverse of what they appear to predict. It may indicate a long life to come.'

'You seem very familiar with witchcraft and divination,' says Digby. He is annoyed. Things ought to be what they seem – no more and no less.

'We magistrates have to be familiar with the black arts, do we not?'

'You may understand the black arts better than I do, Sir John, and you may be a great deal older than I am, but I understand this part of the world. However things are arranged in Essex, to send somebody a skull, here in Suffolk, is very much a threat, not an obscure compliment. If I were you, I'd take it as such and be careful where you go and to whom you talk.'

'Did the servants see who left it?'

'I would have told you at once if they had. This object was there by the front door when I first ventured out early this morning. It had a label bearing your name. Nothing else. No key as to its true, rather than its apparent, meaning. Mother Catch might be able to help you, if you think there is more to it than that.'

He seems pleased with this last suggestion, but this message is a little crude for such a neat and inoffensive sorceress. I don't think it was her. And, if she knew who had sent it, then professional etiquette might prevent her telling me.

'The sacking feels dry,' I say, touching it. 'No dew on it. It cannot have been there long. It was perhaps already daylight when it was left. Somebody else may have seen the person coming this way, as the sun rose, clutching something in a bundle of coarse cloth.'

'That I couldn't say,' says Digby. 'I simply tell you I found it there.'

This too has annoyed Digby. I am deliberately making complicated what should be very easy. Rather like my investigation of his father's death. I have been told by the skull to leave Eastwold, and if that's what the skull thinks, then that's what I should do.

'I'll convey it to the vicar,' I say. 'I have no further use for it myself.'

'Mister Pepys will be most agitated until you are back,' says Digby. 'The election begins just after dinner. We shall row out to the hustings at one o'clock.'

I take out my pocket watch. 'Six hours,' I say. 'You'd be surprised what a busy magistrate can get done in six hours.'

'I shall place it in the crypt,' says Wraith with a sigh. 'But the sea will take it back.'

'As you predicted in your sermon,' I say.

'It is already beginning. Another section of the cliff fell last night. Toby Dix's house is gone. He has no written proof of his tenure, so he loses his vote.'

'I'd say his immediate concern will be that he has no home. The vote is less important, surely?'

'That depends on whether he has already been paid his fifty Pounds.'

'I suppose so,' I say. 'Has he a roof over his head tonight?'

'He transferred most of his goods to Dowsing's house before the collapse. I imagine he will stay there until he can rent another cottage. Tutepenny's is vacant. That is an unexpected blessing.'

'Do you know who might have wished to kill Tutepenny?' I ask.

'Nobody would have wished to kill him,' says the vicar. 'Perhaps somebody had to, but I doubt that they took pleasure in it. There was beauty in his soul, though it was edged with darkness where it had brushed against evil. Nothing washes out the Devil's stains, as I am well aware.'

'He knew something about Mary Pettus's death and burial.'

'Tutepenny was there for neither event.'

'He was nevertheless talking to me about it. He worried we might be overheard. Then he died. You too know something about Mary Pettus. What is it? If you think we are indeed doomed, then it would be as well to unburden yourself now – for the sake of your soul in the next world, if you have no concern for justice in this one.'

He smiles his sweetest smile. This is his area of expertise, not mine. 'We are all going to die,' says the vicar patiently. 'It matters little when that is. Then, on Judgment Day, and every one at the very same moment, we shall be called to account. For some, an extra few hours of life may have given time for repentance. For others, it may have provided an opportunity to experience a completely new sin that had never previously been brought to their attention. But for most, an extra week, an extra month, an extra year of this earthly existence will prove to have been no account when compared with the long procession of days that follow the Last Trump – an eternity of bliss amongst the angels or unbearable agony in the ever-lasting fires of Hell.'

'I would still like to know.'

'To what end? You have no power to grant me absolution. And your enquiry into the death of Admiral Sir Robert Digges is not of the slightest interest to me. Allow me to go now.

I must place this poor fellow in the crypt, just as you request. Then look to your own soul, Sir John. Examine it carefully. You have lived a long time with men such as Arlington. You may have less time to repent than you imagine.'

I find Pettus on the beach. From down here, the damage of last night is much clearer. Rubble from Dix's house lies across a broad swath of flat, damp sand. I notice a few possessions that he failed to save – a mass of firewood, a large cooking pot, now very dented but perhaps still repairable, the remains of a cupboard too big to carry easily in the early hours of the morning and now no longer worth carrying.

'I visited your brother-in-law in Lowestoft,' I say. 'He and his family are well. He sends his best wishes.'

'Ah, he is thriving, then? I'm glad to hear it. I have not heard from him for some time.'

'I have made no further progress on your wife's grave,' I say. 'Last night's storm did not bring down any of the churchyard?'

'No, sir. It did not. She has another few days on land. Well, I'm sure you've done your best.'

He shakes his head. He is used to the sea and its strange ways. This will not be the worst thing that it has done to him. Not by a long way.

'I was sorry to hear of Tutepenny's death,' I say.

'A bad business, sir.'

'Can you think of any way in which his death could be connected with your wife's burial?'

Pettus looks at me as if the vicar is not the only madman in Eastwold. I think he actually backs away half a step. 'Sorry, sir? I don't understand your meaning. My wife was buried many years ago.'

'Don't worry,' I say. 'It was just something Tutepenny said to me on Sunday. I must have misunderstood.'

'Of course, sir,' says Pettus, though he still eyes me oddly. Whatever Tutepenny knew, it doesn't seem as if he had shared it with his fellow fishermen. He was good at keeping secrets.

'Do you know who might have wanted Tutepenny dead?'

'No, sir, but I could not tell you even if I did. You know that young Mister Digges has forbidden any of us to speak to you about Tutepenny?'

'I didn't, but thank you for telling me.'

'My pleasure, sir.'

'He wants me out of his town by any means,' I say.

I look up, just in time to throw myself and Pettus to one side. A large boulder, spinning as it descends from the top of the cliff, smashes into the remains of the cupboard, turning it instantly into splinters. The boulder rolls across the beach, unstoppable by anything but the many yards of soft, yielding sand. It slows and eventually comes to rest by the waterline. I look up again. A thin figure dressed in black stands at about the point from which the rock must have come. He is not concerned that I have seen him. Then he goes on his way.

'Things fall all the time, sir,' says Pettus, picking himself up. 'I've had some close shaves. But that's the closest I've known.'

'I don't think it was an accident,' I say. 'I don't think it was an accident any more than the Admiral's death was an accident.'

'Did you see anyone up there then?'

'A tall, thin man, dressed in black.'

'The vicar?' says Pettus.

'He has been warning me of the nearness of my death. He didn't mention that it might be at his own hands.'

'He is mad, but surely not that mad?'

'I agree it's unlikely in a clergyman,' I say.

'There are others who wear black in this town.'

'True,' I say.

But it did look like the vicar. It looked very much like him.

'I was called straight away when the body was found,' says David Larter. 'He was in his cottage, stabbed through the heart. Quite a lot of blood, as you might expect.'

'Any sign of a struggle?'

'No. He must have been taken by surprise – or he trusted the person who did it until slightly too late.'

I nod. I've made the same mistake myself.

'Witnesses?' I ask.

'None have come forward. Not yet, anyway.'

'Time of death?'

'He hadn't been dead long when I was summoned at about ten o'clock yesterday. I'd guess seven or eight o'clock.'

'There should have been people around by then – somebody who might have seen somebody near the cottage?'

'You'd have thought so, but no witnesses have come forward. The perpetrator must at least have been somebody whose presence in the town was unremarkable – not a stranger.'

'And the weapon?'

Larter goes to a cupboard and takes out a short naval cutlass. 'It was still in Tutepenny's chest, as it happens. There were signs that the killer had tried to extract it, but failed. Perhaps he panicked and fled. Digby Digges identified it as belonging to his father. It had been missing, he said, since his father's death. He thinks his father took it out with him the evening he died. He'd assumed it was lost at sea with the other items that the Admiral had with him and is unable to account for its reappearance now.'

'But, if the Admiral was murdered, as we think, then his killer could simply have taken it away with them after the killing?'

'Yes. Why not? It might have suited their purpose that the Admiral appeared to be unarmed – that he really had just gone for a sail.'

'In which case, whoever killed the Admiral killed Tutepenny.'

'That's possible. I've just had an interesting thought, though. I'd decided the wound in the Admiral's chest was from a fisherman's knife, but it could have been from any fairly broad blade penetrating a short way. A naval sword like this one, for example. It would have given the same width.'

'The killer might have been another sailor?'

'Well, somebody who owned a cutlass.'

'Digby said that you suggested the wound in the Admiral's chest might have been made by the fishermen who dragged his body out of the sea and needed to cut their net to free him.'

'His suggestion rather than mine. That's possible too, though not likely. All I can be really sure of is that the Admiral's stab wound, however made, wasn't fatal. There was water in his lungs. He drowned. Unlike Tutepenny, whose body is laid out at his cottage, if you wish to inspect it. No doubt at all how he died.'

I shake my head. 'I've promised not to make enquiries about this murder,' I say. 'And I'm a man of my word.'

'We've been warned not to speak to you,' says Benefice.

I nod. 'So I'd heard.'

I am of course still in credit with Benefice by several

Shillings. Sometimes investments of that sort take a while to pay a dividend. Perhaps today is the day when this one pays out.

He fills a tankard and pushes it in my direction. 'You'll want to know about Tutepenny, then?'

'If you don't mind. David Larter thought that the same man – or at least the same weapon – may have killed the Admiral and Tutepenny?' I say.

He shakes his head. 'I can't see that at all. Tutepenny was well liked. He had no enemies here. The Admiral was hated by everyone. Many here had good reason to want him dead.'

'Including Tutepenny?'

'Yes.'

'Digges had him flogged. You must have known. Why didn't you tell me?'

'In case Tutepenny had killed the Admiral.'

'Is that what you thought?'

'It's what I'd have done in his place.'

'But Tutepenny is dead now.'

'Yes, nothing can harm him further.'

'Why did the Admiral do it? The flogging?'

'Something Tutepenny had said, so I was told. He had been a favourite of the Admiral's – remarkable in itself because the Admiral had few favourites. Sometimes when that happens a man may forget himself and overstep the mark – I mean become too familiar.'

'That might be cause for a reprimand, or even a demotion, but surely not a flogging? What on earth can he have said?'

'I don't know. I wasn't there. I'd already lost my leg by then and heard about it by chance some time later. Not from Tutepenny himself. He never spoke of the flogging or the cause of it. Nor did he speak of revenge. Ingratitude, yes. He spoke of that. But not revenge. It wasn't his way at all. If he'd had a dozen cheeks, he'd have turned all of them, one after the other, to receive another slap.'

'Yes, Pettus's brother-in-law described him as a philosopher. The vicar said something about the beauty of his soul. He also said it was edged with darkness, or something, where it had brushed against evil.'

'Plenty of that round here,' says Benefice. 'I've spoken to one or two friends, by the way. They're willing to try moving Mary Pettus's coffin. But I think that the weather is likely to be too bad today. They'll come and find you when it improves.'

I look out of the window. The blue sky that had accompanied my gift of a skull has gone. Clouds cover the sun. A stiff breeze has sprung up.

'You think a storm is on the way?'

'I'd tell Mister Pepys to vote early, if he suffers at all from seasickness. It could get quite choppy out there.'

Pepys has been pacing up and down awaiting my return.

'I informed you very clearly that there was a transfer to countersign. How can you vote for me unless you are a qualified burgess?'

'I apologise, but the matter is quickly rectified,' I say.

'You don't need to read through it like that.'

'I never sign anything without reading it.'

'It is a gift of a freehold. It can be in no way to your detriment.'

'There may be onerous covenants.'

'There are none. Why should I waste my time writing covenants when you are to return the property to me by tonight?'

'The only reason I am alive now is that I have made a habit of not believing everything I am told. I shall finish reading this faster if I am not interrupted again.'

I finish reading the document then allow Pepys to pace the room for another five minutes.

'Yes, that appears to be in order,' I say. 'Thank you for your very kind gift. Where is Harbour Street, by the way?'

'Does that matter?'

'I thought we might inspect my new residence on our way to the Guildhall. Since I shall be owner for such a short time, this may be my only opportunity.'

'This is not a matter for humour, Sir John. I have not taken all this trouble for your amusement. The future of the country hangs on what will happen over the next few hours. You have a small part to play, but a noble one, in the history of our struggle with the Dutch.'

I wonder if levity was Tutepenny's crime – a gentle reproof about the Admiral's treatment of his crew, perhaps. That would merit a whipping without doubt. But they are both dead and we'll probably never know now.

'Don't worry,' I say. 'However Spratchett behaves, you should get home with a vote or two to spare. Benefice's advice is that we should go early to the polls. It would be a shame to have gone to all this trouble and be unable to reach the Guildhall in time for us both to cast our votes.'

From my Lady Grey's most excellent poem
The Election

Thus came the day when voters cast
Their votes, as they had in the past,
At Eastwold's famed but damp Guildhall
The home of crab and barnacle.
Our men had spent all they could spend on
Votes – but which could they depend on?
Some memories are sadly short,
And love's just punk when it is bought.

Chapter 20

Election Day in Eastwold

The sky is low, wide and threatening. A stiff breeze blows in from envious Holland and the waves are crashing with a loud, continuous hiss on the sandy shore. It is hard to know whether what blows in our faces is spray from the sea or the first of the rain. It's cold, whatever it is. We have gathered here on the beach in order to be able to sail or row out together to the place where we shall vote, in accordance with ancient custom. The fishermen stand in a little group to one side. They are looking up at the sky and are not happy with what they see.

'Can we delay until tomorrow, Mister Sprachett, sir?' says John Pettus. 'I wouldn't be setting out in this weather to fish. Not for the biggest shoal of the year. The smaller boats could be swamped if we try to take everyone out at once.'

'Today is the day named for the poll,' says Spratchett solemnly. 'We must obey the writ as delivered to us by order of the King's Majesty. We have five boats – all as seaworthy as they need to be. That will be more than enough.'

Cooper and Bottulph, neither of them electors but summoned from their homes beyond the walls to convey their
betters to the Guildhall, regard each other uncertainly. They
don't like that sky either, but Spratchett employs them and
could employ others in their place. They may as well drown
quickly as starve slowly.

Pepys takes out a sheet of paper. 'Would now be a good
time to address the electors?' he asks. 'How long do we each
have to speak?'

'You can say what you like for as long as you like,' says
Spratchett. 'But you'll be talking to an empty beach very
shortly. Didn't you hear what Pettus told you? There's a storm
on its way, no doubt about that.'

Pepys still holds his speech in front of him. He has spent
some time on it. But I think everyone here has already made
up their minds, to the extent that they are permitted to do so.

'Very well,' he says, carefully folding the paper. Then he
pauses and points. 'Dix is here merely to take us out to sea, I
trust?' he says. 'He no longer has a house or a vote.'

'He's voting,' says Spratchett. 'He had a house when the
writ was issued. Anyway, you all know that he has been living
within the walls and has voted in previous elections. He needs
to provide no more proof than anyone else. I say that his
vote is good.'

The other fishermen nod, more out of sympathy with
the homeless Dix than as champions of one or other of the
candidates.

'What does the returning officer say?' says Pepys.

A tall thin figure in black emerges from the crowd. He
sneers at Pepys's flowing periwig and his well-cut breeches and
decides it all tallies with what he has heard from elsewhere.

'My ruling as Town Clerk,' says Peacock, 'is that Mister Dix is notoriously a burgess and can vote. To feign ignorance would be ridiculous and make an ungodly mockery of the dignity of this election.'

'I must protest,' says Pepys. 'This is most irregular.'

'Are you calling my judgment into question?' asks Peacock.

I take Pepys to one side. 'I think you still have a majority,' I say. 'You have your vote and mine. Digby. Benefice. David Larter. Henry Cavendish. That's six. Cavendish has his own vote, Solomon Larter, and probably Spratchett, plus Dix and Pettus if they follow their master's orders. That's five. If you annoy Peacock too much, he may just decide to vote for Cavendish rather than abstain. Or you can stand on the beach and argue if you prefer. The storm may not break for another half hour and we may not all drown on the way back to the shore.'

'Very well,' says Pepys. 'I withdraw my objection, Mister Peacock.'

'What is Sir John doing here?' Spratchett calls over to us. 'He does not live here and is not an office holder.'

'Ah . . . indeed,' says Jacob Cavendish. 'I do not see how he can be a burgess, with the greatest respect to him.'

'On the contrary,' says Pepys smugly. 'I have gifted him this very morning a fine freehold within the borough.'

'Harbour Street,' I say.

I doff my hat to Jacob Cavendish and he returns the compliment. He bears me no grudge personally. Nevertheless he asks politely: 'Do you permit that, Mister Peacock?'

'May I inspect the transfer, Sir John?'

'Careful, Peacock, the ink is still wet,' says Solomon Larter as I hand it over.

Peacock gives the briefest of smiles and glances at the transfer. He returns it to me with a bow. 'Yes, I permit Sir John to vote, in respect of his ancient freehold by the harbour. Long may he live to enjoy it.'

'Ha! Six votes to five,' Pepys whispers to me. Then he turns to the Town Clerk and says: 'Very well, Mister Peacock. I don't think we need to delay any longer, do we?'

'Not at all, Mister Pepys. You may all go to your boats, gentlemen. And may God guard and protect you on your journey. A safe and profitable voyage to you all.' He clutches at his hat and successfully prevents it blowing away down the beach.

Pepys boards our boat adroitly, running up the narrow plank that has been provided, being accustomed to embarking and disembarking under conditions much worse than these. I follow, then Digby, a little cautiously. Bottulph pushes us out with a hand from one of his friends, then clambers aboard. Peacock and Spratchett have boarded a larger sailing boat, as befits their dignity in these proceedings. Solomon Larter, being an elected MP, travels with them. Jacob and Henry Cavendish, any political differences lost for the moment in family unity, board Cooper's boat. Henry must have ridden down this morning. If the storm breaks, he'll have difficulty riding back this afternoon. Pettus rows Dix and Benefice. Dowsing takes David Larter, who is as ever observing everything with a sort of cynical detachment. He leans back in the stern, closes his eyes and stretches out his legs, as if he were listening to the vicar's sermon in church.

Driven by the growing wind, the large sailing boat tacks neatly enough and is soon well ahead of the rest of us. About half a mile offshore, it checks its pace and circles a couple of times until Peacock judges himself, I have no idea how, to be above the Guildhall. It drops anchor. We are not far behind. The smaller boats have to be allowed a chance to make up ground, and we pitch and toss uncomfortably while we wait for them. Salt spray blows up and over our heads. We are all now quite wet. Pepys is sick over the side and Digby looks distinctly unwell. Perhaps his father was right to breed him as a landsman. It is beginning to feel chilly out here and an uncomfortably long way from solid ground. I am very aware how much water is underneath us. Its green depths look cold and uninviting. I would not wish to have to swim to the shore.

'Don't worry, sir,' says Bottulph. 'I've been out in worse, though not on purpose. I'll get you back safely.'

'I'd be very grateful for that,' I say.

Pepys nods and is sick again.

When everyone has finally caught up, the Town Clerk stands in his boat, clinging to a worn but convenient piece of rigging to maintain his dignity.

'Very well, gentlemen,' he says, his voice struggling against the wind. 'Who will you choose as your Member of Parliament?'

'Cavendish,' calls Spratchett from behind him. 'A true Cavalier and a fine English gentleman.'

'As I thought,' mutters Pepys. 'The man is a scoundrel. We were unwise to let him force Dix on us as a voter. But we shall have the final laugh and win the day in spite of him.'

'And no damned courtiers in Eastwold!' Spratchett adds. This meets with a worrying amount of public approval, but he does employ many of those present.

I notice that Bottulph in our boat, perhaps out of politeness, does not join in but simply nods thoughtfully. He has no vote anyway.

Peacock surveys his small, bobbing armada. 'In which case I declare—'

'Pepys!' yells David Larter, against the rising storm.

'Pepys!' This time it is Henry Cavendish. Jacob, in the same craft, scowls at him, but I doubt that his cousin failed to give him some warning.

'We need a poll, Mister Peacock,' calls David Larter from his rowing boat.

'Very well, gentlemen,' says Peacock, who expected no other outcome from his original question. 'A poll it shall be, if that is your wish. Please approach me on foot, one by one, and cast your votes.'

This last seems part of a ritual that dates back to when votes were cast on dry land. Nobody is getting ready to walk on water.

'Mine first,' says Solomon Larter. 'I have that right as the sitting Member. I, Solomon Larter, Member of Parliament for this borough, do vote for Mister Jacob Cavendish.'

Peacock notes this, with some difficulty in a rocking boat, on a sheet of paper.

'I have the right to speak next,' says Spratchett. 'I also vote for Mister Cavendish. So do Dix and Pettus.'

Peacock looks at him with the mildest of reproofs and calls out: 'You must each vote yourselves, Mister Dix and Mister Pettus.'

'Cavendish,' says Pettus, a little reluctantly, I think.

'Cavendish,' says Dix. He seems to show no gratitude for having had his ability to vote confirmed earlier. I think he simply wishes to get back to dry land, before the storm breaks, and not drown.

'Very well,' says Peacock, counting carefully, 'that is four votes for Mister Cavendish and none for Mister Pepys.'

'I vote for myself,' calls Jacob.

'Five for Mister Cavendish,' says Peacock. He makes another note.

'And I vote for myself!' shouts Pepys.

'Who did you say you voted for?' asks Peacock, cupping an ear.

'Oh for goodness' sake! I vote for me – who else would I vote for, you stupid man?'

'Ah! Five votes for Mister Cavendish and one for Mister Pepys.'

'I vote for Pepys,' I say.

'So do I,' says Henry Cavendish.

'So do I,' says David Larter.

'Five Cavendish, four Pepys,' calls Peacock. 'Any more votes?'

'I, Ezekiel Benefice, do cast my vote for Mister Samuel Pepys, thanking him for his custom and his generosity. I look forward to voting for him in future elections on similar terms. I also have some excellent brandy in the boat here, available to all at very reasonable prices, to celebrate his victory.'

'Five votes each and bad brandy for those who have good money to throw away,' says Peacock. 'Anyone else?'

'I vote for Mister Cavendish,' calls Dowsing.

'You don't have a vote, Mister Dowsing,' says Peacock. 'So keep quiet, you old fool.'

Dowsing waves a piece of paper, not unlike my own.

'I have been gifted a freehold by Mister Spratchett.'

'I object,' says Pepys. 'That should have been declared on the beach.'

Spratchett looks at Peacock. 'He votes for Cavendish. Write it down. Go on!'

'That vote is invalid,' says Pepys.

'I allowed your friend with a house by the harbour,' says Peacock to Pepys. 'I must now allow Mister Dowsing's claim, if the transfer is valid. I know of no rule that says that a voter must declare himself in advance. Proof at the hustings is all that is needed. Did you convey a freehold to Mister Dowsing, Mayor Spratchett?'

'Yes,' says Spratchett. 'I rather think I did.'

'Then that would seem entirely in order. I accept and note Mister Dowsing's choice of candidate. You may stop waving that paper now, Dowsing. You'll get it wet, and I think Mayor Spratchett will want it back later. That is now six to five in favour of Mister Cavendish.'

All eyes turn to Digby but Spratchett seeks to forestall the draw that now appears inevitable.

'Aren't you going to vote, Peacock?' asks Spratchett.

'What's it to you, Spratchett?' Peacock asks. 'I'll vote or not as God directs me and according to my conscience.'

'You think God wants to see that damned courtier elected? Are we going to be shamed as the lapdogs of the Duke of York? Are we to hang our heads as the geese of Suffolk? Will you vote with us like a man? Or are you just going to stand there, giving us a never-ending sermon out of your Puritan arse?'

Spratchett has made the mistake that I counselled Pepys against. He thinks Peacock will respond well to having his religion and person insulted. He has also apparently forgotten that he displaced Peacock as Mayor. The corn chandler smiles like a man who has been waiting ten years for something good that has finally turned up.

L. C. TYLER

'Better a courtier on the make than a down-at-heel Cavalier who led us to our ruin. You want me to vote, do you, Spratchett? Very well, I cast my vote for Mister Pepys. That is six votes each and I hope it has made you content. Do you wish to vote now, Mister Digby? You are in a position to break the deadlock.'

'I do so wish,' says Digby. He turns and looks at Pepys. 'I, Digby Digges, of the Priory hard by Eastwold and of Market Street within the walls, do cast my vote for Jacob Cavendish.'

Pepys's jaw drops open. Well, at least we now know whether Digby saw Pepys and Silvia in the garden last night.

'Are there any further voters here?' asks Peacock. 'Any transfer documents that we have overlooked? No? I ask you all once if there are any other votes . . . I ask you all twice if there are any other votes . . . I ask one final time. No? Then, fellow burgesses, the poll is now dry, to use an odd phrase for a day such as this. I declare Mister Jacob Cavendish duly elected as Member of Parliament for the ancient and illustrious borough of Eastwold, founded by King John, of happy and glorious memory. The wind is getting up, gentlemen. I suggest that we all make for the beach as rapidly as we can. And God grant you all a safe return from your homes under the sea to your homes on dry land.'

We are understandably silent in the boat going back. Bottulph is very aware that all has not gone according to plan and keeps his eyes on the misty outline of the beach ahead of us. Pepys knows why Digby has turned on him but has no wish to admit that he knows. Digby similarly has no wish to state out loud the reason for his change of sides. Not in public. It does him no credit, however you look at it. Of course, people will soon start to speculate as to why he turned on the Admiralty candidate anyway. Perhaps he would have been better off voting for Pepys and retaining his dignity. Only I am reasonably content as we make our way towards the shore. Pepys can scarcely say that I didn't warn him, though I have no idea what part I shall play in the story that he has to tell the Duke of York when he gets to London. Perhaps my unnecessary accusations against Spratchett and my rash and foolish acceptance of Dix's status as a burgess will feature prominently.

I think that Pepys may appreciate the skill with which Bottulph brings the boat in to the beach amongst the crashing waves. It would be easy to upset the craft under these conditions, but the bows slide up the gently shelving sand and we come to rest. Digby seems not to care whether we land safely or are dashed to pieces. They both march off up the beach, ignoring each other, leaving me to tip Bottulph five Shillings for preserving our several lives. I watch the other boats come ashore one by one. Henry Cavendish generously shakes his cousin's hand. David Larter also pats the victorious Jacob on the back. The fishermen touch their hats to their new Member of Parliament.

But I don't think they will be roasting an ox on the beach tonight. The rain that has threatened all afternoon comes suddenly, as a vast sheet of stinging water. I run along the beach after Pepys and make my way up the steep and now slippery path to the top of the cliffs. The vicar is standing there, at almost exactly the point from which the rock was sent down this morning. Rain is streaming from his clothes and his long white hair is plastered to his face.

'Cavendish won,' I say.

'What?'

'Jacob Cavendish. He won by seven votes to six. He is your new Member of Parliament.'

'Why should you think I wish to know that?'

'You are standing there. I thought that you hoped to discover the result of the ballot.'

He shakes his head and stares out to sea. 'I told you,' he says. 'God is coming for us. Did you not see him out there? That is where he is, I promise you. There is no escape. You may run back to the manor house, but he will seek you out. He will stick his little finger through the window and extract you as you extract a winkle on a pin.'

I didn't know God could do that, but as ever I bow to Wraith's greater knowledge.

'If I were you I'd go home and get dry,' I say. 'It would be a shame to die of pneumonia just when God came knocking.'

From my Lady Grey's most excellent poem
The Election

You men who only vote on land
Will never truly understand
The pleasure you might all obtain
When voting on the foaming main,
By virtue of a freehold given
Just for the day, which fishes live in,
Gliding through each cosy chamber.
Where should dwell your own dear dame or
Children with their smiling faces
You will find just dabs and plaices!
'Tis a fit place for being taught or
Recalling vows are writ on water!
Men failed to vote as they contracted?
Perhaps because of scenes enacted,
Last night in a shady bower.
Alas, it was a fateful hour!
For our brave naval candidate
Has sealed his parliamentary fate.
You see, not e'en to save his life
Can he ignore another's wife . . .

Chapter 21

My wife is obliging

M y wet clothes are drying in a distant part of the house. I am sitting in front of a fire in our room, dressed in my other breeches and shirt, drying my hair with a towel.

'I fear for Digby,' I say. 'The sort of rough music that Lowestoft folk mete out to wife beaters can also be inflicted on cuckolds.'

'That would be unfair,' says Aminta. 'Pepys is most adept. And the Admiral was deceived in much the same way.'

'Being deceived runs in the Digges family,' I say. 'Perhaps the town will be understanding.'

'I think, in any case, we should be more concerned for Silvia.'

'You think Digby will take his revenge on her?' I ask. 'Now he is undeceived?'

'No – or not as his father might have done. That is not in his nature. My fear, as we said, is that Silvia is the murderer, for all that she has fashionable hair. There is no doubt that she was badly treated – only she could tell us how badly. She had good cause to kill the Admiral and the opportunity. I think, up until yesterday, Digby had done everything in his power to protect her from accusation. But perhaps he will now have second thoughts about that. Digby may be about to turn King's evidence.'

'I agree that, if he did so, things would not look good for Silvia. No court in Eastwold would convict her, of course, whatever he said, but the trial would take place in Bury St Edmunds or Ipswich, not here. I am not convinced of her guilt, but I cannot say what a jury from another part of the county would make of it – the death of a naval hero at the hands of a member of his own family.'

'So, if her husband accuses her . . . ?'

'A husband can't give evidence against his wife in court, but if Digby started to say in public that he knew Silvia had killed his father, it would be difficult for me to ignore. That's what I've been sent here to find out. I would have to arrest her.'

'But Silvia would never have killed Tutepenny,' says Aminta. 'The Admiral, yes – I'd have done it myself – but not somebody as kind and self-effacing as Tutepenny. The killer has to be somebody else, whatever Digby fears may be the case.'

'Perhaps Spratchett killed Digges after all,' I say. 'He wouldn't have hesitated to kill Tutepenny if he needed to cover up the crime. Just another fisherman and not even one who worked for him.'

'I don't think so,' says Aminta. 'Spratchett is Mayor and probably the richest man in Eastwold. Why should he jeopardise any of that? Of the esteemed dignitaries of Eastwold, Solomon Larter is the more likely. Let's not forget that his nephew David was covering up for somebody, and Solomon Larter had good cause to kill Digges.'

'I honestly think that David Larter could have been covering up for Silvia as much as for his uncle,' I say. 'And the dispute over ditches had run for years. It wasn't new. It would be difficult to say why he should have suddenly acquired the urge to kill Digges. Peacock wrote accusing David Larter, of course. He might have done that to cover up his own crime – there's no doubt he hated Digges. But he also hated Larter and Spratchett and they are still alive. Anyway, Peacock would have been much better off just keeping quiet if he had killed him. And again, he'd resisted taking vengeance for years.'

'The same applies to Jacob Cavendish,' says Aminta with a sigh. 'His grievance was in the past, not the present. The Admiral had humiliated him in many ways. He'd deprived him of his home. The town was aware that Jacob couldn't even protect his own daughter from her father-in-law. That would have been an embarrassment for a former follower of Prince Rupert. But we now know that Silvia appeared to have solved that problem herself. She was no longer in danger. Which is why I also think that it can't be Digby.'

'Digby?' I say. 'Well, we can't ignore that possibility that he is just covering up for himself. Digby was out on the beach when the Admiral was killed. But, for him too, the need to defend Silvia had already passed. Digby's eyes may have been opened to his father's faults over the past few days, but I don't doubt that he did respect him in the past. It would have taken a great deal to make him turn on his father – it would have had to be something that could be rectified in no other way.'

'Alexander and Barbara?' says Aminta. 'They needed the Admiral's money.'

'I still haven't discovered if the estate was entailed,' I say. 'But, even if it was, they would have inherited only if Digby died as well as the Admiral. Better for Alexander that the Admiral lived and loaned him what he needed – I think that there is no possibility of a loan from Digby, or not if Silvia has any say in the matter.'

'What about Jacob's cousin, Henry?' asks Aminta. 'He also knew how badly Silvia had been treated and seems a more determined character than Jacob.'

'He had as much reason as Jacob to dislike the Admiral, but he has an alibi, he claims, that his patients will willingly confirm. Having made the journey myself, I agree that he had too little time to commit murder here when he was living so far up the coast.'

'Could it have been Tutepenny, as Pepys proposed?' asks Aminta.

'It's as likely as any of the others, with the same objection that he'd waited an extraordinary amount of time before deciding to get his revenge.'

'It's strange that the Admiral left Tutepenny money in his will,' says Aminta. 'Benefice also served under him but received nothing.'

'Yes, Tutepenny, the vicar and Catch were remembered in the will,' I say. 'A strange trio of legatees. Of course, Tutepenny knew nothing about his bequest – he couldn't have killed him just to get the money.'

'And if Tutepenny killed the Admiral, why did anybody need to kill Tutepenny to keep him quiet?'

'There's Benefice, of course,' I say. 'He had a curse placed on the Admiral and he resented the Admiral's interest in smuggling. Digby said that his father might have been going after smugglers that evening – hence, it would seem, taking his sword. Perhaps the Admiral attacked Benefice and he defended himself?'

'But surely Benefice wouldn't have killed Tutepenny?' says Aminta.

'I agree. He would not have killed Tutepenny, however much Tutepenny knew. Of course, Benefice is one of the few who had an urgent need to kill the Admiral, if he was indeed defending himself, but the problem we keep coming back to with everyone else is why they should choose to do it *then*. And that applies to Silvia as much as to the rest. However much they had hated the Admiral, whoever killed him had held their hand for far too long. But something happened to change things utterly – for one of them anyway. Something that gave the killer a new and more urgent reason to kill.'

'Unless the murderer was a madman,' says Aminta.

'Well, we have one of those. I think Wraith tried to kill me this morning, so I don't doubt he is capable of murder. But if Wraith, or any of them, had killed the Admiral, how would Tutepenny know? I cannot believe Tutepenny's death is unconnected with the Admiral's, since his sword was used. Well, all I can say is that somebody must have killed the Admiral and somebody must have killed Tutepenny, since it is undeniable that they are both dead.'

'No, I think we are closer than that to discovering the killer. And it has to be one of the people we have been talking about. I think the reason is staring us in the face – we just can't see it yet.'

'Perhaps we shall discover that when we exhume Mary Pettus,' I say.

'If you exhume her. She will have to survive tonight's storm. By tomorrow her body may have been swept far out to sea.'

'I hope not. Give me another day. If I can find out nothing of use – and Digby does not actually denounce his wife from the cliff top – I will write exactly the report that Pepys and his master hoped I would write. I shall say there is no evidence that it was not an accident. Perhaps that is for the best, anyway. We can then go back to Essex and onwards to London. There is a limit to how much time the Sheriff can expect me to spend on this.'

'Two days,' says Aminta. 'You can have two more days. See what a helpful and obliging wife I am?'

A violent gust of wind rattles the windows. Yes, the storm is not yet over and by tomorrow the landscape may have changed a great deal.

Chapter 22

Mister Pepys does not eat breakfast

Pepys did not appear for supper last night, pleading tiredness, and this morning has asked that a draught of small beer should be sent up to his room. The rest of us are eating breakfast awkwardly. It is sometimes difficult to extrapolate from one's own family life to that of others, but I would say that Digby and Silvia had an argument last night and that Silvia secured a total victory. Silvia appears quite cheerful, chatting brightly and ensuring that we have enough to eat. Digby sulks openly, tapping his fingers on the table and staring out of the window. He accepts coffee but declines everything else. This does not trouble Silvia in any way. Aminta's attempts to engage Digby in conversation – to discuss the election or the gale that battered the house last night – are met with a single word or are ignored completely. If this is indeed how he behaved as a boy, then he would have been a trial to even the most sweet-tempered Puritans in his family.

'We heard the wind a great deal last night,' I say to Silvia. 'It shook our windows.'

'It was one of the worst gales I can remember,' she says. 'The Steward reports that several trees have blown down in the park. Digby will, I am sure, be going out later to inspect the garden and decide what needs to be rectified – or left as it is. It is a pity, but sometimes damage is done in a garden and it just has to be accepted, would you not agree, my dear?'

'If you say so,' says Digby.

There is anger in his voice, but there is also something that I have often noticed when questioning people on Lord Arlington's behalf in dark cellars: fear. Yes, Silvia's victory has been total – no mere temporary advantage to be brushed off by the enemy and forgotten, but a campaign-ending rout.

'I wonder how they have fared further up the coast,' says Silvia, unconcerned. 'My cousin Henry lives there and will be returning today. But of course, Sir John, you have been to Lowestoft recently yourself – the day poor Mister Tutepenny was killed. My husband encouraged your visit.'

'Yes, that's right,' I say. 'I think Lowestoft is better protected than Eastwold. They may not have suffered the same damage.'

She nods. 'I have told Digby that any losses here at the Priory will be small compared with those who live on the edge of the cliff. We have not forfeited our lives or our home. That is a blessing.' She smiles at Digby, defying him to say that the destruction of the Priory would have been welcome, but he continues to stare out of the window. The sun breaks through the clouds, but I think he does not notice.

I too decide to examine the world beyond the dining room and, assuring Silvia that I have eaten more than well enough, I head for the garden. There is a crystal freshness in the air and there are puddles of clear, clean water on the gravel paths. Several branches have fallen and whole beds of flowers have been flattened by the rain. But it will all recover. In a month's time nobody will notice anything amiss – at least, not outside the house. The walled garden, on the landward side of the house, will have survived even better, I imagine, than the open lawns and beds. I unlatch the gate, only to collide with Pepys, who is about to leave the enclosed space that I am trying to enter. He stops, mouth open, uncertain whether to attack or retreat.

'Good morning,' I say. 'My commiserations on your defeat yesterday. It was not to be foreseen.'

'Yes,' he says thoughtfully. He does not curse Spratchett or berate me for mismanaging his affairs. Of course, we both know the real reason for his failure to win the seat, and it has nothing to do with Spratchett or my investigations.

'I'm sure that the Duke will not blame you,' I say. 'I should be happy to write to him, or to Lord Arlington, and say that it was entirely due to the unexpected and inexplicable defection of Mister Digges, who chose at the last moment to support his father-in-law rather than you – an unfortunate but, with hindsight, an understandable thing for him to have done. I mean that he felt obliged by family ties to do so.'

'Thank you,' he says absently. 'That would be kind. Very kind. The Duke may misinterpret my loss as a lack of zeal in his service.'

I feel strangely sorry for this Pepys in defeat. He is bearing his losses in a more dignified manner than I expected. Of course, it is still entirely his fault.

'You will, I suppose, leave now at the first opportunity? I mean you must have duties in London?'

'In London?' he says, as if he had forgotten there was such a place. 'Yes, I suppose I do.'

'Aminta and I will also depart shortly. I must finally fulfil my promise to take her shopping.'

'Depart?' says Pepys.

'Yes, probably the day after tomorrow. I'll spend another day or so completing my report on the Admiral's death, of course, but it may be that I'm unable to discover more than I already have. Aminta has been very patient and she has kindly given me two more days. My wife has a touching confidence in my ability to resolve this puzzle in that time, but there are many people who could have killed Digges and no conclusive evidence for it to be any one of them.'

'Just two days? But it may take much longer than that to secure a conviction.'

'Surely my job is to discover the murderer and then cover the whole matter up?'

'Do not be facetious, Sir John. This is not time for levity.'

'I assure you that I would not joke about such things but I fear I go round in circles. Peacock hoped that Solomon Larter was the killer. Alexander Digges still rather hopes that it is Silvia, and I think that David Larter dreads that it is. Benefice feared it was Tutepenny. I increasingly believe Digby has been covering up something, but whether it is on behalf of his wife or his father-in-law, I could not say. Whoever killed the Admiral did so just as he stood to win the prize that he so much valued – to be the Member of Parliament for Eastwold. But I don't understand why he had to be killed then, any more than I understand why the vicar will not let us re-bury Mistress Pettus. Perhaps Tutepenny knew and that might help us, but I suspect that it would not, because nothing leads anywhere in Eastwold – every path merely takes you to the cliff edge.'

Pepys shakes his head impatiently. 'It is essential that the Admiral's murderer is caught and punished – however long that takes. You owe it to the King, who has graciously overlooked your previous allegiance to the Republic. You owe it to the Sheriff, who placed such trust in you. And you owe it to your host, Mister Digges, who has looked after you and your wife so well and offered you every possible assistance – assistance that you have frequently and most churlishly rejected. The killer, Sir John, must be found and hanged! He must feel the full force of the law, with whatever forfeiture of office rightly accompanies that.'

It is the possible forfeiture of office that clarifies matters for me.

'You think Jacob Cavendish killed the Admiral, don't you?' I say.

'Isn't it obvious? Only a moment ago, you rightly said that Digby feared it. Who would know better what was going on within his family? The Admiral had usurped Jacob's position in the town. You saw him skulking at the back of the church in tattered lace while the Digges family flaunted their finery in his former pew. What shame must he feel every Sunday? How jealousy must gnaw at his soul as he recites the Creed from such a base position! You have seen the house that he now lives in and compared it with this veritable paradise from which he was ejected. The Admiral mistreated Jacob's daughter, and he was able to do nothing about it. How must he have felt about that? How must it have gnawed his once-proud Cavalier soul? And finally Digges was standing for Parliament – standing for a seat that was rightly the property of the ancient and respected Cavendish family!'

'This is the first time you have mentioned that the Cavendishes have any sort of ownership of the seat,' I say. 'I was under the impression that you thought you would better represent the borough.'

'Indeed, I would! I speak as he must have imagined things – not as a reasonable man, such as you or I, might think. I would most certainly make a better Member of Parliament for the borough and for the nation. And I still intend to, once we can get this result overturned on the grounds of Cavendish's patent guilt. But I do not say any of these things from a personal point of view. It is in the interests of the *country* that Cavendish's election should be set aside.'

'I have no evidence at all that Jacob Cavendish is a murderer, even if his son-in-law fears that he is. I agree Jacob might have done more for Silvia. But not all former Cavaliers believe that fighting solves anything. Henry Cavendish actually said to me that a man might kill without a thought in battle but recoil from the slightest discord in happier times. I can sympathise with that. I think I can see why Jacob might have suggested to his daughter that she took refuge peacefully in Lowestoft. Henry in fact condemned Jacob's actions, but there is a very fine line between cowardice and plain common sense. I think Jacob felt that he had killed enough men for one lifetime. And he no longer needed to resent the loss of the Priory, when his daughter had regained it. As for the election, I now think he would have beaten Digges, just as he beat you.'

'You don't think that he killed the Admiral then?'

'He is no more and no less likely than the others. I'm sorry, Mister Pepys, but I don't recommend that we try to overturn the election result on the basis that Jacob Cavendish is a murderer. There is no evidence to convict him.'

'I disagree. I have already explained his motive very clearly. Any twelve fools on a jury could see that it might be true. I am sure that one of the fishermen, for a fee, would swear that he saw Cavendish near the beach on the night the Admiral was killed, as he may well have been in fact. That should be conclusive. It is the plain unvarnished truth, almost.'

'Which fisherman?' I ask.

'I'd be happy to leave that to you. I'm not a rich man, Sir John. But as long as your fisherman is reasonable, we should be able to come to an arrangement.'

'Benefice?' I ask.

'Perfect. A worthy ex-seaman who had served his country in an admirable fashion, happily giving up a limb for his beloved King. Who could doubt the word of a simple, honest tar? I knew I could rely on you.'

'The problem,' I say, 'is that, while everyone here hated the Admiral and would overlook his killing free of charge, they are, for the most part, decent, fair-minded folk. They won't willingly see somebody like Cavendish trepanned. Not by you. Or me. Benefice is a rogue and he sells bad brandy at a Shilling a bottle, but he has a code of honour that you would scarcely guess at.'

'Ha!' says Pepys. Within this brief exclamation he wishes to convey Benefice's undoubted veniality, my own regrettable naivety and the precipitous decline of moral values in England since the current king was welcomed back with open arms. Of course he may not be wrong in any part of that. I won't know until I push the purse of golden coins across Benefice's greasy table and see precisely how wide is his smile.

'Even if you will not consider the interests of the nation, as any patriot should, you ought at least to consider your own, and what your master, Lord Arlington, may offer you if you succeed.'

'I am not looking for reward or preferment of any sort, Mister Pepys.'

'You are happy as a country magistrate?'

'I am happy as the husband of one of England's most illustrious playwrights and as the father of young Master Charles Grey, who even now eagerly awaits my return, so that he can show off whatever new vices his grandfather has taught him in my absence.'

Pepys sighs. 'I too loved my wife,' he says.

'Of course,' I say.

'The other women – they meant nothing to me. Nothing at all. You do understand that?'

I consider asking if that included Silvia Digges in the garden the night before last. Probably. Silvia would have been unwise to count on being able to run away with Pepys, if that is any part of her plan. Again, I wonder if Venetia made a similar mistake twelve years ago. Perhaps it was, as Jacob hinted, she who wished to flee and Isaac Cavendish who flatly refused to give up his peaceful life on the Suffolk coast.

'Each time,' Pepys continues, 'every single time, I swore that it would be the last. Each time, I felt that I had the strength to resist temptation in future. That I'd never do such a thing again. And yet when the time came and the opportunity arose, how easily I fell . . .'

'I understand,' I say.

'Do you? Your circumstances and mine are not the same.'

I shrug. He's right. Our circumstances could scarcely be more different. But I do understand. Aminta would understand too. She wouldn't approve, but she would understand.

She's a playwright, after all. Human nature is her stock in trade just as the law is mine. Alexander Digges will most certainly appear in one of her future plays as a comic Puritan. But if she bases a character on Pepys, then it will be a tragedy that she is writing – a man who had so much in his grasp but chose to throw the most important part of it away, almost without noticing what he was doing. Standing here, in the sunshine after the storm, I think that Pepys has almost forgotten yesterday's defeat. That is not important to him. It is a minor check that he will recover from, by getting Cavendish arbitrarily hanged or otherwise. But from the loss of Elizabeth Pepys there is no way back. The bridge is broken. The road is for ever closed.

'So, Pepys now wishes you to remain?' asks Aminta.

'Yes, I say, 'to ensure that Jacob Cavendish is arrested for the Admiral's death. Or, if that cannot be done in two days, then to confirm that there is some other good reason for annulling the result of the election.'

We have escaped from both Pepys and the Diggeses and are walking along the beach. The fine, wet sand is spattered with all manner of debris from above – bricks, branches of trees, whole shrubs, cobblestones. The sea has taken another great bite, but this time no inhabited houses have been harmed.

'I was worried about Silvia, but now I begin to fear for Jacob Cavendish unless you help him,' says Aminta. 'Pepys will find a way to bring him down, just as he offers to raise you up.'

'Jacob's welfare is my concern? I think not.'

'He fought alongside my father.'

'So did half the country.'

'I mean it. And he is Silvia's father.'

'Yes, Pepys has already damaged her family enough. Silvia deserves our care. But I promised to take you to London.'

'And so you shall. The delay has been useful. Before we left Essex, I thought that I needed to order two new dresses while we were there. Now I have been given time to think about it, I realise that three is the minimum I shall require.'

I kiss her. 'Order four. And some pearls. And have your hair dressed as the ladies do in France. We pass this way but once. If Pepys could still order dresses for his wife, he'd do it by the dozen.'

'Samuel Pepys seems to have had a very good influence on you,' she says.

'I'll see if I can return the compliment,' I say, 'but I somehow doubt it.'

We have reached the point where the church looms above, high on the cliff. I look up. The graveyard is smaller than it was yesterday by several feet. Whereas, before, just the end of Mary Pettus's coffin was visible, now almost a third of it juts out above our heads. Mary herself is still concealed in a seemly manner. But that is not what I am looking at.

'Are those bones sticking out underneath the coffin?' I ask.

'I don't think they can be Mary's. Her coffin is still intact.'

'So Mary was buried on top of somebody else?'

'I doubt that the bones were slipped under Mary's coffin last night,' says Aminta. 'I think that, twelve years ago, somebody must have taken the opportunity to drop an inconvenient body there while the grave was still unoccupied. Mary's coffin followed very shortly afterwards.'

'If the vicar knew, it would explain why he did not wish the grave to be disturbed. Had last night's storm taken as much from the churchyard as it did a few weeks ago, then it would all have vanished in a single night. Bones from several graves might have been scattered over the beach. Nobody would have been any the wiser who had been concealed where.'

'That is very unlucky for somebody.'

'Yes, isn't it?'

'Time to visit the vicar, I think.'

Chapter 23

I pay a visit to the vicar

'Bones?' says the vicar? 'Of course there are bones in the churchyard. Citizens of Eastwold have been buried around the church for hundreds of years. In earlier times their graves were not marked as they are now. The position of a burial was known only so long as the buriers were still alive. Of course, our registers show who is buried here, but only since Thomas Cromwell's time. And even they are vague about where in the churchyard a grave might be. Almost every time we dig a new grave we find some sign that others have laboured there before – a fragment of a skull, a tooth, the plate from a coffin, a ring.'

'It is difficult to tell from the beach,' I say, 'but my belief is that these bones are recent ones, laid precisely in the bottom of the newly dug grave – not old bones from an interment centuries ago that just happened to be nearby and overlapped onto the new grave. It is essential that we exhume Mary Pettus's coffin and examine what lies beneath it.'

'And what of the exhumers? Mary Pettus could fall to the beach at any moment. The sand around her is about to release her from its grip. Can you not hear each grain trickle away?'

'I have a group of fishermen,' I say, 'who have pledged to try, in spite of the danger.'

'The cliff will come down the moment the ground is disturbed,' says Wraith.

'I shall be there digging with them, if they are still willing,' I say.

'You wish to die too?' asks Wraith.

'I would not ask others to take a risk that I would not take myself,' I say.

He shakes his head. 'No, you will outlive me,' he says. 'I have asked the Devil that very question and he has told me. You will watch the life being squeezed out of me. Thus it shall be. The Devil obfuscates, but he does not lie.'

'I am of course very impressed by your bravery in promising to sacrifice your life, and the wellbeing of your wife and child, to establish the origins of some bones that quite possibly have no bearing at all on the death that you have been asked to investigate.'

'Thank you,' I say.

'I cannot speak for our little son, Charles, but I shall hold your memory dear during the long, but happily uneventful, years that will follow the interment of whatever parts of your body we are able to retrieve from the beach.'

'That is very kind,' I say.

'But,' Aminta continues, 'I think there may be a simpler way of discovering the owner of those bones.'

'Really?'

'Yes. It is just possible that there is somebody in the village who already knows exactly who it is lying promiscuously beneath Mistress Pettus.'

'Who?'

'Her house is a ten-minute walk the way we are already going. It is a small diversion for us and probably worth it to reduce the length of my widowhood by a year or two.'

Mother Catch seems to be expecting us.

'I have already boiled the water,' she says. 'And the pot is on the table. We can talk about whatever it is you wish to talk about over tea.'

'You knew we were coming?' I ask.

'There would be little point in being reputed a witch if you could not do small things like that.'

'Really?'

'No, not really. I was making tea anyway and heard you coming up the garden path. You see how easy it is to get people to believe in witchcraft? But people will believe very easily the things they want to believe and strain at an obvious truth when they do not.'

She carries her teapot over to where the kettle is boiling and adds the water to the tea leaves. Then she returns the pot to the table, beside three delicate blue and white porcelain bowls. The bowls are probably Chinese and show small figures moving around in a stylised garden, with large exotic plants and buildings with roofs at strange and wonderful angles.

'Now, what can I tell you? Do you wish to know about the future?'

'No, we wish to know about the past,' says Aminta.

'Yes, I thought you did,' she says.

I am about to say 'really?' again, but decide not to. I am beginning to understand how witchcraft works.

'How far back do you need to go?' she asks.

'Twelve years,' says Aminta.

'Ah – so that is the death of Venetia Digges?'

'And Mary Pettus,' says Aminta.

'True. Mary Pettus died a few days before Venetia Digges.'

'So, would they have dug her grave before Venetia died?'

'Why do you think I would know that?'

'Because your father was churchwarden,' says Aminta.

'He did not talk to me about every burial. A girl is of course interested in her father's work, but one grave is much like another.'

'There is something about Mary Pettus's grave that is unlike most others,' says Aminta. 'She was buried with somebody else just below her coffin.'

'Ah, that,' says Mother Catch. 'I think the tea should be ready now. I suppose you want to know whose body it is?'

'Yes, please,' says Aminta.

'Isaac Cavendish,' she says. 'But I'm sure you've both guessed that already. I mean, he had to be somewhere, didn't he? Do either of you add sugar to your tea? I am told some are doing so in London. It revives the spirits more, but I think you lose some of the flavour of the tea leaves. There is a loaf of sugar on the table there, and tongs to break off as much as you need.'

'You are certain it is Cavendish in that grave?' I ask.

Mother Catch considers this while I sip from the porcelain bowl of fragrant, unsweetened tea.

'At about the time that Mistress Digges died, my father complained to me about an irregular burial that the vicar had made him carry out. It troubled him a great deal – then and later.'

'Did he speak to anyone else about it?'

'Yes, I think he spoke to my aunt. They were close. He would have gone to her for advice, because I was at a loss to know how to counsel him. I believe, in the process of seeking her views, he made some sort of confession to her – told her more than he had told me. Then she cut him out of her will.'

'He never named the person whom he had buried?'

'No, not to me. But Isaac Cavendish vanished at about that time. It was odd that nobody ever heard from him again, wherever he was supposed to have fled to, don't you think? And my aunt was quite enamoured of Isaac Cavendish. A lot of women in the town were. My father really should have taken that into account when speaking to her. We all knew about Isaac and Venetia Digges, of course – we accepted that she had first rights to him – but we didn't think it would last long. I mean – Mistress Digges' infatuation with Jacob Cavendish hadn't lasted. Jacob was married himself then, with a daughter – Silvia Digges as she now is – so it was perhaps as well that it ended when it did. But my father should have been aware that Isaac was the one person in the town that my aunt would not forgive him for burying illegally.'

'And that is why the vicar would not inter your father in consecrated ground?' I ask.

'Yes, my father lost both a pleasant home in this world and the many advantages of a churchyard burial when faced with Judgment Day.'

'But you say that it was the vicar who requested the deceit?' I say.

'The vicar will also be buried outside the churchyard. He will punish himself too. He is a fair man.'

'Did your father say how Isaac Cavendish died?' asks Aminta.

'No, but he may not have known himself,' says Mother Catch. 'I doubt if he would have dared to ask – and I'm sure that Wraith would not have told him. Wraith is a strange clergyman, even for these times.'

'Wraith implied he communicated with the Devil,' I say. 'He had learned from some supernatural source that I would witness his death.'

'It is highly likely you will outlive him, bearing in mind the difference in your ages. Some say Wraith has sold his soul. I do hope not. Satan never pays what it's really worth. It's like selling your corn to Peacock. He knows there's nowhere else you can easily go if you don't like his terms.' She reaches out, snips a small piece of sugar off the loaf and drops it carefully into her cup.

'Tutepenny said that Wraith's madness dated from that time,' I say.

'The guilt, I suppose – burying somebody illegally and without any rites or ceremony – it must be very trying for a vicar. It crept into his sermons. They dwelt in great detail on the fires of Hell. I don't know where he got most of it from. Not the Bible. But nobody really listens to sermons, do they? They are a chance to let your mind wander pleasantly in between the prayers and psalms. I think it was a year or two before anyone remarked on it.'

'Has he preached a sermon before like the one on Sunday?' asks Aminta.

'Predicting the destruction of everyone in Eastwold? I think not, but, as I say, he may have done and we simply didn't notice.'

'So that was what Tutepenny wanted to tell me?' I say.

Mother Catch takes a sip of her tea. 'He had worked out that Isaac Cavendish was buried there? Yes, it's possible. He knew that the vicar's madness dated from the time of Mistress Pettus's death, that Mistress Digges also died then, that Cavendish disappeared just as Mary Pettus was being buried . . . He would have put those things together. Of course, others would have known those facts too, but Tutepenny was an intelligent man, who had seen a great deal of the world. I imagine you regarded him just as a fisherman, but you scarcely knew him. If he had had friends to help him to better things, who knows what he might have become? A bishop? A judge? And the Admiral trusted him. Of course, Digges did nothing for him in return – such was his way – but I know that the Admiral respected his ability. I imagine that's why Tutepenny was killed. It doesn't pay to be both clever and lacking powerful friends.'

'You have been very helpful,' I say.

'Well, knowing the questions you would ask me, it was not difficult, my dear.'

I look at her. Yes, I think she really did know we were coming. The three teacups – no more, no less – must have been on the table long before we set foot on her garden path.

'But this is exactly what we need!' exclaims Pepys. 'Jacob Cavendish may or may not have killed the Admiral, but it would seem there is every chance that he killed his brother and Venetia Digges. You say that Isaac had supplanted him in Venetia's affections. We know that Isaac was a cautious man – but Jacob was one of Rupert's cavalry officers. Rupert's men never thought before they acted. Never. They were incapable of it. The idea of Venetia drowning herself when Isaac rejected her always seemed a little far-fetched, as did Isaac killing her in a fit of rage. And the Admiral was elsewhere. But Jacob was in Eastwold and if he had caught Isaac and Venetia together and about to flee the country . . .'

Pepys pauses thoughtfully. I do not draw any parallels with what occurred in the garden only two nights ago. It would be instructive for him, but unkind.

'Yes,' I say. 'That is possible.'

'Jacob Cavendish, as a member of the family that had ruled over this village for centuries, would have been able to persuade the vicar that he should allow the secret burial of his brother's remains, so that Isaac would appear to have fled after Venetia's killing. Edward Catch, out of a long and devoted loyalty to the family and the vicar alike, would have acquiesced, however reluctantly. Only afterwards would they have regretted their actions – as, from what you say, the vicar still does.'

'And Tutepenny's death?'

'That is easy. Tutepenny was clever enough to realise what had happened. Jacob Cavendish overheard him talking to you about the Pettus grave. He knew that Tutepenny would shortly meet with you and tell you everything. So he killed him.'

'Why would Cavendish use the Admiral's cutlass to kill Tutepenny, rather than a cavalry sword?'

'To throw you off the scent if you got this far! He is no fool.'

'And how does he get his hands on the Admiral's cutlass?'

'How can we be sure that's what it is? There must be hundreds of naval cutlasses along this coast – all of much the same pattern and easily obtained.'

'And the Admiral's death?'

'Does that matter?'

'Please forgive my mentioning it, but it is what I was sent here to investigate.'

'The circumstances have changed somewhat. The Duke would now be wholly indifferent to whether it was murder or an accident. We seek to overturn an undesirable result, not make it safe.'

'It would be odd if I made no report at all.'

'Very well. Tutepenny killed him. He had long held a grudge against him for his flogging and his ingratitude. Now he saw the Admiral about to be elevated to Parliament. He sent a note asking Digges to meet him on the beach. The Admiral went down there with his sword. Tutepenny attacked him, seized the sword, stabbed him, drowned him and took the sword home with him. Which – if you insist on the cutlass now with David Larter being the Admiral's – is how Jacob Cavendish was able to use the sword in his turn, when he assaulted Tutepenny at his house. It was already there. He had only to pick it up and use it. I think that clears everything up very nicely. Are you happy now?'

'I agree that it is plausible. And since Tutepenny is already dead, there is nothing more to be done?'

'Well, Cavendish needs to be arrested, of course, and the election result nullified. But there is happily nothing more to be done about the Admiral. You may say in your report that Tutepenny had good cause to hate Digges and that, believing the Admiral was about to have fresh honours heaped upon him, he decided that he could abide it no more. Being a somewhat simple soul, he struck, little caring that he would be found out as soon as you and I applied our greater skill and cunning to the matter.'

'Simple? But we have already agreed that Tutepenny is reputed an intelligent and, indeed, a kindly man.'

'But you surely do not need to mention that?'

'An unnecessary complication?' I ask.

'A story should be clear and straightforward. It should be evident all along who is good and who is bad. There is no need for anything in between.'

'I shall tell my wife. I think she often complicates things by suggesting that good and evil, wisdom and foolishness, are more difficult to separate than you imply.'

'The stage is another matter.'

'I bow to your greater knowledge. You have spent far more time amongst actresses than I have.'

I know that I have resolved to be kind to Pepys, but I too sometimes yield to temptation, however much I know I may regret it later. But this time Pepys does not seem to notice.

'Indeed,' he says. 'I know the theatrical world very well. It is my greatest love, except perhaps for music. How long do you need to gather witnesses to Cavendish's guilt?'

'To which murder?'

'I thought we had settled on Isaac Cavendish, Venetia Digges and Tutepenny? But I have no wish to cause you unnecessary work or delay your decision. Just one of them would be sufficient – or indeed the Admiral, if that is easier. I am happy to leave it to your judgment.'

'I have not said that I agree Cavendish is guilty of anything. But I shall see if I can find out more. If Wraith is feeling cooperative, then perhaps it will not take very long.'

'Do you think Wraith will be?'

'Probably not. Now I consider the matter, I think it must have been Wraith who sent me the present of a skull the other day. It puzzled me for a while who was trying to warn me of my impending death, but Wraith has skulls in abundance in his crypt. He could have easily spared one. And he, or somebody very much like him, tried to kill me yesterday by pushing a boulder off the cliff. It was odd that he tried to end my life with so little attempt to avoid detection, but it is further proof that he is not well disposed towards me.'

'However ill disposed he might be, I am surprised that he showed his intentions so openly.'

I shake my head. 'On the contrary. Oddness is quite normal for Eastwold.'

Chapter 24

I re-examine my witnesses

The vicar is outside the church. He stands perilously close to the edge of the cliff, examining a large crack that runs through the flint wall, from the ground to the roof. His right foot is dislodging a certain amount of sand, which is falling in a golden stream to the beach, but he either does not notice or does not care.

'The storm took only a little of the churchyard,' he says, 'but it has caused part of the cliff below this wall to collapse. More will follow, even if there are no further high seas. When the first part of the wall goes, it will pull the rest with it. By next Sunday the building will be open to the four winds.'

'You sound pleased,' I say.

'Yes. I sometimes think that Peacock is right. These buildings are more of a burden than they are an asset. God is indeed everywhere. This is the last church in Eastwold. Once this goes, they will have to worship in the open air, with God's beauty all around them.'

'That will be very pleasant for us all.'

'Except when it snows. Then, I think, not. But most of the time they will not miss this damp ruin, full of dead sinners and their boastful, lying monuments.'

'I should be careful. You may awake one morning to find that you are a Puritan.'

'No, it is too late for that. I am already damned.'

'Mother Catch fears you may have got poor terms when you sold your soul to the Devil.'

'My soul was never worth much.'

'What was the price?'

'A dozen years of peace.'

'That seems cheap.'

'It didn't then. Twelve years seemed almost forever. Anyway, if you ask too much then he will always trick you. That is how he works. He uses cunning words. You think at first they mean one thing but later you realise their true import.'

'My wife does the same in her plays. It's not difficult. Sometimes she does the same thing with me at home. She's good with words.'

'You would do well not to mock the Devil, Sir John. He hears you! Like the rat under the floorboards, he is never far away.'

'I'll be careful.'

'Not you! If you were careful, you would have left days ago. The town has long been doomed. You, as yet, are not.'

'Did you send me a present of a skull to tell me that?'

'I don't recall.'

'Did you try to kill me with a rock from the cliff top? I ask only out of interest. If it wasn't you then it was the Puritan Peacock – I'm sure you wouldn't want him blamed for your own misdeeds.'

'I certainly did nothing to stop the rock falling. It was a strangely solid thing in this world of sand – but it has always been there. I like to think one of our Pagan ancestors placed it on that spot, having dragged it across country, to sit watching over the sea. But when it arrived here the sea must of course have been no more than a distant reflection on the horizon. The sea came to meet it, bit by bit, year by year. And finally they were together. The slightest tap was all it needed. Whether it hit you was God's decision alone. I was simply curious to know His will. I was pleased, on balance, that He chose to spare your life.'

'So, you were working with God yesterday?'

'God and the Devil are better friends than you would imagine.'

'Milton says they fell out. I'd assumed he had that on good authority. Did Jacob and Isaac Cavendish fall out?'

'Why do you ask?'

'The body under Mary Pettus's coffin. It's Isaac Cavendish. Jacob may have killed him and put the body in the grave with your help and Edward Catch's help.'

Wraith smiles. 'Who has told you this nonsense?'

'The part about the burial is from somebody who would know; the rest is from somebody for whom it would be convenient. You are perhaps the only person alive who knows for certain. It would save me a great deal of time if you told me.'

Wraith looks me in the eye. 'Listen to me, Sir John,' he says. 'Whatever I know about Venetia Digges, I have kept secret for twelve years. What possible reason could I have for telling you anything now, when it is far too late to help anyone?'

'It would help Mister Pepys. He badly wants Jacob Cavendish to be the murderer. I think he may stop at little to ensure that happens. Alternatively, if you know that Jacob is innocent, I'd like you to tell me now, so that I can stop Pepys hanging him. You can still save the life of an innocent man.'

'So I could. If I chose to do so. Which would you prefer, Sir John? Guilty or not guilty?'

'The truth.'

He shakes his head. 'I swore something twelve years ago. I will not break the oath I swore. Not for you. Not for the King, who swears half a dozen oaths every hour.'

Well, that's true enough.

'There was a time,' I say, 'when being a clergyman exempted you from many laws of the land. A convicted priest needed to fear nothing more than an inconspicuous branding on the thumb. Not now. If you are guilty of murder – if you are an accessory to murder – you can hang with the rest of them.'

'That's right,' he says. 'The benefit of clergy will not save me. But, do you know? I think the Devil just might step in. My twelve years isn't quite up.'

'Maybe you got a better deal than I thought,' I say. 'But don't count on it. I'll be back.'

I decide to travel in my own coach. A horse would take me there faster but I have still not recovered from my last ride.

Alexander is about to leave for his fields again after dinner. He shows no pleasure in seeing me again or in seeing my coach, which he must regard as one of the many temptations of the Devil that he would dearly love but cannot afford.

'Very well, Sir John,' he says, when we have found a sufficiently secluded spot, away from my coachman's ever-attentive ears and Barbara's general disapproval of playwrights and their husbands. 'To what do we owe this signal honour? I assume you wish to question me further about my brother's death?'

'I thought that it would be good for my soul to revisit such a charitable and Christian household.'

'I'm not sure that I like you very much, Sir John. You imagine that you can mock the pious and the God-fearing with impunity – you think that we do not see the contempt beneath your easy smile. You should know better. You were at Cambridge University at a time when there was some piety about the place. You had the advantage of studying under godly doctors and divines. But you behave as if—'

'I had attended the University of Oxford? Then I apologise for my levity. But I can assure you that, deep down, I remain loyal to the principles in which I was brought up. It's just that God seems no longer to favour Puritanism as much as He did. Unless you think He does, but is powerless in the face of Arlington's and Clifford's preference for vestments and incense?'

I do not think that these conciliatory remarks have endeared me to Alexander Digges. I think he would like me to go. And so I shall. But not yet.

'Have you come here just to annoy me?' he asks.

'No, I have also come to try to solve a mystery dating back twelve years. I wanted to talk to you about Venetia Digges.'

'A harlot.'

'Well, that's certainly what her monument says about her. "And of Jezebel also spake the Lord, saying, The dogs shall eat Jezebel by the wall of Jezreel". But the vicar thinks that few of the monuments tell the honest unvarnished truth, so the wording may flatter her.'

'For once a monument speaks plainly. It is a fitting tribute to her.'

'Your sister-in-law seems to have had an understanding with both of the Cavendish brothers?'

'You have seen her epitaph.'

'It is not explicit.'

'It is explicit enough. Very well, though it shames me to admit this of my brother's wife, she did indeed have an understanding, as you call it, with both. At first, according to rumour in the town, she favoured Jacob, but he was married – I doubt that worried her, but I think it caused him to have second thoughts. Then it was Isaac.'

'With such a brutish husband is it any wonder that she sought protection elsewhere?'

'Brutish? You speak of my brother, Sir John.'

'I do indeed. An unpleasant, wife-beating brute. Did you do nothing to check his behaviour?'

'He was within his rights. As a lawyer you will be aware that the law was on his side.'

'I stand corrected. An unpleasant but perfectly legal brute. So who killed Venetia Digges?'

'Why, Isaac, of course. Just as the Coroner ruled. Some people here would have liked it to have been my brother who killed her, but he was miles away, with half the court to vouch for him.'

'Your brother was lucky his ship was delayed,' I say. 'Or he might have risked the same accusations that Jacob may soon face.'

'Lucky? I don't know what you are implying now, but it's all well documented. Ask Pepys. He'll have access to the records of Robert's voyages.'

'I agree that the Admiral has a cast-iron alibi. But Jacob Cavendish doesn't. He was in Eastwold when Venetia died. Could he have killed both Isaac and Venetia?'

'Nobody killed Isaac. Isaac fled.'

'Not very far. We think we've just discovered his remains, in Mary Pettus's grave.'

'Have you? What should I care, Sir John, if one Cavendish wishes to murder another? Good riddance to him, I say. Good riddance to them all. What about my brother's death? Isn't that what you're supposed to be looking at?'

'Yes. But I have made less progress than I hoped.'

'So, you waste your time on the death of that harlot?'

Perhaps Alexander is right. This is simply a waste of time. What if Jacob Cavendish did kill his brother? If there were witnesses they would have come forward years ago. Without witnesses, it is simply idle speculation that will take me nowhere at all. It is time for me to write the report that Pepys has always wanted and turn my coach towards Essex.

'So when will you arrest Silvia?' asks Alexander.

'For your brother's murder?'

'Yes.'

'Why do you think it was her?' I ask. 'Do you know something against her that you did not mention when I was here before?'

'I know nothing that you do not already know. I have merely thought about it, as you should have done yourself. Sir John, the Cavendish family have been plotting to regain the manor ever since my family bought it – quite legally – from them. Silvia never loved my nephew. You saw, as I did, how she was behaving with that Admiralty clerk. That is your final piece of evidence, if you like – it was certainly mine. I warned Digby against Silvia, just as I had warned my brother against Venetia, many years ago. Jacob's plan is quite clear to me now. First, marry his daughter to Digby. Then the pair of them would kill Robert and Digby and regain his lost estate.'

'Both father and son? Surely not?'

'You must know yourself that Silvia was always visiting that Mother Catch – she never made any secret of it. Witches know how to poison people. Luckily for Robert, he was away at sea and out of her clutches. But she enchanted Digby so that he obeyed her every word. Is that natural, Sir John? The husband obeying the wife? Is that what the Bible commands us to do? Wives, submit yourselves unto your own husbands, as unto the Lord! I see only the Devil's work in a husband ruled by his wife.'

'It may be commoner than you think. But the Admiral was not poisoned. He was drowned.'

'When she found he was too clever for her potions, she tried a more direct way. And she succeeded. You must have worked out for yourself that she could have met him on the beach, stabbed him, then drowned him.'

Well, yes, obviously. I have thought of that.

'Alone?' I ask. 'Or are you saying that Jacob and Silvia killed him together?'

'She could never have overcome Robert on her own.'

That would also explain Tutepenny's death, if he had proved a threat. Silvia might not have killed him. Maybe Jacob would.

'But her plan, as you describe it, has so far succeeded only partially. I am happy to say that Digby is alive and well.'

'As you say – he has survived so far. But now my brother is dead, Digby has lost his main protector. Silvia would like to be rid of her husband, so that she can run off with that Pepys, just as Venetia sought to run off with Isaac Cavendish.'

Does this explain the fear on Digby's face? Has he long suspected the same thing?

'How does she intend to kill Digby, then? In the same way that she killed the Admiral?'

He shakes his head. 'I've worked that out too. She will get you to do it.'

'Me?'

'She will get you to hang him for his father's murder.'

'She will struggle to do that. Digby is the last person I would suspect,' I say. Then I pause. Is any of that really true? Digby was, after all, out on the beach when his father was killed. He knew where his father was going. Nobody had a better opportunity. Had it not been for his lack of motive and his complete devotion to his father, he should have been amongst the most obvious suspects. And, as for Silvia getting me to hang him, hasn't she been gently pushing me in that direction all the time? She was careful to tell us that she thought the Admiral had been murdered. She told us that he had been stabbed. She ensured that her account of Digby's actions on the evening of the Admiral's death was as incongruous as possible – his delay in leaving, his purported failure to notice whether the Admiral's boat was still there. She reminded me, after Tutepenny's death, that her husband had conveniently sent me off to Lowestoft on the day of the killing. She has slowly built up my case for me. Had it not been for her, I might have happily already written my report confirming the death as suicide. Perhaps Alexander is not being as fanciful as I thought. Very occasionally, you see a plot and there really is one.

'Even when Silvia and Barbara were walking after dinner,' says Alexander, 'Silvia lost no opportunity to drop poisonous hints that Digby had been less well disposed to his father of late. Who else has she spoken to in that way? What other lies has she told?'

'I promise that I shall watch over Digby as if he were my own child,' I say.

'I am serious, Sir John. I am convinced Digby is in the greatest danger.'

'So am I serious, Mister Digges. It is no part of my role as a magistrate to permit murder, even by the strange method you suggest.'

Alexander shakes his head wearily. 'I know that you don't like me or my wife. But we have acted for the best. We brought Digby up as well as we could. Brought him up to be honest and trusting and straightforward. What we would have wanted our own son to be, if we had been blessed with one. Barbara and I – we can't help that times have changed. Do you think that it is a better world now? It seems to us just more cynical and more corrupt, run by fools and rogues for the benefit of their friends.'

'That at least is true,' I say.

'Impossible,' says Aminta. 'We have said that Silvia might have killed the Admiral in revenge for the suffering he had subjected her to – I might have killed him myself. But I cannot believe in this convoluted conspiracy that Alexander describes. Just to regain a house?'

'That was also my first thought,' I say. 'But consider the facts. First Silvia marries Digby, though they seem wholly unsuited to one another. Then, in some way that I do not understand, she gains control over both Digby and his father. Then the Admiral dies.'

'So, your only explanation for her being able to control Robert Digges is not that she might happen to be brave, intelligent and resourceful – it has to be witchcraft.'

'I don't believe in witchcraft. You know that.'

'But otherwise I'm correct? If a death is secret, unnatural and inexplicable, then a woman has to be behind it?'

'What we have both struggled with is the timing of the Admiral's death. It no longer seemed necessary for any of those who might have done it. But this explains everything. He had to die, and the sooner the better, as the next stage in the plan. It also explains why she has been so helpful to us all the way through my investigation. She has been deliberately pushing us towards the idea that the Admiral was murdered by his son.'

'And this is the theory of your fellow Puritan, Alexander Digges? I might have known you would sympathise with him.'

I take a deep breath. 'I agree that you have sometimes warned me in the past of the danger of wishing to believe somebody because I liked them – or not believe them because I didn't.'

'Precisely,' she says.

'But I don't like Alexander.'

'You respect him, though. You respect him for sticking to outdated principles that you have fortunately abandoned.'

'That may be true. But consider this: you have said several times how much you have in common with Silvia – how you were both ejected from your family home by Cromwell, how much your fathers are alike, being Cavaliers who fought alongside Prince Rupert. You are yourself doing exactly what you advise me against.'

'You have missed that we both have arrogant, obtuse husbands. Well, watch over Digby, while we are here, if it pleases you to do so. Once we have gone, I assume that he can be in no further danger of your hanging him? At least you are no longer proposing that you should risk your life, trying to dig up a coffin to enquire further into Isaac's death. Perhaps I should be grateful for that.'

There is a knock on the door. It is Digby's steward. 'There are some fishermen downstairs,' he says. His tone implies that such people would normally be beneath his notice. 'They wish to dig up a body for you. They say that there is still time to do it before the light fades and the weather breaks again, but you must come now. Shall I tell them to go away?'

'No,' I say. 'Tell them I shall be down at once. And, if you would, please then go and fetch the Coroner, Mister Larter. Ask him if he will very kindly meet me at the churchyard. I lost my chance of interrogating James Tutepenny properly. I'm not going to lose my chance of interrogating Isaac Cavendish about exactly who killed him.'

Chapter 25

I meet a former colleague of my wife's father

The rain is already starting to come down as we approach the churchyard – a gentle drizzle that sits on my coat in tiny droplets and hangs like a mist between us and the church. The men are already armed with spades and, in case this takes longer than we think, some lanterns. But at the lichgate the vicar bars our way.

'There will be no digging in my churchyard this afternoon,' he says, holding up his hand. 'These souls were given into the care of God, with my blessing, and only God can order me to hand them over to another party.'

'I am using my authority as a magistrate to counter-mand your previous instructions,' I say. 'Please stand to one side, Vicar.'

'Your authority does not run here, Sir John. This is Suffolk, not Essex.'

'I have a letter from the Sheriff of Suffolk requesting that I investigate a murder for him. That is what I am doing.'

'The murder of Admiral Digges.'

'I am doing precisely that, as you will see in due course.'

'I forbid it.'

'Vicar, I can, if you wish, instruct two of these gentlemen to escort you back to your vicarage and sit with you until this is over. But they'd be better employed digging, so I should be much obliged if you would take a seat on that brick tomb yonder and allow us to do what we have to do. The Coroner is on his way, if you would like further civil authority.'

Wraith would dearly like to kill me, but I am no longer at the bottom of the cliff and he has no more boulders to hand.

'I shall remain where I am,' he says.

'Do so,' I say. 'Stay under the shelter of the gate. I wish I could too. But twelve years ago you made sure that would not be possible. We dig here to correct your mistake.'

We advance almost to the cliff edge. I look over. The drop is not great, but it ought to be enough to kill. I take off my coat and tie a rope round my waist. Pettus ties one round his. The other ends of the ropes are pegged into the ground. If the cliff top does collapse, hopefully we shall not fall too far. If the sides of the grave collapse, the others can pull us out, or at least find us quickly. If we are lucky. And so we start to dig, on opposite sides of the grave. After a while we are untied and two fresh diggers take over. The rain is now falling heavily. Only Wraith, huddled on the seat under the wooden roof of the gate, is at all dry. But he'll be colder than those of us who have been digging. I look at the eastern horizon. It is already becoming dark out there. This is at least light sandy soil, not the heavy clay of North Essex. The men continue to dig; they are now more than waist-deep but they keep up a regular rhythm as another spadeful of earth is thrown onto the growing heap. Another pair ropes up and takes over. Then, finally, I hear a thud as a spade hits the top of a wooden coffin. We are making good progress – and much of the coffin is of course already out of the ground and hanging over the beach. The hole is widened and eventually we are able to get ropes under the wooden box. Now we all have to pull together. Very slowly we edge the coffin upwards. If we get this wrong, if we allow it to overbalance, it will slide off the ropes and hurtle downwards to the sand. We are just easing it onto the surface when the neat figure of David Larter strides through the gate.

'I'm sorry – I was out when your message arrived. Am I too late?'

'Not at all, Mister Larter,' I say, offering him a sandy hand.

Together we stare down into the grave. The feet and lower legs have vanished already, but from the knees upwards we have a complete skeleton of a man, five foot eight or nine originally, still half obscured by soil, lying on his back, dressed in the scraps of a blue velvet suit, white linen shirt, and white stockings. The hands remain completely buried and the arms seem to end abruptly at the wrists. A hat, beaver and with what may have been a fine feather, has been tossed in and rests, flattened beyond any possible repair, on his chest. I think somebody will have regretted doing that, but it wouldn't have been safe to keep it and wear it. His teeth are in good order, under the circumstances, and very white. He grins at us in greeting. He hasn't seen anyone for a while. Long dark hair still attaches to his scalp. He would have been better looking when he went in, but the last dozen years have not been too unkind to him.

'So is that Isaac Cavendish?' I ask.

'Without doubt. I even remember that suit of clothes. And

the hat. Perhaps we could get him out of there? The ground looks none too safe, and it would be a shame if all your effort went to waste. Don't worry if the bones get a bit mixed up. I know where they should all go.'

I tie the rope round me again and give one end to Bottulph. I climb down carefully into the hole. Shouldn't I have given this job to somebody with two properly working legs, especially after that ride? I try not to show my grimace of pain as I bend my knees and start passing bones up to my companions. For some reason I give them the skull first, though I suspect that will not be the critical part of Mister Cavendish. I take up the ribs as a bundle, then the pelvis, then the arm bones, one by one, then I scrabble in the sand to retrieve as many fingers as I can. It is at this point that the ground beneath me gives a sickening lurch. I hear sand and stones thudding on the beach below.

'Come up now, Sir John,' calls Bottulph. 'I don't know if I'll be able to hold you if it all goes at once. I don't even know if it will hold me.'

'Get Dix to help you,' I say. 'We may need the thigh bones.'

I reach down but then there is a rush beneath my feet and I find myself both falling and swinging rapidly towards the cliff face at the end of a rope. I put out my hands to lessen the impact. A reassuring stab of pain round my waist tells me I have been brought up short. I shall fall no further. Then I am being pulled quickly upwards and over the edge onto the greensward. Bottulph and Dix are smiling with relief. I crawl forward a few yards and risk standing.

'I fear I may have lost a couple of femurs,' I say, 'though if you wish to dig in the heap of sand at the base of the cliff you may find them.'

'We lack a number of bones. Femur, tibia, fibula, tarsus and one or two others that need not concern you,' says Larter. 'But I think his assailant may have aimed higher. We have the upper body intact, including ribs, arms and most of the fingers. I'll take a look at this lot and convene a jury tomorrow – say midday. Can somebody give me a hand to bag it all up in a decent and respectful manner? Oh, and don't forget the hat. You'd be surprised what you can sometimes get from clothing, even when it's been in the ground this long.'

'And, equally important, please take Mistress Pettus's coffin into the crypt,' I say. 'The vicar cannot refuse her his hospitality for a day or two before we re-bury her.'

I look over towards the lichgate, but at some point Wraith has slipped away, unnoticed by the rest of us.

I return to the house very wet, but that is not what troubles Digby. He accosts me as I enter.

'Wraith tells me that you and Larter have gone against my express instructions and lifted Mary Pettus's coffin. I have warned you, Grey. I shall not tolerate this. I shall complain to the Sheriff. I shall prosecute those fishermen for desecrating the grave. I shall have you dismissed as a magistrate. My father was well connected at Court. I still have friends there.'

'We found your wife's uncle underneath the coffin,' I say.

Digby is less surprised than he might be. Had he already worked out at some point that Jacob might have killed Isaac? Was that what Edward Catch told Digby on his deathbed?

'You have nevertheless acted illegally. You had no permission to dig there – not from me, not from the vicar, not from the Sheriff.'

'Even so, as the magistrate resident in the town, how do you plan to account for his strange burial?'

'That is my affair and I shall deal with it when I can. You are here only to investigate my father's drowning. Isaac Cavendish's burial, however unorthodox, cannot have any bearing on the death of my father twelve years later.'

'Larter is convening a jury tomorrow,' I say. 'On his authority, not mine. If I were you, I'd be there, Mister Digges.'

'Very well, I shall make my protests at the inquest. I shall ask that he begins by condemning your unwarranted interference in matters that do not concern you. I shall object to the body being exhumed at all without proper permission. And after that, I want you to leave Eastwold and never return.'

I look at Digby, standing in front of me, his fists clenched, his face red. I have told Alexander I shall protect him as if he were my own child. He certainly resembles one at this moment, but he seems determined to dismiss me from my role as his guardian if he possibly can. I can understand why Alexander and Barbara found him a difficult boy to manage.

'It is not that simple.'

'Why?' he demands.

'I went to visit your uncle. He thinks that your wife killed your father and now wishes to kill you, perhaps in league with your father-in-law. He also thinks that she plans to run off with Mister Pepys. I must leave you to judge whether you think that likely, on the basis of what you have seen.'

I wonder if Digby will again insist that his wife is innocent of any malice towards him or his father. But I think that recent events have changed his mind. He still recalls very clearly his wife and Pepys in the garden.

'I don't believe you,' he says eventually, but he sounds far from convinced. 'How does he claim she is going to kill me, anyway?'

'Your uncle thought that she might try to get you convicted for the murder of your father.'

Digby's jaw drops. 'She wouldn't do that.'

'Alexander thinks that she married you only to get the house and the land.'

'He has never liked her.'

'He certainly doesn't like her now. He thinks that she has bewitched you. She and Mother Catch together. Your wife certainly visited Mother Catch, after which she seems to have gained some sort of hold over your father. Only you could say whether she has sought to gain control over you.'

Digby nods. He seems a defeated man.

'Very well,' he says. 'What do you suggest that I do?'

'Fear not, the law is not so easily hoodwinked as your uncle seems to believe. Go to the inquest. Listen to the evidence. But don't raise procedural issues that make it look as if you are trying to block my investigation, just in case people start to think that what Silvia is pushing us towards is actually true: that you really have something to cover up. Or that's what I would advise you to do if I were your lawyer.'

'Thank you,' he says. 'You have considerably more experience than I do of such matters. I think it would be best, would it not, if Silvia did not attend the inquest?'

'On the contrary. We should do nothing to make it seem you were afraid of any accusation she might make.'

He nods, but his face is white.

'You are quite wrong about Silvia,' he says. 'I don't know what she has said to you, but my father's death has affected her greatly. She has not been the same since. I fear that, like the vicar, she may not be entirely in her right mind. You must take that into account if she gives evidence.'

'It may not be necessary for her to give evidence,' I say. 'Isaac Cavendish was her uncle, but the events happened many years ago. It would be for David Larter to call her or not, as he wishes.'

'Of course,' he says. 'Of course.'

He gives me a weak smile. I hope I have not misled him as to whether I can save him or not.

Chapter 26

I make some final enquiries

I had assumed that David Larter would be an early riser, and I am not wrong. He has already lain out as much of Isaac Cavendish as he has on his dining table, reassembling him in the correct order, though sadly without his legs.

'I thought to go down to the beach at first light,' he says, 'but there will be much debris there. I could not be certain which were Cavendish's bones and, in the absence of that certainty, anything they told me might be a lie.'

'Perhaps if you located them in the remains of his blue velvet breeches?' I ask.

'I suppose so. But they would not have been needed. I already know how this man died. Come over here and look for yourself.'

I approach the table. 'Ah,' I say. 'The grooves on the ribs . . .'

'Precisely. As the sword was plunged into his chest, the bones on either side of the blade were damaged.'

'Can you tell what type of sword was used?'

Larter goes to a cupboard and fetches a cutlass.

'This is the sword we found in Tutepenny's chest.' He holds it against the rib. 'You will see that the edge of the blade matches exactly the groove in the bone – and in this rib just below the first.'

'There must be many naval swords of a similar design,' I say. 'Pepys said there might be hundreds along this coast.'

'Well, I suppose he would know. But the fit here is as good as you could ever hope to have.'

'So, was it the same sword that killed Isaac Cavendish and the Admiral and Tutepenny?' I ask. 'No, that's impossible. When Isaac died, this sword would have been with the Admiral, and he was on board his ship, at sea.'

'Then maybe not,' says Larter. 'As you say, there must be a number of very similar swords. But it certainly looks as if he may have been killed with a naval cutlass.'

But it has raised in my mind a doubt that I have long had. Perhaps I have been very wrong about something all along. Which in turn means I have been very wrong about something else.

'Where will you hold the inquest?' I ask.

'At the inn. I have already sent out word so that we can empanel a jury. I think we may start at midday.'

'If it is not an impertinence, I would suggest that you and Digby and I all sit on the bench and take evidence.'

'Is that necessary?'

'I think we may need to ask questions about other events in the town – earlier and much later. Together we may have authority to do it. Or not. And Digby is less likely to try to halt proceedings on procedural grounds if we are beside him.'

'I thought Digby was conflicted? Wasn't that the entire point of your being here?'

'It would certainly be wrong for him to work alone. As one of a panel of three, however, it is less of a problem.'

'I bow to your greater knowledge of these things, Sir John. You are a magistrate. I am merely a Coroner. You will have sat on many cases like this.'

'No, I've never sat on anything quite like the session that will begin at twelve o'clock. But I think that the result will justify any minor irregularities in procedure.'

'I need to send word to Benefice of the revised plan,' says Larter.

'Don't worry,' I say. 'I'm going that way. I'll tell him myself.'

'Three of you on the bench, then?' asks Benefice.

'Yes,' I say.

'Well, that's helpful to know, but you didn't need to come here yourself, Sir John. Mister Larter could have sent anyone with that message.'

'I thought you might be able to clarify one or two things for me before the inquest begins,' I say.

'What things?' he asks warily.

'The Admiral's sword,' I say. 'It wasn't in the boat when you found it?'

'No.'

'Young Mister Digges thinks the Admiral took it with him to the beach.'

'He often had it with him. He was used to carrying it.'

'Let's assume Mr Digges is right, then. In which case, where was the sword in between the Admiral being drowned and the weapon being found in Tutepenny's body? Who had it?'

'I couldn't say, Sir John. The sword that killed Tutepenny was definitely the Admiral's?'

'Mr Digges identified it.'

'I still can't help you, but I agree it's odd that it wasn't with the Admiral or left on the beach where he was killed. Why would anyone take and keep something that connected them to a murder? Maybe you'd like to ask me something easier next.'

'You were living in Eastwold when Venetia Digges died?'

He looks at me suspiciously. That is only superficially an easier question. 'I saw nothing that night. I was up here, at the inn, the whole evening. I told them that at the inquest.'

'And Tutepenny?' I ask. 'He was still serving with the Admiral then?'

'He was a trusted man on board the Admiral's ship.'

'How trusted?'

'What are you trying to get me to say?'

'I'm not sure yet. Isaac Cavendish was killed with a naval cutlass. Tutepenny would have possessed one.'

'It wasn't Tutepenny who killed him.'

'You can't be sure of that. And it would be convenient for a lot of people if it was true. Mister Pepys, for example. But why should we care how Tutepenny is remembered? The Admiral trusted him. Then he flogged him. If there's so little gratitude in the world, why should it bother you and me if he's remembered as Isaac Cavendish's murderer?'

'Tutepenny was here with me that evening. I'll swear to that if I have to.'

'Here with you?'

'Yes.'

'You've never said that before.'

'Nobody ever asked me. Not exactly.'

I suppose I didn't. Not exactly. Still, now I've got it, the information is certainly worth a lot more than the three

Shillings and six pence that I have so far paid Benefice. And it confirms what I had begun to suspect.

'Tell me more,' I say.

'How much more?' he says.

'Enough to convince me that you know what you're talking about. Enough to rule out Tutepenny being a murderer.'

'The evening that Venetia Digges was killed and Isaac fled, as we thought ... I'd been running this inn for two or three years by then. Sailors who'd been with me in the Navy would often call in – I mean if they'd docked at Lowestoft or somewhere along the coast and had a few days ashore and no family in this part of the world. Well, early that evening Tutepenny showed up. I said to him, 'Was the Admiral back with us, then?' Because they were on the same ship and the Admiral wasn't expected until the following day. So, I thought perhaps the ship had arrived early. He looked a bit shifty and said, no, not exactly. I wondered if the Admiral had dismissed him, but thought he'd tell me soon enough if that was the case. So we sat there drinking. I mentioned that Pettus's wife had died a few days before and was to be buried the following day, but he said he wouldn't be able to go to the funeral. He was in town just for a short time, he thought. But he was uneasy. Kept asking me what hour it was. Then he left to go down to the beach. It was dark by then, but there must have been a bit of a moon to see the path. Ten minutes later he was back looking like death. Asked exactly where Mary Pettus's grave was. I told him. Then he said never to tell anyone he'd been in Eastwold that evening. And I haven't. Until now.'

'But, if he was in Eastwold that evening and acted as you describe, then surely it must have been Tutepenny who killed Isaac and Venetia?'

'He had no sword with him, sir,' says Benefice. 'He was away too short a time anyway to meet with Isaac, remonstrate with him then kill the two of them. Afterwards, when we all discovered Venetia Digges was dead, I didn't doubt that he'd stumbled across her body or something, but I'm certain he couldn't have killed her – or Isaac. He wasn't here for that inquest, of course, and nobody knew it might have been worth calling him. So he never gave evidence. And I told them the truth when I said I never went anywhere near the beach that night and saw nobody down there. I wasn't going to get Tutepenny hanged as an accessory, if that's what he was. I might have asked him later what had happened, but I decided there are some things that it's better you don't know.'

'And it was just after that that the Admiral had him flogged?'

'Yes. I don't know when exactly, but some time after.'

'Could Tutepenny have been flogged because the Admiral suspected that he must have been complicit in some way in his wife's death?'

'I don't think he was complicit in any death – or not willingly.'

'Did you know that Isaac Cavendish was buried there?'

'I knew something funny had been going on with Mistress Pettus's grave. I wasn't very happy when you suggested that we should raise her coffin – not while Tutepenny was alive, at least. After he was dead, well that was a different kettle of fish.'

'Thank you,' I say. 'And thank you for your help with the exhumation. I appreciate it. I may have to ask you to repeat some of what you've told me at the inquest.'

'Maybe – if it helps clear Tutepenny's name,' says Benefice.

'I'll try to do a little more than that,' I say.

And for the first time, Benefice looks at me with something close to respect.

'Yes,' says Jacob Cavendish. 'I'd heard that some bones had been found and that they were rumoured to be my brother's. I suppose that explains a great deal.'

'And Isaac and Venetia were enamoured of each other?' I say.

'I've already told you that.'

'You haven't told me that you were similarly attached to her.'

'I wasn't.'

'Others have informed me differently.'

'I thought that rumour had died years ago.'

'Clearly not,' I say.

Jacob takes a deep breath. 'Venetia's life was a tragedy,' he says. 'She married young and her first husband was killed during the war, fighting for the King, leaving her without a penny. When Robert Digges proposed, she accepted, but she found herself ill used when he was home and utterly alone when he was away. She was a strange exotic flower in this drab, sandy place. There are no portraits of her, as far as I know, but you can see a reflection of her beauty sometimes in Digby's face. She had few friends here, but she gravitated naturally towards my wife and myself, as another old Cavalier family. Though this cottage is modest enough, it provided a comfortable refuge for her and Digby from an admittedly grand but undeniably cold and ruinous house. She came more and more often – asked for advice, in her husband's absence, on running the estate and on rebuilding the Priory. Well, it had been my home, so I knew about both the building and the land around it. We'd walk the fields together sometimes, with me telling her what crops grew best where. But in time it became clear that she wanted more than agricultural advice from me. And gossip had started in the town – silly gossip, but I needed to put an end to it. It wasn't fair on my wife or on Venetia. So, we stopped issuing invitations to her. She turned to Isaac, who was more obviously available. I warned him, but he said he would never do anything that was to his dishonour or hers.'

'And did he?'

'I don't know. We became a little distant towards the end, as a result of his association with her. But I never doubted that he would have rejected her before he conspired to run away with her. Even if the body proves to be my brother, I am convinced that Venetia killed herself.'

'Then who killed your brother?'

'I don't know. Digges didn't arrive in Eastwold until a week after Venetia's death. Somebody else who disapproved of their relationship, I suppose.'

'What if I told you that Tutepenny was in Eastwold that night?'

'Who says so?'

'A reliable witness.'

'Are you sure he's reliable?'

'As sure as I am of anything here. I'd advise you to be at the inquest, Mister Cavendish.'

'Of course. If the body is my brother's, where else should I be?'

'So, the inquest is at midday,' says Aminta.

'You've heard?'

'Everyone has heard. I should think that Alexander and Barbara will know by now in their farmhouse. I doubt that

Henry Cavendish will yet know in Lowestoft, but I think the whole of Eastwold will descend on Benefice's inn. He will not have known trade like it since the last inquest.'

'I've talked to Benefice,' I say. 'And I've talked to Jacob Cavendish. I think I've finally pieced everything together.'

I explain to Aminta what I've been told and what I plan to do. She has a smug smile on her face because she has, in some ways, been proved right.

'You'll need a chart,' she says. 'One that covers the whole of the North Sea and the Medway. Sometimes a picture is worth a great deal.'

'Perfect. I hadn't thought of that,' I say.

'Well, I did,' says Aminta. 'And I think I know where the Admiral would have kept them. I'll ask Silvia for the key.'

'Not Digby?'

'From what you say, I think that would not be wise.'

'I agree,' I say. 'Again, you are right.'

'So, I am to be part of Larter's panel?' asks Digby.

There is a note of suspicion in his voice, which may or may not prove to be justified. Even I do not yet know how cautiously he will have to proceed.

'Both of us will be,' I say, with the easy smile that Alexander criticised me for. 'I can't say where the evidence may take us. There is Tutepenny's death to consider here too.'

'Surely not? I mean, what can Tutepenny possibly have had to do with the killing of Isaac Cavendish?'

'Larter thinks the two of them may have been killed with the same sword.'

'Can you really tell that?'

'It's a probability rather than a certainty,' I say.

'Just so ... I don't think we need to confuse matters by pre-empting Tutepenny's inquest.'

'I agree. We need to keep things as simple as we can. But it would be good to have you there beside us, just in case.'

Chapter 27

In which certain persons have a mirror held up to them, in which they may know themselves better

The small inn is packed. Benefice has arranged for Larter, Digby and me to sit on a raised platform and for chairs for Aminta and Silvia to be reserved in the front row. All are equal in the eyes of the law, but gentry get better seats.

'Perfect,' I say. 'I shall be calling both ladies to give evidence, though I am expecting my wife's part in this case to be brief.'

'And the jury, sir? Which of us is to be on the jury? The room is full but I doubt we can muster twelve, once you exclude your good selves, the witnesses and the ladies.'

'I think we might have Dowsing, Pettus, Bottulph, Cooper, Dix, Peacock. That will have to be enough, in view of how few inhabitants of the town we have who are not to be called to give evidence . . . or feature more prominently.'

'I'll let them know, Sir John.'

'Thank you,' I say.

Benefice works his way round the room very nimbly for

a man who has had only one leg since 1653. I think he can probably do most things that his two-legged colleagues can do. But perhaps not climb rigging in a gale. He may have been wise to retire from active naval service when he did and become an innkeeper.

I survey the crowd. Not even another sermon from Wraith could have drawn such an audience. I wonder which of them are in a position to predict what the outcome will be. I think that Mother Catch, already seated in the front row, possibly is, but she has had an unfair advantage. The vicar, not yet present, has been preparing for this day for twelve years. But I may yet be able to surprise him.

'So which of us is to chair this?' asks Digby, when he has muscled his way through the throng. 'As the resident magistrate here, I fear that heavy burden falls to myself.'

'I have already discussed the matter with David Larter,' I say. 'He is willing to concede his authority to a Justice of the Peace. As between the two of us, since I am the more senior magistrate in terms of years on the bench and years on this earth, I think I must claim the right to direct proceedings. As you say, it is a heavy burden. I would not want to subject you to it.'

'But, equally, I would not wish the findings of the court to be invalidated by any procedural irregularity,' he says. 'I think it would be safer to have me chair it and guide you both through some potentially rocky waters – particularly concerning what evidence we are able to consider and what we should prudently disregard.'

'Thank you,' I say. 'But I'll chair it and deal with the Sheriff or the authorities in London when the time comes.'

Digby would like to find further arguments for relieving

me of unnecessary burdens, but he is forestalled by the arrival of the third member of the panel, followed shortly after by Pepys and the ladies. Aminta and Silvia are assisted to their seats, with quiet efficiency by David Larter and much show of metropolitan gallantry by Pepys. While Pepys finds a convenient place to stand and sneer at the burgesses who so recently rejected him, Larter comes over and joins Digby and me. He has a sack over his shoulder. 'Bones and a cutlass,' he says cheerfully. 'Just the necessary bones for the most part, but also the skull to amuse the children, who are easily bored. I'm ready to begin when you two gentlemen are. You're chairing this, aren't you, Sir John?'

I like to pause at the beginning of cases such as this. I survey the room for long enough that they are beginning to fear I may say nothing at all. Then, when I speak, I begin very softly. I find it helps convince them that they need to stay silent themselves if they don't wish to miss anything that they may, one day, want to repeat to their grandchildren.

'I have convened this session,' I say, 'to look into the discovery of a body that we believe to be that of Isaac Cavendish. A previous inquest ruled that he had killed Mistress Venetia Digges and then fled, probably to join the King in exile; but if it proves to be him in Mister Larter's sack, then that view will have to be modified a little.'

There are one or two nods. If he's in the sack, then he wouldn't have been able to travel to Brussels.

'I will ask Mister Larter to say a few words to you all about the identification of the remains.'

Larter, who has already started to lay out the more important bones on the table, looks up. 'I have examined the human remains found under the coffin,' he says. 'Though the skeleton is incomplete I can state that the deceased was about five foot nine or ten and was dressed in a blue velvet suit and a fine beaver hat.'

There are more nods. That was how Isaac Cavendish dressed before he ended up, less fashionably, in sackcloth.

David Larter holds up a small gold ring. 'And on one of his finger bones, caked in sand, I found this. It has the Cavendish crest on it.'

Well, Larter knows how to grab the attention of his audience. That's twenty-five Shillings' worth of evidence. I don't think we'll need to do any more to prove the identity of the skeleton. Jacob Cavendish, standing at the back, looks on impassively as we discuss his brother. He glances across at Elijah Spratchett and at Solomon Larter, who have arrived inadvisably late and have also had to squeeze into any space available, Mayor and Member of Parliament though they are.

'We know that the body must have been buried, and given a light covering of soil, after the grave was dug,' David Larter continues, 'but before the coffin was lowered. That is a period of less than twenty-four hours. The time of burial, if not of actual death, can therefore be judged very accurately.'

'And how did he die?' I ask. I'm sure Larter plans to tell us, but it is important that I establish my authority as chairman to direct people to speak or to be silent.

'A stab wound through the chest.' Larter indicates two rib bones on the table, then passes them to Benefice for onward transmission to the jury. 'You will see, gentlemen, that the bones are scored by the blade as it penetrated. If you now examine the cutlass here, which I am also now passing to Mister Benefice, you will see that its shape matches the notches exactly. Of course, a great number of naval cutlasses might do almost the same, but the match, as I'm sure you'll agree, is as near perfect as it possibly could be.'

'And to whom did the cutlass belong?' I ask.

'This one? To Admiral Digges,' says Larter. 'It was identified by Mister Digges here.'

There are gasps in the crowded room.

'I protest,' says Digby. 'You've said that any number of cutlasses might fit the marks. There is no need at all to attribute the act to my father, who is not here to defend himself.'

'I have not accused anyone,' says Larter. 'That is for the jury to make up its mind on. But the ownership of this particular cutlass is incontestable, unless you have changed your mind. I'm sure nobody would dispute that you would recognise your father's sword.'

'Thank you Mister Larter,' I say. 'Do you have any further questions, Mister Digges?'

'May I see the ring?' He examines it briefly and returns it without comment. He would know the arms of his wife's family well enough.

'I should now like to call Ezekiel Benefice,' I say. 'Once he has returned the cutlass to Mister Larter.'

I swear him in and Benefice repeats to the room what he told me earlier. There is much nudging and raising of eyebrows amongst assembled company – it was worth coming just for that.

'Tutepenny was then under the command of Admiral Digges?' I ask.

'He was his most trusted man,' says Benefice. 'Whenever the Admiral went ashore, Tutepenny would steer the boat.'

'But the Admiral, though expected daily in Eastwold, was

then supposed to be on board his ship, sailing back to the port of Chatham from the Netherlands. Of course, so was Tutepenny. But Tutepenny was here. Where, in that case, was the Admiral? My wife has suggested that we study this chart.'

Aminta stands and, with Benefice's aid, holds up a large map of the North Sea.

'You will observe,' I continue, 'that the route from Texel to Chatham passes right by the coast of Suffolk. The Admiral arrived in Chatham two days after the death of his wife and Isaac Cavendish. Had he paused here in Eastwold – I merely postulate that he might have done – he would have had time to be rowed ashore by Tutepenny, to be rowed back and to reach the Medway easily by the date we know he finally docked. There was some surprise amongst his superiors that it had taken him so long to repair a defective rudder and catch up with the fleet – a commission of enquiry was established. Perhaps the rudder really did break. But the length of the journey is equally explicable if you allow for a diversion to Eastwold.'

'Is that my map?' asks Digby.

'It is. Your wife very kindly loaned it to us.'

'And what are you suggesting?' Digby demands.

'It is not for me to suggest anything. But the jury might consider the possibility, in view of Tutepenny's presence here and the slowness of the Admiral's progress to Chatham, that Digges decided to put in at the beach, just after dark. As those here who are involved in smuggling will know, this can be done discreetly and without causing much of a stir.' From the amount of nodding in the room, it is clear that almost everyone present is able to confirm from personal experience that this is true. 'Whether the Admiral was hoping for a happy reunion with his wife or to catch her with Cavendish, I do not know. But it is very likely word reached him of what was a well-known liaison – either by post or by overhearing something on a previous visit to his home. These things do come to light eventually, in my experience. At least, they do in my own village. Whatever the state of his knowledge, I think he caught his wife and Cavendish on the beach, one of the places they were said to walk together. Thus Tutepenny returned to the shore from a pleasant hour at the inn, only to find his master there with two rather inconvenient bodies. But there was a solution. They could leave his wife's body on the beach, drowned. The more difficult stabbing could be dealt with another way. Tutepenny had been told there was an open grave waiting in the churchyard. Together, he and the Admiral carried the body up the cliff path to the churchyard. But, before they could complete the impromptu burial, they were discovered by Edward Catch. He summoned the vicar. I don't know exactly what conversation followed, but I do know that the upshot was that the vicar ordered Catch to allow the burial and save the neck of his friend, the Admiral. Catch was consumed with guilt for the rest of his life. He unwisely unburdened himself to his sister and suffered the consequences. At the moment of death he saw no point in confessing to the vicar what the vicar already knew only too well. But he did tell the whole story to his local magistrate, didn't he, Digby? The one practical act of contrition he could make was to let you know that he had condoned the death of your mother at the hands of your father.'

I am aware that I may have suggested slightly more to an inquest jury than I should have done. But I am uncertain what sort of enquiry this is. I may still be acting perfectly lawfully.

'What if Catch did confess to me?' says Digby. 'I was able to give him some comfort that Wraith certainly never offered him.'

He gives the vicar a look of pure hatred. I can see why, after Catch's death, Digby decided that he might not go to church as regularly as he had before.

'The three bequests in your father's will puzzled me at first – but there we have it: the vicar, the churchwarden and Tutepenny, all were to be rewarded for their long silence. I now also see why you delayed so long paying Tutepenny. That must've been somewhat distasteful, under the circumstances.'

'You are making a lot of assumptions, sir,' says Digby.

'But not unreasonable ones. In any case, you were not the first member of your family to have concluded that your father killed your mother, were you?' I say. 'Because your wife was a frequent visitor at Mother Catch's, as many others in the town were and still are. And Mother Catch had also worked out your father's secret. I'd wondered how Silvia had tamed the Admiral. But if you tell your father-in-law that you know not only that he is a murderer, but also where the body is hidden, then it can save you a lot of ill treatment, one way or another. That, not curses or poisons, was the magic ingredient she obtained from Mother Catch. Of course, the same knowledge had not saved Tutepenny a flogging – indeed, an incautious reference to it almost certainly occasioned the savage punishment, to teach him to keep his mouth shut. But that was at sea and Tutepenny had nobody to go to. Silvia had more options. She was safe. Isn't that true, Mister Digges?'

'That is merely speculation!' Digby exclaims. 'All this tramping around in the dark with dead bodies and the sudden appearance of Catch. You have no actual proof of any of that.'

'But it is exactly what Catch told you.'

'I am not a witness to be cross-examined in this way, Sir John. You have not sworn me in. I have said that he unburdened himself to me. That is all you need to know. Your own version of events is a mere fantasy.'

Just for a moment I remember my promise to Alexander that I will protect Digby as my own child. But I have no doubt that, if Alexander knew what I now know, he would not suggest a different course of action from the one I have planned. *Fiat justitia ruat caelum.* One thing we share is a respect for the truth.

'Mere fantasy?' I say. 'Then why not tell us exactly what Catch said on his deathbed? You can have scarcely forgotten. What is your objection to enlightening us?'

'He spoke to me as his friend, not as a magistrate. Nor was he then under oath. I cannot be certain that what Catch said to me was true.'

'That is of course absolutely right, and is the reason that the law places a lower value on second-hand evidence from witnesses who have not been sworn in and cannot be cross-examined. Unfortunately, the Admiral, Catch and Tutepenny are all dead, and we cannot question them. And you, we are agreed, were not there yourself when Isaac Cavendish was buried. But we do have one survivor of that fateful evening. Don't we, Vicar? Shall I swear you in next to testify?'

'You most certainly shall not,' Wraith snarls, in a very unclerical manner. 'This is not a properly constituted court. You have no right to chair the panel, sir. And your fanciful speculations have further muddied the waters. You should have left this to Mr Larter, who at least knows how to conduct an inquest. What you are running is neither an inquest nor a Grand Jury nor anything else sanctioned under law. I can rightfully refuse to give evidence at all.'

'Indeed,' I say. 'So you can. Very well put, Mister Wraith. A most rational response. You're not as mad as people say, are you?'

'What do you mean by that, Sir John?'

'I mean that it was very convenient for you that signs of madness began to appear just after the double murder. You were undoubtedly an accessory after the fact and you knew it. There is no benefit of clergy for murder – we agreed that earlier. But a plea of not guilty by reason of insanity? That is another matter. So, you began to prepare your defence. Your last sermon was a masterstroke of fabricated lunacy. So was your hurling a boulder at me in broad daylight – I mean, only a madman would think he could get away with that, surely? Anything really to strengthen your case, even at the expense of my own death.'

'You think you're very clever, don't you?' says Wraith.

'It's more that he is well advised by his wife,' says Aminta.

This too meets with some approval from the spectators, and not only the women.

I turn from the cleric at bay to my still-indignant fellow magistrate. 'You would think, Mister Digges, that the vicar would be clearer in his refutation of my theory. After all, he was only has to take the stand and swear that nothing of the sort happened. Who would doubt the word of a vicar? But he prefers not to say anything, one way or the other. I shall have to leave the jury to make of that what they will.'

'You're finally happy to let the jury make up their own minds on something?' says Digby. 'You don't wish to treat them to more idle speculation of your own?'

'Not for the moment,' I say.

'Very well. Then, before they come to any conclusions, they should note that the vicar has in no way corroborated your strange version of events. He has merely stated his right to silence in a court that you have no right to chair. I demand that you yield the chairmanship to me, so that we may proceed in a more orthodox manner.'

'Again, thank you for your kind offer, Mister Digges,' I say. 'It is much appreciated. I should now like to call Mother Catch. I take it that nobody here has any objection to my swearing in a reputed witch?'

There are puzzled shakes of the head. Why would anyone want to object to that?

I swear her in on the Bible. The book does not burst into flames. The ground does not open. Demons do not appear.

'You are right,' she says. 'My aunt did say something very much along the lines you indicated. I was not shocked. You must remember my calling – people tell me a great deal that is considerably stranger than anything you have heard so far.'

'But you informed nobody?'

'No, not until Silvia Digges visited me for salve for injuries that she had suffered. I asked her how she came by them. She explained. It was no surprise. I already knew something of the Admiral's character from others in the town who had visited me, though I naturally cannot say who they were.' There is a collective sigh of relief at this last statement. Mother Catch smiles benignly at her assembled clientele and continues: 'I gave young Mistress Silvia some salve at a small discount from the usual price and I also told her that her father-in-law was a murderer and that she could get him hanged whenever she liked. I thought that that knowledge might help prevent a recurrence of the problem.'

'And did it?'

'Yes, I believe so.'

'Could Mister Digges have come by the same knowledge?'

'He may well have overheard a conversation within his house. I imagine that there would have been several between Mistress Silvia and the Admiral. They may have been quite loud.'

'So, befriending Edward Catch at his hour of need may not have been an act of pure charity on the part of young Mister Digges?'

'No, I think he may have already had suspicions that he wanted confirmed. He was careful that I was not called to my father's cottage. Nor was the vicar sent for. I think he may not have wanted my father to confess to anyone else.'

'Thank you, Mother Catch,' I say. 'Do either of my colleagues on the bench have any questions?'

'Nothing from me. I think you are doing very well,' says David Larter.

'I must object again most strongly to the direction your questions are taking,' says Digby. 'You are making a wholly uncalled-for attack upon my character. My understanding was that the three of us were to hear this case together, as equals. You have deceived me.'

'So I have,' I say. 'Do you wish to ask Mother Catch a question, Mister Digges?'

'No.'

'I call Silvia Digges to the stand,' I say.

'I object,' says Digby.

But his wife is already on her feet.

Silvia is dressed in lilac silk and much lace. Her hair is,

as my wife has previously explained to me, in the very latest French fashion. She places a white hand on the book and swears very prettily – soft as a dove but as clear as a bell in the silent room. Aminta is right that an old Cavalier family always adds tone to any event.

'Did you visit Mother Catch for salve?' I ask.

'I did. And she did give me a small discount, as she says. The information about my father-in-law was free of charge.'

'Good,' I say. 'Let us turn then to the night of the Admiral's death. Where was your husband?'

'He went to the beach.'

'When?'

'Shortly after the Admiral left. But Digby delayed for a few minutes – I don't know why – and failed to catch up with his father.'

'How long was he away?'

'An hour or so. Perhaps a little more.'

'How was he when he returned?'

'Very wet.'

'Just wet?'

'Agitated.'

'Because he had not found his father?'

'So he said.'

'I think we should end this questioning now,' says Digby. 'You have overstepped the mark, Sir John. You know perfectly well that a wife cannot give evidence against her husband. Husband and wife are legally one entity and nobody can be forced to give evidence against himself.'

'I believe that all she has said so far is that you went to the beach and returned alone, understandably worried.

You said much the same thing yourself at your father's inquest, and under oath. Are you saying you lied?'

'Of course not.'

'Then in what way is this evidence against you, Mister Digges? Unless you know what she is going to say next?'

'I can see where this is leading,' he says. 'Everyone can see what you are doing. Whatever my wife says will have to be discounted – either now or later.'

'I, however, am not your wife,' I say. 'I am related to you in no way that I know of. So I shall allow your wife to stand down and I shall simply tell you what happened. I do feel sorry for you in so many ways. Your mother, whom you loved greatly, died when you were twelve. Your father was away at sea. You were sent to live with your Puritan kinsmen. Nobody here will envy you any of that. But slowly you began to wonder if the stories you had been told were true. They told you that Isaac Cavendish had murdered your mother and fled. He never returned – perhaps that was not surprising. But no message ever came from him. Nobody ever reported that they had seen him at the Court of the exiled King. You must have wondered why. And the epitaph put up by your father, the Admiral … That didn't seem to blame Isaac Cavendish in any way at all, did it? It didn't even say that your mother had been unlawfully killed. And you overheard things – things spoken by your wife to your father. Things that you scarcely wanted to believe but that finally made sense of your entire childhood. Then, a month or so ago, Edward Catch lay dying and you finally got proof of the thing you had most feared. Your father had murdered your mother. Those endless, dreary days of your Puritan upbringing had been completely unnecessary. You could have tried to bring your father to justice, but how? Your best witness, Catch, was now unfortunately dead and the vicar was accounted mad. And I think, in spite of what Catch told you, you still had no idea of Tutepenny's role until you overheard what he told me in the churchyard. You therefore believed that you alone could avenge your mother. So, you wrote your father a message to get him to come to the then deserted beach – to the exact spot where your mother had been found. You, not he, took his sword, delaying your departure by a few minutes while you collected it. But there was no urgency – you knew exactly where he would be. There on the beach, by his boat, you told him all you knew – you would not have been able to resist that. Then, you tried to stab him. Of course, you did it badly – you are, as you have said, no man of action – but the shock had weakened him. He collapsed. Or did he fall to his knees to beg for forgiveness? I don't know but, in response, you came up with the happy notion of holding him under the water – that was, after all, the punishment that fitted the crime of drowning your mother. And you may not be a swordsman, but you are very strong. You dragged your father into the more than adequate waters of the North Sea, then his lifeless body into the boat. You dumped him somewhere not too far off the shore, perhaps above the Guildhall, where he had hoped to celebrate his victory in the election. Finally, you beached the vessel a little way up the coast, so that it would seem he had had an accident while sailing. Of course, your wife worked out almost immediately what you had done. She knew your father was a murderer. She knew what your likely response would be once you found out. She knew you were on the beach at the right time. You returned soaking wet. She made no objection when the Coroner's jury found that the death was accidental – perhaps some trace of love remained in spite of your abject failures towards her. Sadly, a letter was sent to London by somebody in the town – admittedly under a misapprehension – suggesting that the jury had misunderstood matters. I was dispatched here. Did you urgently consult the vicar at this stage? You hated him almost as much as you hated your father, but it would do neither of you any good if I reopened the matter of your father's death, which would quite possibly lead to discussion of your mother's twelve years ago and the revelation of your motive for your father's murder. You would certainly have agreed that you both needed to avoid the discovery of Isaac Cavendish's body. You had to stop the exhumation of Mary Pettus. But I pressed on, ignorant of all of that. The vicar's response – a badly aimed rock – did nothing for your cause. You needed me dead, preferably, but he was content if it only reinforced his plea of insanity.'

'And Tutepenny?' asks Digby. 'I thought I was here because you might need to consider his death as well. Next you will be stretching the credulity of the jury to its limits by claiming that I killed him too!'

To be fair, it's a nice try to muddy the waters. But I don't think I shall be expecting too much of the jury in what I say next.

'Tutepenny also knew your father had killed your mother,' I say. 'He'd actually seen her body on the beach. I have already alluded to your overhearing our conversation in the churchyard. Afterwards, I foolishly confirmed the key fact to you over dinner – not the part about the burial of Mistress Pettus but that Tutepenny always rowed the Admiral ashore. So finally you knew he'd also been there that night. You realised from the start that you would be a suspect, other than for your complete lack of a motive. Tutepenny was about to give me the piece of evidence I needed to understand not just *why* you killed your father but why you killed him *then*. I'd also been puzzled why anyone would have wished to kill somebody as inoffensive as Tutepenny. But in your eyes, he was as guilty as the rest of them. He deserved to die. You sent me to Lowestoft before Tutepenny could tell me more – it was the only thing you could think of to get me out of the way. Then you took up your father's cutlass again and paid Tutepenny a visit. You left the sword sticking in him, which was a mistake. I assume you couldn't easily pull it out and panicked. But I've already said that you have no idea how to use a sword.'

'This is ridiculous! It is like one of the contemptible comedies that you now get at London theatres. I can scarcely recognise anyone you mention as a real person. They are just hideous caricatures.'

There is a cough from Aminta's direction. His attempt at literary criticism has not been well received. I suspect that it is the Puritan in him that has implied that all comedy is contemptible, but if Digby gets out of here alive, Aminta may finish the job tonight.

'My storytelling may be bad,' I say. 'I agree that I have left the stage scattered with corpses as in the tragedies of our grandfathers' time. But which acts and scenes of my drama do you wish to deny?'

Digby opens his mouth. Will he admit to murder? Will he curse me to Hell? Will he raise some long and carefully constructed procedural objection to the composition of this court? I shall never know. Outside there is a most theatrical rumble of thunder. The door of the inn flies opens. A fisherman whom I do not recognise staggers in soaking wet. While we have been absorbed in the hearing, the storm has resumed.

'The church!' he calls to all of us. 'The cliff has collapsed. The whole east wall is gone!'

'My mother's coffin,' Digby says, almost to himself. 'Wraith, we have to save her remains. You owe me that much.'

'How bad is the damage?' Wraith asks the fisherman.

'You can't go to the church, sir. The roof is about to fall in. You'll have to leave those who are buried there to their fate.'

'Nonsense,' says Wraith. 'Three sound walls will hold it up for hours yet. Who will help us? We'll need to raise the stone just below her monument, then we can lift the coffin out.'

Nobody seems anxious to assist. Perhaps they have decided that Wraith is just strengthening his plea of insanity. But I think he really plans to atone for his actions twelve years ago. He has wronged Venetia Digges. Like Catch, he has seen a final chance to make amends.

'Very well then, just the two of us,' says Digby.

The crowd parts, like the Red Sea, to let them through. They've never seen people going willingly to their deaths before. There is no attempt to stop them. Their madness has made them objects of awe and wonder. The door closes behind them. It is through the window that we view the second flash of lightning, then the thunder explodes again.

'We shan't see them again on this earth,' says the fisherman to nobody in particular. 'Unless they return as ghosts, which I hope not. Too many of those in this town already. May God have mercy on their souls.'

'It's just as the vicar said in his sermon,' says somebody.

'That was the whole town,' his neighbour points out, 'not just the church.'

I turn to where my small jury sits. 'Your decision, gentlemen?'

They go into a huddle for a minute. Then Dix says: 'Mister Isaac Cavendish was murdered by Admiral Sir Robert Digges, and his body disposed of with the aid of the vicar and church-warden. The Admiral was murdered by Mister Digby Digges. Are we to rule on Tutepenny, sir? Or on Mistress Venetia Digges?'

That's thirty seconds per murder. I've seen juries deliver verdicts faster than that, when so instructed by the judge, but it's as good as it needs to be.

'No, you've heard only part of the evidence on Tutepenny,' I say. 'His inquest will have to wait for another day. And the inquest on Mistress Digges has already taken place. It was clearly wrong, but I believe I have no powers to reopen it without higher authority. I therefore declare this hearing closed. Thank you, gentlemen, and God save His Majesty the King.'

'We should go after Digby,' says David Larter, glancing out of the window. 'He is a double murderer and should be brought to justice. So should Wraith for his part in concealing the earlier killings.'

'Leave them,' says Aminta to me. 'If they wish to die that way, then let them. You may not mind if you die or not, but I'd like some company in the coach going back to Essex.'

'No, Larter's right,' I say. 'We can't let them die while trying to raise part of the church floor. On balance, entering an unstable church seems less risky than exhuming a body on a cliff top. We got away with that. Wish us luck. And it would be kind if you went back to the house with Silvia. She'll need your support.'

Chapter 28

The death of a minor prophet

Outside, though it is early afternoon, it is already almost as dark as night. The clouds are thick and swirling and deep black. So strong is the wind that Larter and I can scarcely maintain our balance as we follow the path along the top of the cliffs. We are soaking wet within minutes – so wet that we know that pressing on will get us no wetter than we are already.

Digby and Wraith have already vanished into the sheets of rain that are being driven by the gale. My hat sails away into the sky and hangs there before tumbling down towards the beach. I realise how wise I am not to have adopted a periwig, or I should have also lost my hair.

Larter points ahead of us. 'The path along the cliffs has gone,' he says. 'The sea has already taken another twenty or so feet. We need to go a little inland. Follow me.'

We dodge along a passageway between two ruined walls and find ourselves on a deserted cobbled street. There are house fronts down both sides, but on our right the houses no longer have any backs to them and those on the left have wisely been abandoned by their owners. Their glassless windows frame the storm clouds that are scudding over the sea.

'Everyone moved out five years ago,' says Larter, 'but the ocean decided to stop where you see things, with the job half done. I think it will all go today, on both sides of the road. I wonder whether by nightfall there will be anything left of Eastwold above water except its town council and two Members of Parliament.'

We turn a corner and find ourselves on the open cliff top again and a view of the church ahead. A flash of lightning shows that not only has one entire wall already gone, but the crypt below the church is now partly exposed in the cliff face. I think of Mary Pettus's body, which lies there with so many others, but there is nothing to be done.

'Is that Digby in the church?' I say, pointing.

Larter rubs some of the rain out of his eyes.

'It can't be anyone else. And Wraith. Do you see, there?'

Yes, there are two shadowy figures moving inside the church.

They are standing in front of Venetia's monument as if discussing, calmly and logically, what might be done. I suspect that the stone they have to raise is too heavy for the two of them alone and without equipment. There is another flash, then a long, long roll of thunder.

'We have to get them out,' I say. 'Standing in the nave like that is merely inviting the roof to fall on them ...'

'You're seriously planning to go into what remains of that building?'

'If we have to. Whatever their intention now, they deserve a proper trial. Digby has had no chance to give his evidence. Perhaps he could show that he acted in self-defence – his father was known to be a violent man. Perhaps Wraith really is mad. Perhaps they both are. I never saw such calm in the face of such danger.'

Then we hear a sound that grows and grows in volume, the sound of impossibly vast millstones grinding together. The cliff below the church is collapsing again, slabs of rock and individual sand grains racing over each other, faster and faster, to see which will reach the sea first. The south wall sags, then the lead roof starts to fall. It pauses for a moment as if it can't quite make up its mind, then its timbers buckle in a wave all the way along the length of the building and it crashes decisively to the ground. I don't know if Digby and the vicar are even aware of what is happening until it hits them. When the dust settles, there is just a massive heap of debris in the nave of the church.

'I'll go back to the inn,' says Larter. 'We'll get shovels. There's just a chance that we can dig them out. Nobody should have to die trapped under rubble like that.'

I have no idea whether he believes either that anyone can have survived in there or that the fishermen will come to their aid if they have, but even as he speaks, the cliff crumbles once more. There is the same despairing cry of stone on stone and, above it all, the final clanging of the great bell as it tumbles from the tower and spins away over the cliff. When we can finally see the church again, there is nothing standing but the west wall. The rest – Wraith, Digby, the memorial to Venetia Digges and the tomb of the knight and his lady – all has gone.

'It was very foolish of you even to think of trying to arrest the pair of them,' says Pepys.

He has changed into dry clothes. I am wrapped in a heavy silk dressing gown, once the property of the late Mister Digby Digges, sometime magistrate of the county of Suffolk and owner, for a few brief weeks, of Eastwold Priory.

'Well, in the end, we didn't,' I say.

'Let's hope the roof killed them instantly when it fell,' says Larter. 'I don't like to think of them entombed under that stone and lead, even for a few minutes.'

'Wraith at least escaped being tried as an accessory to the murder of Venetia Digges,' says Pepys.

'Interestingly he would not have been tried,' I say. 'An accessory cannot be convicted unless the principal is found guilty. And, the Admiral being dead, that would have been impossible. Wraith sadly did not realise that the Admiral's murder freed him.'

'And, as a result, he allowed himself to become an accessory after the fact to the Admiral's death?' asks Aminta.

'True,' I say. 'I suppose he was. He doubtless knew that Digby was the murderer and assisted him to the extent of trying to kill me by means of a boulder thrown from the cliff. Ah well, that's what comes of selling your soul to the Devil. He plays with you as a cat plays with a mouse.'

'It is of course six votes each now,' says Pepys, rubbing his hands. 'The vote of Mister Digges, as a convicted felon, is invalid. We shall need to run the election again.'

'I have no intention of going out in a small boat for another week at least,' I say. 'The sea will be far too rough. By the time it is calm again, I shall be in London. So, that's five to six against you, I'm afraid. In any case, Digby Digges was not a convicted felon when he voted.'

'Was he when he died?' asks Larter. 'I don't think so. I

mean, I know what the jury said, but what sort of jury was it? A Coroner's jury? A grand jury? A petty jury? It makes a difference. You never quite said what you were doing.'

'Oh, I just gathered all of the suspects together in a parlour and let things run their course. Eventually the guilty parties gave themselves away.'

'I can't see anyone doing that again,' says Larter.

'No, nor can I,' I say.

Chapter 29

In a carriage, still slightly too far from Clavershall West – early April 1670

The rain has gone. The flat Suffolk countryside is damp and green and misty, but the sun is breaking through the clouds. Our coachman, up on his box, has unfortunately started to sing a merry song. He knows the first verse quite well but hums a lot during the later ones. I hope he will reach the final chorus very soon.

'In the end,' I say, 'I think we had rather less in common with Silvia and Digby than you imagined. Our home life is considerably more tranquil.'

'Let us see what disasters we discover on our return to Essex. I always worry what my father will have got up to. He learned bad habits fighting under Prince Rupert. I hope he has not taught too many of them to our son, Charles.'

'We must remember to give him Jacob Cavendish's best wishes,' I say. 'And to tell him that one of his former comrades is now a Member of Parliament.'

'Pepys will not proceed with his challenge?'

'He says there are other seats along the coast that he can contest. And, in return for Pepys's not challenging the result, Jacob has agreed to vote for the necessary taxes to rebuild the fleet. They are good friends, I think.'

'Didn't Jacob swear to the electors that he would oppose the taxes?'

'Yes, but he's elected now and considers he paid more than enough for his seat. It will be a while before he has to worry about what his constituents think. And Pepys has also promised to speak to the King about restoring property lost by Cavaliers under Cromwell.'

'Will the King listen?'

'On that? No.'

'But surely it doesn't matter?' says Aminta. 'Now Digby is dead, Silvia has the Priory outright, as her own property? Unless it was entailed, as Alexander had hoped . . .'

'No, it was not. God has again spared Digby's uncle and aunt the temptation of wealth. Interestingly, however, had Digby been convicted and hanged, much of his property would have reverted to the King. I wonder if Silvia realised that.'

'Why should she have considered it? You mean you think she was actually conspiring to get him hanged, exactly as Alexander said?'

'Perhaps not conspiring exactly,' I say. 'But Digby had proved a great disappointment to her – especially in failing to stand up to his father, when she was so in need of protection. She had to turn to David Larter to defend her as her husband should have done. That wasn't really forgivable. I think that, when we arrived, she was still undecided whether to denounce her husband as a murderer or let him get away with it. It does her no credit, but I fear it was the prospect of running off with Pepys that made up her mind that it wouldn't bother her that much if Digby were hanged. Thereafter she was quite helpful in what she told us, from sharing her suspicions that it was murder to giving us such an enlightening account of Digby's movements on the night of the murder. Digby could see what she was doing. Towards the end he was very worried indeed.'

'I've never understood what other women see in Pepys. But there was no question of Pepys marrying her. He's told me: he won't remarry. He is loyal to his dead wife in a way that he never was when she was alive.'

'Well, as things have worked out, Silvia at least has the house. Unlike Pepys, I don't think she has any loyalty at all to her former spouse. And if she decides to marry again she can only improve on Digby.'

'David Larter seems to be an admirer of hers,' says Aminta. 'He has been her protector in the past. He also went out of his way to ensure that you did not suspect Silvia of murder – the failure to mention the knife wound, for example. And he badly needs a new residence, with his own so close to the sea. Yes, that might work well for both of them.'

'You think that people should marry simply in order to obtain a pleasant home?' I ask.

'It very much depends on the property concerned. And of course location is everything.' Aminta smiles and gives my arm a gentle pat. 'It wasn't just your house, my dear husband. You have many other excellent qualities.'

I look out of the window at the sun shining on a distant line of willows. Our coachman has lapsed into a contented silence and somewhere high above us I can hear a lark singing.

'Good,' I say. 'I'm very pleased to hear it.'

From my Lady Grey's most excellent poem
The Election

And thus our merry Cavalier
Has won the thing that he held dear
And though the Clerk has lost his seat
He's got a vote to build the fleet
And gratify his royal master.
All shall live happy ever after!
A few have died – yes, that is true.
And some are given cause to rue
They trusted, even for one hour,
A candidate intent on power.
One final word, then, from a poet
Whose work you've read (I think I owe it
To you as man or wife or spinster):
Take care whom you send to Westminster . . .

Notes

Rereading my books I am often aware how much they have been influenced by the events that took place during their production – migration, Brexit, social media witch hunts and the rest of it. I cannot see much Covid in this one, though it was written when the country generally and I personally were (intermittently) locked down. But maybe 2020, Covid and Brexit are in there somewhere, if only in the form of a world being nibbled away and made narrower. Or in Aminta's final injunction not to trust those who are after your vote. But you didn't need me (or Aminta) to tell you that.

Eastwold is, of course, loosely based on Dunwich in Suffolk, where the sandy coastline has been receding rapidly for almost as long as written records exist. Dunwich was once a port 'equal if not superior to London'.[1] In 1229 King Henry III was able to demand forty ships from Dunwich 'well equipped with all kinds of armament, good steersmen and mariners'.[2] Like Eastwold, Dunwich received its first charter from King John, for which it had to pay 200 marks and 5000 eels. It too had an ancient guildhall, which was swept away in a storm on the night of 1 January 1386, along with the churches of St Leonard, St Martin and St Nicholas. Though the town shrank, and eventually (like Eastwold) had only a dozen or so voters, it continued to send two MPs to Westminster until 1832. Voters would, exactly as I describe, row out to a point above the town hall to record their votes. My description of the exact stages of a poll is, however, taken from an election in Essex at about the same time as the story is set.

Chicanery of all sorts was common in late seventeenth-century elections, including the practice of temporarily conveying property to people so they could vote, with conveyances brought 'wet to the polls', the owners not even knowing where their residences were. Votes manufactured in this way were known as faggots.[3] The Admiralty did control, or attempted to control, certain coastal seats, and the voters (like those of Eastwold) objected from time to time to being fobbed off with 'courtiers'. Dunwich failed to elect the Admiralty's candidate Thomas Allin in 1671, but later accepted his son. Aldeburgh rejected Samuel Pepys in 1669 'although this was more a reflection on the candidate than on the patron'.[4]

Polls were leisurely affairs, often run over three or four days, which gave candidates the opportunity to chase up, or invent, supporters. There was no secret ballot – hence voters being completely open to intimidation or bribery. Money might be paid to individuals or given for public works or laid out on entertainment. 'No election seems to have been complete without a vast amount of eating and drinking.'[5] Candidates constantly expressed somewhat hurt surprise at the expense they were put to – especially when they had already bribed

the voters liberally at the previous election. James Herbert
wrote to his constituents in Queenborough in 1681: 'I have
had the happiness to serve twice for your corporation through
the favour of some of my friends amongst you. Yet by the
opposition of others, it was upon terms so severe as a stranger
might have expected it.' When Pepys was elected as MP for
Castle Rising in 1673, it cost him £700 (well over £100,000
in today's money). Candidates sometimes cast lots, the loser
agreeing to stand down, to avoid the growing expense of
opposing each other.

Elections and Parliament were an easy target for satirists.
Lord Rochester wrote:

> A parliament of knaves and sots
> Members by name you must not mention
> He keeps in pay and buys their votes
> Here with a place, there with a pension

Aminta's poetic account of the Eastwold election is therefore
completely in character for the times. I should add, for
those who think it is simply doggerel, that she is writing
hudibrastics – mock-heroic iambic tetrameters, in the style
of Samuel Butler's *Hudibras* – which were very fashionable in
the 1660s and 1670s. The same style was later used by Swift as
an effective vehicle for satire, though without Butler's rather
contrived rhymes. So, there you are. Now go back and read the
poem with greater respect.

As ever, the stranger the fact that I mention, the more
likely it is to be true. Pepys's doctor did try placing pigeons
on Elizabeth Pepys's feet. Not surprisingly, it had no effect on
her health. Pepys did own a silver fountain pen – probably one

of the first in the country. MPs actually were sometimes given a horse by their constituents on which to ride to Westminster.

Society in 1670 was of course very different from today's. I have tried neither to hide those differences nor to criticise behaviour simply because it does not conform to twenty-first-century standards. If anyone feels I have been unfair to seventeenth-century men, however, I would direct them (for example) to Elizabeth Foyster's excellent paper 'Male Honour, Social Control and Wife Beating in Late Stuart England'.[6]

One of my regrets, with regard to the year in which the book was written, is that I never got to visit Dunwich that summer as I had intended. Perhaps a stroll through the town and a visit to the museum would have inspired a chapter or two, or at least shaped Eastwold more clearly in my head. But Dunwich is Dunwich and Eastwold is Eastwold. The book was never intended to provide an accurate portrait of a real town and a visit might have constrained my imagination as much as inspired it. And in 2020 I had more than enough constraints.

References

1. Allan Jobson, *Dunwich Story*, Southwold Press, 1951
2. Paul Vallely, 'Britain's Atlantis: the search for our lost capital', *Independent*, 22 Jan 2008
3. Joseph Grego, *A History of Parliamentary Elections*, Chatto and Windus, 1892
4. Mark A. Kishlansky, *Parliamentary Selection*, Cambridge University Press, 1986
5. Richard Morris, *Essex's Excellency: The Election of two Knights of the Shire for the County of Essex 1679*, Loughton and District Historical Society, 2007
6. Elizabeth Foyster, *Transactions of the Royal Historical Society* Vol. 6 (1996), pp. 215–224, Cambridge University Press

Additionally I consulted and have made use of:

David Underdown, *A Freeborn People*, Clarendon Press, 1996.

House of Commons Information Office, History of Members' pay from the 13th Century.

B. D. Henning, The House of Commons, 1660–90 (1983).

R. L. Bushman, 'English Franchise Reform in the Seventeenth Century', *Journal of British Studies* 3 (1963) pp. 36–56.

Merrill Crissey and Godfrey Davies, 'Corruption in Parliament 1660–1677', *Huntingdon Library Quarterly* 6 (1942–43) pp. 106–114.

Godfrey Davies, 'The By-election at Grantham 1678', *Huntingdon Library Quarterly* 7 (1943–44) pp. 179–182.

J. E. C. Hill, 'Parliament and People in C17th England', *Past and Present* 93 (1981) pp. 100–25.

Acknowledgements

Too Much of Water could not have been produced without the assistance of a lot of other people. My thanks are due as ever to my agent, David Headley, for his constant support and advice; and to Krystyna, Amanda, Sarah, Beth, Joanne and everyone at Constable for their invaluable help with various stages of the production of this volume and of the earlier ones in the series. Nor should I forget, in a Covid year, how dependent we all were on NHS workers and all who ran essential services, including those who delivered our groceries every week and ensured that I didn't starve as I wrote. Finally, my gratitude to my wife, Ann, for her love and encouragement during a year of lockdown – and to the rest of the family (seen mainly on Hangouts calls during the past twelve months), Tom, Catrin, Rachel, Henry, Ella, Ieuan and the very newest one, Reggie, to whom this book is dedicated. Hopefully, by the time he is old enough to read it, the Covid pandemic will be a distant memory.